THE EMERALD CHASE

Also by Cap Daniels

The Chase Fulton Novels Series
Book One: *The Opening Chase*
Book Two: *The Broken Chase*
Book Three: *The Stronger Chase*
Book Four: *The Unending Chase*
Book Five: *The Distant Chase*
Book Six: *The Entangled Chase*
Book Seven: *The Devil's Chase*
Book Eight: *The Angel's Chase*
Book Nine: *The Forgotten Chase*
Book Ten: *The Emerald Chase*
Book Eleven: *The Polar Chase*
Book Twelve: *The Burning Chase*
Book Thirteen: *The Poison Chase*
Book Fourteen: *The Bitter Chase*
Book Fifteen: *The Blind Chase*
Book Sixteen: *The Smuggler's Chase* (Winter 2021)

The Avenging Angel – Seven Deadly Sins Series
Book One: *The Russian's Pride*
Book Two: *The Russian's Greed*
Book Three: *The Russian's Gluttony* (Fall 2021)

Stand-alone Novels
We Were Brave

Novellas
The Chase Is On
I Am Gypsy

THE
EMERALD CHASE

CHASE FULTON NOVEL #10

CAP DANIELS

ANCHOR WATCH
PUBLISHING

** USA **

The Emerald Chase
Chase Fulton Novel #10
Cap Daniels

This is a work of fiction. Names, characters, places, historical events, and incidents are the product of the author's imagination or have been used fictitiously. Although many locations such as marinas, airports, hotels, restaurants, etc. used in this work actually exist, they are used fictitiously and may have been relocated, exaggerated, or otherwise modified by creative license for the purpose of this work. Although many characters are based on personalities, physical attributes, skills, or intellect of actual individuals, all of the characters in this work are products of the author's imagination.

Published by:

ANCHOR WATCH
PUBLISHING
** USA **

13 Digit ISBN: 978-1-951021-02-3
Library of Congress Control Number: 2020936454

Cover Design: German Creative

Printed in the United States of America

Dedication

This book is dedicated to . . .

The incomparable Dawn Lee McKenna

When I began what would ultimately become my career as a novelist, a guardian angel was sent to me from God Himself. There's simply no other explanation for how Dawn Lee McKenna ended up in my life. For reasons I'll never understand, Dawn read my first novel in this series—at the time, it was the only novel in this series—and she decided to help me. Perhaps she saw some tiny glimmer of true writer potential in me, or maybe she just felt sorry for me. Either way, the impact this magnificent woman has had on my life can never be measured.

Dawn and the great Wayne Stinnett conspired to catapult my writing career by telling their readers about this "new writer on the scene" and recommend they give my books a chance. They put this conspiracy of theirs into action on the day I launched my second book in this series by announcing through their mailing list and Facebook pages that they'd read my work and that it wasn't bad. I'll confess: I cried when I saw the posts on social media and read their newsletters with my name in big bold print. Prior to that moment, I'd sold exactly one hundred fifty-five books, total. In the two days after Dawn and Wayne recommended my work, I'd sold three thousand one hundred sixteen books, and my life changed forever.

Sometime after the launch of my second book, The Broken Chase, I met Dawn for the first time in person. We'd shared hundreds of emails and dozens of phone calls prior to that moment, but holding each other in our first hug is something I'll never forget. I've turned to her with the most ridiculous questions imaginable, and she's never laughed at me. She remembered the days of selling a handful of books and knowing nothing about how to be a real writer, and she answered my questions with patience, kindness, and grace. Along with her guidance, wisdom, and recommendation, the greatest and most priceless gift has been her beautiful, faithful friendship. We've come to love each other as if our souls were cut from the same star. Her friendship and character are two of the most steadfast constants of my life since I became a professional novelist, and I find myself turning to the faith she has in me as a writer when I question my ability to pen another line. She's been an inspiration beyond imagination for me and continues to represent the best of what humanity should be.

Dawn Lee McKenna is a brilliant storyteller, novelist, wordsmith, and poet, but behind the public persona of the remarkable writer she is, deep in her heart—where it truly matters—she is the kindest, most beautiful, selfless angel this world will ever know. Until the day we die, she'll call me "Looootenant Dan," and to me, she'll always be my Guardian Angel.

Dawn, I love you and treasure your friendship. I only wish I had some way to truly express how much you mean to me.

Special Thanks To:

My Remarkable Editor:
Sarah Flores – Write Down the Line, LLC
www.WriteDowntheLine.com

Since the first book of this series, Sarah has become such an integral part of the creation of my work that it is impossible to determine where my creation ends and hers begins. She continues to be the greatest teacher I've ever known and a magnificent friend. Through eleven novels, she has turned my error-filled stories into books enjoyed by thousands of readers all over the world. I treasure her friendship, respect her professionalism and talent, and wonder at her unending devotion and dedication to making me a better writer one book at a time. I never want to do this without her.

My friend:
Tonya Ray, Speech Pathologist Extraordinaire

Tonya is not only a dear friend, but also the wife of the real-life Stone W. Hunter. She has devoted her professional life to serving children suffering from conditions affecting their ability to speak. She has taught me more about the science of speech pathology than I ever imagined learning. She is one of the most sincerely caring, kind, and generous people I know. Her devotion to her craft is admirable and unparalleled. The character of Tonya in this novel is a larger-than-life personality who is full of energy, brilliance, and expertise. The fictional character I created is modeled after her, but I'll never possess the ability to capture the magnificent true-life character of Tonya in any fictional creation.

The Emerald Chase
CAP DANIELS

Chapter 1
Camping Trip

When the president of the United States of America calls, most people, especially people like me, answer the phone. The thought of the president calling me, a simple kid from Georgia, was almost too much for my brain to comprehend, but the world into which I'd been thrust was a world in which the unexpected was the norm.

I pressed the phone to my ear. "Chase Fulton here."

I'd spoken with the president five times on the telephone and once in person prior to that afternoon's call, so I'd come to know his tone. He was, as one would expect of the leader of the free world, rightfully confident and self-assured. When he spoke for the first time, his voice possessed neither of those qualities.

"Chase, it's the president. Is your team available, and how quickly can you be mission-ready?"

"Yes, of course, Mr. President. We can be ready in twelve hours . . . perhaps sooner, depending on the nature of the mission."

Standing in my hangar with my team around me and listening intently, I pointed toward a champagne flute and then made a slashing motion across my throat. Every member of the team placed their glasses back on the tables. Champagne and our line of work didn't blend well.

"That's good," the president said. "I can't brief you on the phone, Chase. How quickly can you be on deck at the Hagerstown Regional Airport?"

I stared at my newly rebuilt P-51 Mustang, *Penny's Secret,* and tried to mentally measure the distance from Saint Marys, Georgia, to Maryland, and came up with roughly six hundred miles. "I can be there in less than three hours, sir."

"Meet Major Redford at the Civil Air Patrol building on the northern side of the airport. What will you be flying?"

I admired my airplane, its nose adorned with the image of my beautiful wife. "My North American P-Fifty-One-D, sir."

"Well, that should be easy enough to pick out. I'll see you in three hours. Oh, and bring your analyst."

The phone went dead, and a dozen pairs of eyes stared intently.

"Cotton, I need you to change the oil while it's still hot. I have to be in Hagerstown, Maryland, in three hours."

Cotton Jackson was the Picasso of airframe and power plant mechanics. He rebuilt my Mustang after I'd gotten her shot up in a battle with a Russian spy ship. The president's call arrived only minutes after I'd flown *Penny's Secret* for the first time after the rebuild. The brand-new engine had fewer than six hours on it, and I was about to fly it six hundred miles—I still assumed—with my analyst, Skipper, in the back seat.

Cotton didn't question or hesitate. He pulled out his toolbox and went to work. The rest of the team huddled up, obviously anxious to hear what I had to say.

"Obviously, that was the president. He has a mission for us, but he wasn't willing to brief it on the phone. He wants me in Hagerstown, Maryland, ASAP. I told him I could make it in less than three hours. If my geography is right and Cotton gets the oil changed, I should make that without any issues."

"Is that all he said?" Clark Johnson asked.

Clark, until recently, had been not only my partner, but also my teacher. A former Green Beret and brilliant covert operative, Clark taught me how to stay alive when everything in the environment wanted me dead. After being abandoned on the Khyber Pass by Brinkwater Security after an ambush in which he'd broken his back, Clark endured many arduous surgeries to repair his wrecked spine. He also defeated an infection that almost took his life. Unable to continue as a field operative with me, he'd been promoted within our organization to manage the missions my team and I would execute.

"No. He told me to bring Skipper."

Skipper, the young woman who was practically a sister to me and the best and brightest young intelligence analyst in the game, stood, mouth agape. "Me? Why would the president want me there? And how does he even know I exist?"

I laughed. "I don't think there's much about us he doesn't know. Whatever he wants from us, it obviously involves you, so hit the head and grab us a couple of bottles of water."

My wife, Penny, raised an eyebrow. "Seriously? That's all he said? Come to Hagerstown and bring Skipper?"

"Yeah, that's all he said."

Forty minutes later, the oil was changed, and Skipper and I were airborne out of Saint Marys and headed north at three hundred fifty miles per hour.

"So, what do you think this is all about?"

I looked up into the mirror to see Skipper staring back at me from the back seat. "I wish I knew. He said he couldn't discuss it on the phone."

She nodded. "You do know why he wants us to go to Hagerstown instead of D.C., right?"

"No. I haven't got a clue."

She smiled. "Hagerstown is fifteen miles from Camp David."

"Oh, that makes all of this a little clearer."

We landed on runway nine and asked the ground controller for progressive taxi instructions to the Civil Air Patrol ramp.

The controller said, "Turn left at Bravo, cross Alpha, and taxi straight ahead to the ramp. The CAP is at the north end."

"Thank you, ma'am."

We followed her instructions and shut down beside a National Parks Service Jet Ranger helicopter. As we climbed out of the Mustang, a man in his mid-thirties approached, wearing a green flight suit. "You must be Chase and Elizabeth. I'm Major Mike Redford. Welcome to Hagerstown."

I shook his hand. "Nice to meet you, Major. Can you tell us what's going on?"

He smiled and walked toward the chopper. "All business . . . I like that. Come on, let's go."

We climbed aboard the Jet Ranger, Skipper in the back, and me in the left front.

Major Redford went through the startup checklist. "Okay, Mr. Fulton, you have the controls if you'd like. Climb to fifteen hundred on a hundred and ten degrees, and you'll soon get to do something only a handful of civilian pilots will ever do."

I pulled the mic to my lips. "Hagerstown Ground, this is Forestry Five-Five on the Civil Air Patrol ramp, request taxi to Alpha for VFR departure to the east."

"Forestry Five-Five, Hagerstown Ground, altimeter three-zero-zero-one, wind calm, taxi to Alpha via Bravo."

"To Alpha via Bravo, Forestry Five-Five." I then did a terrible job of hover-taxiing the helicopter across the ramp and arriving somewhere in the vicinity of taxiway Alpha. I didn't hit any hangars or parked airplanes along the way, but that's the only positive outcome of my sloppy effort.

"Been a while since you flown anything with rotors?" Redford said.

"The last time was in a stolen chopper in Latvia, if I remember correctly."

"Well, you obviously survived it, so here's hoping your landing is better than your taxiing."

I keyed the mic. "Hagerstown Tower, Forestry Five-Five, ready to go taxiway Alpha at Bravo."

"Forestry Five-Five, Hagerstown Tower, wind calm, taxiway Alpha, cleared for takeoff."

I eased the collective upward and the nose downward, and climbed away from the airport as if I knew what I was doing.

Seven minutes later, Major Redford pointed toward an open field. "See that big LZ just beyond the skeet shooting range? See if you can put us down there nice and easy without breaking anything. If you pull it off, you'll be the first civilian in this century to land a helicopter at Camp David."

Determined to make it look like I'd done it before, I approached the grassy field at sixty knots and gently bled off speed as the Earth loomed larger beneath the nose of the chopper. All of the big pieces were still attached to the helicopter when I finally got it to stop moving, but it wasn't what anyone would call a textbook landing. I was proud to be the only civilian to have done it since the turn of the twenty-first century, two-and-a-half years before.

"Not bad, Mr. Fulton. I think we'll be able to use the chopper again."

I shut down, and the three of us climbed from the helicopter. Major Redford stayed with the chopper while Skipper and I climbed aboard a waiting golf cart driven by a guy who probably had a valid set of secret service credentials in his pocket. We pulled up in front of a surprisingly normal-looking, single-story house with a cedar shake roof and manicured landscaping. The agent, who still hadn't said a word, motioned for us to follow him. He deposited us on the flagstone patio where the president of the United States was sitting in a cast-iron chair at a table that could've been bought at Walmart.

The president set his drink on the table and stood. "Welcome to Camp David and the Aspen Cabin, Chase. Thank you for coming."

I offered my hand and turned to introduce Skipper. The president ignored me and reached for her. "And you must be Elizabeth Woodley, also known as the infamous Skipper. I'm so happy you came."

Skipper didn't spend much of her life speechless, but standing three feet in front of the most powerful man in the world tends to leave most people in awe. She was no exception.

"Uh, I mean . . . thank you. I guess."

The president laughed. "We're pretty relaxed up here, Ms. Woodley. There's no reason to be nervous. Won't you have a seat. Can I get you a drink?"

Skipper froze, staring straight at me, and whispered, "The president just asked if he could get me a drink."

I was only slightly more at ease than Skipper, but I kept my composure. "No, thank you, Mr. President. We're fine."

He motioned toward a pair of chairs that matched his. "Please, please . . . sit. We have a lot to discuss."

We took our seats and waited for him to start the briefing.

A butler, the best-dressed man we'd seen since arriving, appeared with a pair of glasses. "Sweet tea?"

Skipper and I accepted the offered glasses, and I took the gesture to mean I would be flying again soon and wouldn't be served anything matching the president's cocktail.

"So," the president began, "I'm sure you're wondering why I asked you to come out here in the middle of the woods to talk about a mission."

"I am curious, sir."

He cleared his throat. "Well, it's a complex situation, to say the least. Do you know what the term *ecoterrorist* means?"

Chapter 2
Pull!

"Do you shoot, Chase? For sport, I mean."

I watched the president stare into his glass before raising his eyes to meet mine. "I enjoy shooting, sir, but I can't say I do it for sport."

He swallowed the final ounce of honey-colored liquid. "Then come with me . . . both of you. Are you both right-handed?"

He stood, and we followed suit.

"Yes, sir," I said. "We're both right-handed. But Mr. President, you didn't have us fly all the way up here on a moment's notice to shoot with you."

He walked from the patio toward the golf cart. "No, I certainly did not, but I've also not found anyone who can give me a run for my money on the skeet field. The secret service can strike a match with their sidearms, but hand them a shotgun, and they look at it like it's from outer space."

We followed him into the golf cart and arrived at the skeet field five minutes later, near where I'd pitifully landed the helicopter.

"I like the gag with the Forestry Service chopper," I said.

The president turned, his brow furrowed. "Gag? What do you mean?"

"I mean, painting a presidential helicopter up like a Forestry bird is genius."

"It's no gag," he said. "Camp David is a national park, and all national parks fall under the Forest Service, which falls under the Department of the Interior, and of course you know what that means." He looked at me expectantly.

"I'm afraid I don't know what that means."

He put his hand on my shoulder. "Son, where do you think your paychecks come from? The Department of the Interior has been the largest funnel of covert operations funds for decades. Nobody questions the budget of the National Park Service, but imagine writing an eight-million-dollar check to you from the State Department's checkbook. Why, it wouldn't take two weeks for the House Oversight Committee to pounce all over that one."

I stared at the man as if he'd just told me there was no Santa Claus.

He laughed. "Oh, my boy, you're damned good at catching and killing the bad guys . . . and even running Russian spy ships aground. But you've got a lot to learn."

"I suppose I do, Mr. President."

He elbowed me out of the cart. "Come on. Let's break some clays." He unlocked an armory of shotguns of every shape and size and ran his finger across the stocks until finally settling on one. "Here you go. This one should fit you just fine. It's a Krieghoff K-Eighty. The Germans were no match for your Mustang, but they build a fine shotgun."

He fitted Skipper with a Benelli automatic. "The Italians aren't too shabby when it comes to their scatterguns, either." The president handed me a small, yellow remote control with three buttons. "We start here at station number one, with our backs to the high-house and our belly buttons pointed toward that low-house window over there. I'll call for the bird, and you press that first button." He loaded a pair of twelve-gauge shells into his own Krieghoff, sighted down the barrel, and called, "Pull!"

I pressed the button, and a bright orange clay pigeon flew from the window above his head.

He pulled the trigger, and the clay exploded into black and orange powder. "Now press the other button on the top when I call." I nodded, and he bellowed, "Pull!"

With a press of the button, a clay flew from the low window from the distant house. The president patiently waited for the bird to fly to our side of the field, and he crushed it about ten feet in front of us.

"That's impressive, Mr. President."

He thumbed open his shotgun, and the spent shells flew across his shoulder. "Now, let's try for the pair. This time, press the bottom button. Pull!"

I pressed, and the two launchers fired simultaneously.

The president demolished the high-house bird and followed up the shot with another on the incoming clay, splitting it in half. "Ooh, I almost missed that one." He discarded the spent shells and stepped from the station. "Come on up here, Ms. Elizabeth. Load two shells . . . never more than two."

Skipper did as he instructed and took her place on the firing station.

"Now, when you call for the bird, you look for it to appear and imagine it has little feet dangling down from beneath it. Then, shoot that sucker right in those imaginary feet."

"Whatever you say." She mounted the gun. "Pull!"

I pressed, and an instant later, Skipper had killed her first clay pigeon. She wasted no time sighting on the low-house window and called, "Pull!"

I pressed again, and the clay came. Skipper couldn't wait for the bird to come to her and shot before it made half of its flight. The undamaged bird sailed past and landed unbroken on the grass.

"Dang it. I wanted to break it," she said.

The president laughed. "Don't worry. That's the best part of this game. You get one do-over. Just load one shell this time and call for that low-house bird again, but this time, be patient and let him come to you. Break him right out here in front of you, where it's nice and easy."

"Pull!" she said.

The bird came, Skipper was patient, and the clay exploded twelve feet in front of her.

"Now, shoot the pair."

She missed the high-house bird but crushed the incomer.

We shot our way around the field. I broke nineteen, Skipper hit fifteen, and the president ran the full twenty-five. We shot three more rounds, and at the end of the fourth round, the president had broken ninety-eight out of a hundred. I broke eighty-six, and Skipper finished with an excellent score of seventy broken birds on her first attempt at skeet shooting.

"Well, I guess I was wrong about you giving me some competition," the president said, "but with a little coaching and some practice, I'd have my hands full with you."

"I was just being polite, Mr. President. I didn't want to out-shoot you on your home field. That would've been rude," I said.

"Ha, rude indeed. Now I suppose we should talk about these ecoterrorists." He lowered his chin and looked over his shooting glasses. "Eco or not, they're still terrorists."

We locked the shotguns away and rode the golf cart back to Aspen Cabin.

"Chase, my brother's wife is a Meriwether. Her people are from Austin, and they've done very well for themselves in a number of businesses through the years. Cattle, real estate, and of course, the oil business." He paused as if waiting for a reaction, but I gave none. "Anyway, the oil business gets a lot of bad press, and a lot of people like to say it's the devil's blood, but for now,

Chase, it's the best mass fuel source the world has. That's not likely to change in my lifetime, but it may in yours. There are some smart people looking for alternative sources of energy—solar, wind, etcetera—but nothing, and I mean nothing, comes close to crude oil when it comes to satisfying the world's thirst for energy. This is not a speech to sell you on the merits of the oil business, mind you. I'm telling you this so you can understand why this particular issue is so delicate."

I crossed my legs. "I'm listening, Mr. President."

He coughed and repositioned himself in his chair. "There's an oil rig two hundred miles off New Orleans called the Pan America Rig. It's an old rig, but one of the most productive in the Gulf of Mexico. It pumps a hundred thirty thousand barrels of crude and over a hundred twenty million cubic feet of natural gas every day."

I watched him as he awaited my reaction. "I don't know anything about the oil business, sir. I'm afraid those numbers don't mean anything to me."

He shook his head. "The numbers aren't all that important. It's a highly productive rig and has been for years. It's expected to continue producing in that range for another decade, or maybe longer. Take it from me, Chase, that's a lot of oil. Just the oil alone, not including the natural gas, is over four million dollars per day."

I let out a low whistle. "That brings it into perspective."

He took a long breath and let it escape his lips slowly. "That brings us to the point. The rig is under siege."

"Under siege?"

"Yes. There's a group of ecoterrorists who've overtaken the rig, and they're holding the entire workforce hostage."

"Why?"

The president huffed. "To make a point. Oil is bad, and it's ruining the environment. They're threatening to blow up the rig if I don't cease all offshore drilling in the next thirty days."

"Why hasn't any of this been on the news?" I asked.

He closed his eyes. "For the first time in modern history, we've been able to keep something out of the media, but it's only temporary, I'm afraid. There's no way to keep it quiet forever."

"I see. Can't you order a SEAL team to retake the rig? I'm sure the SEALs could do it in a matter of hours."

"Therein lies the rub, my boy. If I send a team of SEALs in to rescue the oil rig workers and they end up killing some, or all of the terrorists, I'm on the political hook for using the U.S. military to save one of my sister-in-law's family's oil rigs. Two thousand four is an election year. I don't have to tell you what the other side's campaign slogan will be if I do that."

The reality of the world into which I'd willingly stepped was about to come crashing down around me. Dominic Fontana, who happened to be Clark's father and my previous handler before Clark's promotion, warned me about getting caught up in politics, but I didn't listen. Both he and the president were right. I had a lot to learn.

"What are you asking me to do, Mr. President?"

He licked his lips. "I'm asking you to take a meeting with Meriwether Energy Systems, and to give some very serious consideration to cashing their check . . . their very large check for doing whatever is necessary to liberate that oil rig. I can't be seen having a hand in any of this. I'm sure you can understand that."

"Mr. President, I have a team of four men, including myself, a sniper, a giant, and a former combat controller. I don't have the manpower to pull off something like that."

He smiled. "But you have something other teams don't have. . . ." He pointed at Skipper. "You have her."

Skipper spoke for the first time. "What do I have to do with any of this? I'm just an analyst. I don't know anything about rescuing an oil rig full of hostages."

His smile didn't fade. "You may not know how to rescue them, but from what I hear, that brain of yours can do things a thousand SEALs couldn't do. Just take the meeting and consider their offer. That's all I'm asking." He leaned forward in his chair and locked eyes with me. "Do this for me, Chase, and you can call the score even."

The president had lent me a boatful of Navy SEALs as guardian angels when the Russian Foreign Intelligence Service was trying to kill me. He'd tasked a nuclear submarine to spirit Hunter, Anya, and me out of the Black Sea. He'd even given me a three-million-dollar Mark V fast patrol boat. Just like Dominic had warned, my chickens had just come home to roost.

"I'll take the meeting, but I can't promise I have the assets to pull off a mission like this."

"That's all I can ask, Chase. Thank you for coming all the way up here just to shoot a round of skeet with me. Maybe next time, you can bring Ms. Penny and spend the weekend. That is, of course, if we win the election next year."

* * *

I opted to have Major Redford do the flying on the way back to Hagerstown. I had enough to think about without trying to convince my brain I could fly a helicopter.

Back in the Mustang, Skipper and I leveled off at fourteen thousand feet with the oxygen cannulas under our noses.

I glanced into the mirror and met her eyes. "So, what do you think?"

She rolled her eyes. "I think the same thing that happened to me in Miami is happening to you now."

Five years earlier, Skipper had been held against her will by a Miami pornographer. With the help of Anya Burinkova, a Russian SVR officer, I rescued her and watched a scared, confused little girl grow into a brilliant woman with a brain the size of Montana and a natural talent as an intelligence analyst. She'd become an invaluable part of my team, and even though she occasionally still sounded like a kid, I trusted her with my life and valued her opinion.

"I get the same feeling. But I'm stuck."

"No, *you're* not stuck. *We're* stuck. We're all in this together."

The reasons I was thankful for Skipper just kept piling "I'm afraid this one may be more than we can handle. There's only so much the five of us can do."

"You've forgotten how to count," she said. "You, me, Singer, Mongo, Hunter, Clark, and Anya make seven. I don't know how many so-called ecoterrorists it takes to hold an oil rig hostage, but I think the seven of us could handle two or three dozen."

"I love your confidence, but you'll be in the ops center, Clark will be in his office, and I don't know how I feel about taking Anya on this one."

Skipper said, "You don't have to trust her, but she did save my life . . . twice."

Chapter 3
Classified

Back at Bonaventure Plantation, my home and base of operations for whatever I'd become, I called a meeting.

"I know, I know. All of you are dying to find out what happened this afternoon, but before we get into that, there's some housekeeping that has to be done." Every eye in the library focused on me. "I've been asked to take a meeting with a company in Texas."

The anxiety on the faces of my team made my stomach turn inside out. "This one is delicate. It's going to involve a potential operation that can never, under any circumstance, be discussed outside the team."

I locked eyes with Anya Burinkova, the former Russian SVR officer who'd not only been sent to seduce, entrap, and potentially kill me six years before, but had also been the woman I'd fallen head-over-heels in love with before naiveté gave way to reason and reality. "Anya, I'm not sure I can brief you in on this one—at least not yet."

She pressed her lips into a solid, horizontal line and nodded. "I understand. I am sorry I put you in position like this." As silently as a cat, she rose from her seat and slipped through the heavy oak door.

I waited to hear her footsteps grow faint, but she made no sound beyond the door. "As I said, this one is touchy. It'll get highly political and may not be directly in defense of the country. If anyone wants out, I'll never hold it against you. You can walk out now or anytime, but regardless, everything about this mission is classified and shall never leave this circle. Understood?"

Hunter, my partner and former Air Force combat controller, was the first to speak. "Chase, everything we do is exactly what you're describing. We don't talk. I won't speak for the rest of the team, but as for me, if you're in, I'm in."

Singer, our Southern Baptist sniper, licked his lips. "Is it illegal?"

I blinked repeatedly, unsure how to answer him. "I don't know yet, but maybe."

He nodded slowly. "Okay. I'm with you and Hunter."

Mongo, our resident giant and Anya's most recent love interest, shot a look at the door and bit his lip. The moral battle the big man was fighting inside himself was obviously tearing at him more violently than any combat he'd ever endured.

I raised my finger. "Don't say anything yet, Mongo. I understand. Just give me your word that you'll listen to my briefing before you decide."

"That's not necessary, Chase. My loyalty is to you first. I'm in."

Clark, our handler and technically our boss, said, "Do you think you and I should have a talk privately before you do whatever this is?"

I shook my head. "No, but I understand why you'd say that. If we do this, it's off the books and not an official op. I won't be asking for support or approval from the Board."

The Board was the highest echelon of the organization for which I worked. All decisions about sanctioned operations came from them.

Clark raised his eyebrows. "It doesn't exactly sound like you're doing this of your own free will, College Boy."

I sighed. "Let's just say I have some debts to pay, and if I do this, the slate is clean."

Dominic warned me about making deals with the president, but I didn't listen. I was learning the hard way not to dance with the devil.

"Okay, I get it," Clark said. "I can't say I'm in yet, but I'm definitely not out either. Let's hear your sales pitch."

I took a long, deliberate breath. "There's an oil rig in the Gulf of Mexico called the Pan America Rig. It's been seized by a group of ecoterrorists, and they're holding it and the workers hostage. The rig belongs to a Texas company called Meriwether Energy Systems."

Hunter interrupted. "As in Caroline Meriwether, the president's sister-in-law?"

"Yeah," I muttered. "That's the one."

Clark exhaled a long, exasperated breath. "Oh, for God's sake. You can't be serious. The president ordered you to rescue the hostages to save his sister-in-law's oil rig?"

"No, he didn't order me to do anything. He simply asked me to have a meeting with Meriwether Energy and listen to what they have to say."

He slapped his knee. "I can tell you what they're going to say. They're going to offer you a huge check with a bunch of zeros at the end to risk our lives saving their cash cow in the Gulf."

I let him rant. Interrupting him would serve no purpose.

"Clark, I told him I'd take the meeting. That's all. Nothing beyond that . . . yet."

Disappointment overtook his face. "This is a bad idea."

"I'm taking the meeting, and I want you with me. All of you. We're a team, and we'll make this decision as a team. If anyone wants out, the door is open with no hard feelings. Trust me, I'd understand if you walked away now."

No one moved.

"Okay, I'll make the call tomorrow. Be ready for wheels up and bound for Texas by mid-morning."

Everyone stood to leave the library—everyone except Clark, of course. He pulled the door closed after the other three disappeared. "Just listen. The first part is coming from your boss. The second part is coming from your friend and former partner. Got it?"

"Sure," I said. "I expected to hear from both of those guys."

"First, this is a terrible idea. Everything about it is terrible. There's no way for this to turn into anything good. You crawled in bed with a dog, and now you're scratching fleas of your own." Clark closed his eyes for several seconds and then smiled. "Now, if we get to save a couple hundred oil rig workers and kick the shit out of a bunch of wannabe gangsters, I can't think of anything that'd be more fun."

I chuckled. "I know, but you're a broken-down old man. You'll have to watch from the cheap seats."

* * *

Alone with Penny, I broke my own rule about keeping the briefing inside the circle. "I'm going to Texas tomorrow to meet with an oil company about a problem they're having on one of their oil rigs in the Gulf. The president asked me to take the meeting."

"Do you know anything about oil rigs?"

I loved how she rarely minced words. If she thought it, most likely, it would come out of her mouth.

"I don't know anything about oil rigs, but I owe him, so I'm taking the meeting."

She frowned. "There's more to this than you're saying."

"There always is," I admitted. "In this case, it involves some hostages on the rig, and the company who owns the rig belongs to the president's sister-in-law's family."

"Oh," she mouthed.

* * *

Twelve hours later, I was on the phone with Thomas Meriwether, CEO of Meriwether Energy Systems.

"Good morning, Mr. Meriwether. My name is Chase Fulton. I met with your brother-in-law outside of D.C. yesterday, and he asked me to give you a call concerning the Pan America."

"What time can you be in Austin, Mr. Fulton?"

I like men who don't waste time with unnecessary pleasantries, but Thomas Meriwether didn't waste time with anything.

I said, "The only airplane I have that can carry my team is a Caravan, so it'll take me seven hours."

He didn't hesitate. "Where are you?"

"I'm in Saint Marys, Georgia."

"I'll have the Citation there in two hours."

I found the rest of the team on the gallery overlooking the North River. "We'll be wheels up in two hours. Meriwether is sending a Citation jet to pick us up."

No one seemed surprised, but Mongo stood over my six-foot-four-inch frame like a giant oak and whispered, "We need to talk."

"Sure, let's take a walk."

We walked across the yard and planted ourselves in a pair of Adirondack chairs beneath the gazebo.

"Okay, let's hear it," I said.

He glanced toward the house, then back at me. "I've been with her every day for over six months, Chase. I bugged her phone, put a key tracker on her computer, and never let her out of my sight. If she's feeding the Russians anything, she's doing it telepathically."

"So, you trust her?"

He answered immediately. "I do."

My eyes wandered toward the house. "She's been trained to manipulate men. You know as well as anybody what the Russians are capable of."

"I do, and I'm not saying Anya couldn't manipulate anyone she wanted, but I've seen no signs of her doing anything to gain my trust. I really believe she's glad to be an American."

"Are you saying we should take her with us to Austin?"

"No, not necessarily, but I'm saying don't rule her out if we need an extra gun-toter on this one."

I let his words soak in. "Okay, we'll take the meeting, and if we take the job, I'll consider bringing her in. If this thing is what I think it is, we'll need all the shooters we can find . . . and then some."

* * *

The Meriwether Energy Systems Citation taxied to a stop on the ramp, but the pilots didn't shut down the engines. A fifty-something man in a well-tailored suit descended the stairs and motioned for us to come aboard. We did, and the pilots were taxiing before the door was secured.

"Good morning, gentlemen. My name is Langston. I'm one of the security executives at Meriwether. Thank you for coming. We'll be back in Austin in less than two hours. Enjoy the ride, and if you need or want anything, Deborah will be serving as soon as we level off in cruise."

Clark tapped my knee. "We've got to get us one of these."

"We can't afford one of these," I said.

He scanned the interior of the luxurious jet. "Maybe they'll give us this one if we get their rig back in one piece."

"Maybe."

Langston was right. We were in a blacked-out Chevy Suburban two hours later, being whisked through the streets of Austin.

Meriwether Energy Systems consumed a twenty-six-story building on Cesar Chavez Street, overlooking the Colorado River. We were ushered to Thomas Meriwether's office on the top floor, and Thomas welcomed us as if we had something he badly wanted. Unfortunately, *we* didn't have it—the terrorists had it. But I was pretty sure we could get it back for him if his sales pitch and offer were strong enough.

Chapter 4
It's Not an Offer

"There's no reason to beat around the bush," I said. "Let's get to it. You've lost an oil rig, and you want it back, right?"

Thomas Meriwether dug the heels of both hands into his temples and clenched his eyes. His thousand-dollar haircut didn't survive the encounter with grace. "No, no, we've not lost it. We've merely . . ." He sprang to his feet, stormed to the floor-to-ceiling window, and pounded his fist against the heavy glass. "You'd think having a damned brother-in-law in the White House would garner enough favor to get a platoon of SEALs. I mean, these people are terrorists, for God's sake. This thing could be over in an afternoon."

I leaned back in the most relaxed posture I could assume. "Is that what you want, Mr. Meriwether? A platoon of SEALs?"

He spun on his heel, the lines on his face deepening with every breath. "I want those animals off my rig. Do you have any idea how much those bastards are costing me? Over four million a day in crude and two-and-a-half million in gas. Seven million dollars a day."

As it turned out, there was one way I could appear more relaxed. I placed the heel of my left boot on top of his desk and crossed my right leg over my left. "Let me guess. We're not what you expected."

He motioned wildly toward us with his outstretched hand. "Just look at the lot of you. You're a bunch of mercenary cowboys."

"Have you got something against cowboys, Mr. Meriwether? Something tells me the great state of Texas has a different opinion of them than you do."

Back to pounding on the window he went. I had the feeling he'd jump out if his pounding resulted in a hole big enough for him to fit through.

"Look at me, Mr. Meriwether. I agree with you. The SEALs could have your rig back in your hands in a matter of hours, but that's the fastest way to ensure your brother-in-law will be out of a job next January. We're not SEALs. We're also not mercenaries or cowboys. What we are is five guys." I pointed at each of my teammates, in turn. "That's Singer, he's Mongo, that's Hunter, and he's Clark. You already know my name, but what you don't know is that in this room, there are one hundred forty-four combat missions and over a hundred years of downrange experience between us. We've been shot, stabbed, blown up, left for dead, and abandoned in parts of the world you've never heard of. We've been a lot of places and done a lot of nasty things, but there's one thing none of us has ever done. . . ." He turned from the window, and I pointed at Singer. "How many missions have you failed?"

Singer cast his eyes toward the ceiling and then shook his head.

"Mongo, how about you? How many have you failed?"

The giant shrugged. "None, boss."

"And Hunter, what's your failure rate?"

He motioned toward the other two with his chin. "I'm tied with them at zero."

"And finally, Clark. How many check marks do you have in the failure column?"

Through his trademark crooked smile, he said, "I don't even have that column, let alone any checks in it."

"You see . . ." I slid a nameplate on his desk around with the toe of my boot. "Thomas J. Meriwether the Third, in our line of work, failure means death." I pointed toward Mongo. "You see, he's got a Russian supermodel waiting at home for him." Moving my gaze to Singer, I said, "And that man has a Baptist church choir and a monastery full of Jesuit monks to go home to."

Singer said, "They're not Jesuits, Chase. They're Trappist monks. But the choir is Baptist."

I motioned toward Hunter. "Him . . . well, I have no idea what he has to go home to. All he does is fight and train to fight. And Clark there, he's the old man of the team. He's got more bullet holes in him than you've got fingers. He's also got a gorgeous girlfriend who's barely half his age, and she can't wait for him to come home. And me, I've got a pecan plantation and the prettiest North Texas girl you've ever seen waiting for me, so none of us has any interest in dying anytime soon. What that means to you, Thomas J. Meriwether the Third, is that we don't fail. If you want a platoon of SEALs, we're not your guys, but if you want your rig back. . . ." I stared through the wall of glass overlooking the Colorado River. "Well, if you want your rig back, stop beating on that window, and tell us what's going on out there in the Gulf. If you're honest with us, we'll tell you whether or not we can do it. If we can't, maybe you can keep lobbying for those SEALs."

Instead of returning to his high-back leather chair, Meriwether leaned against the front of his desk and stared down at my boots still propped on the edge.

I didn't budge. "Who has your rig, Thomas?"

He looked away. "I don't know. All I know is they're good. They've silenced all communication from the rig—internet, sat-phones, the whole nine yards. Nothing is getting off that rig, and nothing can get near it."

He walked back around his island-sized desk and spun a monitor toward us. With a dozen keystrokes and a few mouse clicks, a video of an offshore oil rig filled the screen, and the speakers crackled as a computer-generated voice said, "Listen closely. I have taken your environmental disaster of a monstrosity that you call Pan America. I control every inch of the facility. I have one hundred seventy of your slaves, and production has been halted. It will not restart . . . ever. These are my demands. Notice, I did not say terms. Terms are negotiable. Demands are not. You will halt production from all twenty-four of your off-shore, planet-killing, greed-feeding factories of filth, and your brother-in-law will declare a moratorium on all offshore oil pro-duction within thirty days or I will sink this rig and all one hun-dred seventy of your slaves with it. If you make any effort to approach the rig, I will destroy it. If you notify any law enforce-ment or military entity, I will destroy your rig. If you make any effort to subvert or deny my demands, I will destroy your rig. Thirty days . . . not a minute longer." The screen went dark.

"One hundred ninety million dollars a day," Meriwether said. "That's what it costs to stop production. One hundred ninety million dollars per day. If he sinks the Pan America, it'll cost a billion dollars and a year's time to replace it."

"Tell me their names," I said.

Meriwether scowled. "I told you I don't know who they are. That message is all I have."

"No, Thomas. Tell me the names of the one hundred seventy employees being held hostage on the Pan America Rig."

He jerked his head as if he were having a seizure. "What dif-ference does *that* make?"

"How many of them have families?" I demanded. "I'm quite sure those families would think it makes a great deal of difference if the CEO of Meriwether Energy Systems knows the names of the men and women being held hostage on *his* rig."

Back to his feet he jolted. "You're focusing on the wrong thing. These people want to make a political statement."

I pulled my feet from his desk and let them crash to the floor. An instant later, I was towering over him with my chin only inches from his five-thousand-dollar bifocals. "If these people wanted to make a statement, they wouldn't have demanded your silence, and they wouldn't have sent a computer-generated video voice message. They'd have posted it all over the internet and called every news outlet they could find. The last thing in the world they would demand is silence."

He took a step back. "Just what are you suggesting, Mr. Fulton?"

"I'm not suggesting anything. I'm saying plainly that you know a lot more about what's really going on out there on that rig than you're telling us. Remember what I said. If you're honest with us, we'll tell you whether or not we can help. You're hiding something. Now, what else do you know?"

He licked his lips and ran a manicured hand through his salt-and-pepper hair. "Greg Peterson, John Hampton, his son Junior Hampton, Gary Carter, Carolyn Stillwater, Jason McCarter, Pete McClinton. How many more names do you want? I can't name everyone on that rig. I have over ten thousand employees. But I can name every man and woman on that rig who've been with us for more than five years."

I stared down at him. "Exactly when and how did you receive that video message?"

"Four days ago, on a CD. It was delivered by a courier and addressed specifically to me. My secretary opened it and found another sealed envelope inside the outer package, marked personal and confidential for my eyes only."

"Do you still have the packaging?"

"I don't know. I still have the inner envelope, but I don't know about the larger packaging."

I turned to my team, and one by one, locked eyes with each man. They all responded with a single, sharp nod.

"We'll need everything, including the name of the courier company and the courier, if possible. I need a complete list of every human on that rig, their families, addresses, phone numbers, and medical conditions. I need the address of every house, condo, or treehouse you own, as well as every email address and telephone number you have access to. If you withhold any information we request, try to hide anything from any member of my team, or lie to me about one single thing, we walk away, and you owe me the full fee, plus expenses."

Meriwether fell into his chair. "How do I know you won't take my money and run?"

"Because I don't get paid until I return your rig to you."

He placed his hands on his desk. "How much?"

"One percent," I said.

"One percent of what?"

I returned to my seat. "One percent of what it would cost to replace the Pan America Rig."

"That's ten million dollars. You must be out of your mind."

My boots found their spot on top of his desk again. "No, ten million dollars is one percent of what it would cost to build and install a new rig. The cost, as you so eloquently put it earlier, would be a billion dollars plus a year's time. A year's time at seven million dollars in lost production per day is about two-point-five billion dollars. Add that to the one-billion-dollar construction cost, and that brings the total to three-point-five billion dollars. Our fee is one percent of that figure. That's just thirty-five million dollars . . . plus expenses. We'll cap the expenses at five million. You'll make that in less than a week of production after we get your rig back."

His eyes narrowed, but mine did not. While he stewed in the financial calculations, I hooked a Birdseye Maple humidor with my boot and pulled it toward the edge of the desk. Inside were a couple hundred high-quality, hand-rolled Cuban cigars. I bit the tip from a gorgeous Maduro Diadema that must have been ten inches long, and I toasted the foot with my XIKAR lighter. The aromatic white smoke billowed, forming a plume over my head instead of the angelic halo I'd hoped for. I carefully selected the Diadema, a size cigar that is only lit when the smoker has no time constraints and can spend ninety minutes enjoying the experience.

Meriwether's elbows landed on his desk with a thud, and the heels of his hands found his temples once again. From the color of the man's forehead, his blood pressure must've been off the charts.

I slid a business card across his desk. "The five million goes into the first account. I'll draw against that for expenses. The thirty million goes into the escrow account at the bottom. The remaining five million will be adjusted based on how much of the expense account we use, and you can write me a check for the balance when we're finished."

"You have me over a barrel, so to speak, Mr. Fulton. Is there any room for negotiation in your offer?"

"It's not an offer, Thomas. It's the price. If it's too steep, you can always call the White House and place an order for that platoon of Navy SEALs."

I lifted the humidor from his desk, opened the lid, and offered a cigar to each of my team. No one declined. When I turned back to Meriwether, he had the telephone handset pressed against his face, and he was reading the account numbers to someone who apparently had the ability to wire thirty-five million dollars to the Cayman Islands.

When he replaced the phone in its cradle, I said, "That Citation jet you sent to pick us up . . . Do you own or lease that?"

He shook his head as if he didn't understand the question.

The spacious office was filling with white cigar smoke.

Meriwether squinted. "It's a lease."

I took a long draw from my cigar and slowly allowed the smoke to float from my mouth. "Good. That'll save you some money. We'll take the jet and crew, minus Langston, of course, for the entirety of the operation."

"Fine," he muttered.

"Oh, there is one more thing. We'll need the personnel files of everyone in your security branch and complete financial statements for all of the officers of the company, including you."

"That's going to take some time. It's not like we have that information just lying around."

I pulled the cigar from my mouth, spinning it slowly between my fingers and admiring the quality of the roll. "No problem. I'm sure I have at least an hour left in this fine cigar. I assume you prefer we start right away, so let me know when that information is available."

Chapter 5
I-O-K

The files and financials I needed weren't as difficult to round up as Meriwether predicted, and we were airborne aboard our new Citation jet before I'd finished my Cuban Diadema.

Clark sat with his boots off and his feet propped in the seat across from him. "I knew you'd figure out a way to get us a Citation."

I followed his lead and removed my boots, assuming a similar posture. "This one's not ours."

He looked around the opulent cabin. "It is 'til we get that rig back."

Deborah strolled by. "Would you gentlemen care for anything?"

I looked up at the uniformed flight attendant. "I forgot you were part of the crew. I'd love an old-fashioned with some good bourbon."

She nodded and turned to Clark.

"I'll have what he's having, except hold the old-fashioned part. Just the bourbon for me, please."

"Don't get used to this," I said. "It's only temporary."

He pretended to count on the tips of his fingers. "I don't

know. With thirty-five million bucks in the bank, this thing is just a drop in the bucket."

I raised my eyebrow. "The thirty-five million exists only *if* we get the rig back."

Deborah materialized between us with two tumblers, and just as quickly, she vanished.

Clark raised his glass toward mine. "How many check marks do *you* have in that failure column, College Boy?"

I touched my glass to his. "Thanks to you, that column is clean."

He looked around the cabin again. "Yep . . . just a drop in the bucket."

* * *

Back at Bonaventure, Skipper wasted no time reaching for the personnel files and financials. "I'll have a summary for you ASAP."

I held the briefcase containing the documents. "We need some satellite imagery before you dive into those."

She snatched the case from my hand. "It's already streaming live on your monitor, and I'm running scans for any shots from the past four days. I'll let you know as soon as I get anything. Now, leave me alone. I've got work to do."

"You're pretty good at this," I said. "But I'd really like to see some shots from immediately before, during, and after the siege."

"I'm on it."

The team, including Penny and Anya, huddled up in the library and I started my briefing.

"Here's what we know. Better yet, let's start with what we believe. Thomas Meriwether told us the rig was seized on Monday afternoon and that this video message he received was delivered by a courier shortly afterwards." I played the video message twice, listening intently to the computer-generated voice.

Everyone in the room appeared to be equally focused on the voice.

Penny grimaced. "Play it one more time."

I did as she asked and waited somewhat impatiently for her to share her thoughts.

She furrowed her brow and stared at the edge of the desk. "I'm not a speech pathologist, but I don't think that's a computer-generated voice. I think I detected a little inflection. Computers don't inflect. I think it's an electronically modulated voice."

Anya was nodding as Penny spoke, and I let my eyes meet hers. "I also hear same."

"Why didn't any of us hear that?" I asked, scanning my team.

"Maybe it's an X and Y chromosome thing," Singer offered. "Those two are missing the Y."

"How can we find out for sure?" I asked Penny.

"Maybe Skipper can dig into it and find out, but I have a friend from Baylor who really is a speech pathologist. If she heard it, she'd know instantly."

"I suppose there's no chance your friend has a security clearance, is there?"

Penny frowned. "She works with children with speech impediments, so I can't imagine why she would."

I turned to Clark. "You're the boss. How do you feel about releasing this audio to a set of ears without a clearance?"

He threw up his hands. "I'm not the boss on this one. I'm just a grunt. This one is yours."

I scratched at the two-day growth on my chin. "In that case, let me rephrase the question, Your Honor. I'd like the thoughts of a grunt concerning letting a civilian set of ears hear that audio."

Clark pointed at me. "Now, that's a much better question. If I were in charge, I'd have Skipper give it a shot before we start involving anyone outside this house, regardless of them having a clearance."

Penny hopped to her feet. "I'll get her."

Instead of bounding up the stairs of the antebellum plantation house as I'd expected, my goofy wife stuck her head outside the library door and yelled, "Skipper, get down here! We need you!"

Skipper appeared in the doorway and scowled. "I'm busy. This better be important."

I clicked on the video and turned up the volume. "Give this a listen, and tell us what you think about the voice, not about the content of the message."

When the audio ended, Skipper said, "It sounds like some guy talking through one of those electronic voice-changing things we used to play with."

I glanced at Singer. "I think you were right about the chromosome thing. It still sounds like a computer to me."

Skipper huffed. "Is that all you wanted? I've got a lot of work to do."

"Actually, I want to know if you can run that audio through some software and determine if it is what you thought or if it's a computer-generated voice. And if it is an altered human voice, can you filter out the distortion and give us a clean version of how the voice really sounds?"

Skipper stared at the ceiling for a long moment. "I want to say yes, but it would take a really long time. I can probably find somebody at NSA who could do it."

"No, I don't want to involve the National Security Agency. Do you know any contractors who could do it?"

She shrugged. "I can't think of anyone, but I really need to get back to work on those financials."

I waved her away and looked back at Penny. "Get your friend on the phone."

Penny stepped away.

I said, "I think I can cut the audio to play only the nonthreatening sections so the speech pathologist will only hear the benign parts. If she can clean it up and let us hear how this guy sounds, that may give us some insight into who these guys are."

Clark nodded. "I like it. Now, how about that satellite feed?"

I clicked on the streaming video and turned the monitor around so everyone could see it. We watched the video for several minutes, taking careful note of every detail. One of my favorite parts of any operation was about to happen. Everyone in the room had a specialty, and each perceived the world through the lens of that specialty.

"All right, let's hear it. What did you see?"

Singer, our death-from-a-distance sniper, was first. "They don't have any overwatch. Just the four—I think I only saw four—roving guards."

Clark asked, "How close would we have to get you to take out two of the roving guards?"

"If I'm on a boat, it depends on the conditions of the water. If it's rough, I'd need to be inside five hundred yards. The smoother it is, the farther I could make the shot. Do the rules of engagement on this one authorize us to shoot first?"

"There are no rules of engagement yet. We're still in the planning stage," I said.

Hunter spoke up. "I'd like to see some schematics of that rig, but it looks like we could gain access from beneath without being seen. I know this sounds crazy, but if we could get Anya on that rig from below, I think she could neutralize the roving guards in less than an hour."

Anya glared at him. "Half hour . . . no more."

Hunter bowed respectfully from his seat. "Forgive me, but half an hour is technically less than an hour, so I was right."

Clark intervened. "Cut it out. We need to watch long enough to determine the guard schedules. If they're shorthanded, the guards are going to get tired and complacent toward the end of a long watch."

Mongo said, "Roughnecks—that's what oil rig workers are called. They're not easy people to take hostage. Imagine trying to take a hundred guys like me hostage. Whoever these people are must've made quite a show of force to get the roughnecks to co-operate and not fight back. Of course, not everyone on the rig is a roughneck. There are some engineers and office folks. I guess you wouldn't have much trouble out of those guys, but the boys outside with grease under their fingernails aren't exactly the sub-missive types."

"I hadn't thought of that," I admitted. "Where do you think they're holding all those hostages?"

"If it were me," Mongo said, "I'd lock them inside common areas where they didn't have access to tools or communications gear."

"By the way," I asked, "how do you know so much about oil rig workers?"

"I used to be one. I worked on the rigs between my junior and senior year in high school and for a couple months before I shipped off to boot camp after graduation."

I slapped my forehead. "You've got to tell me these things, Mongo. You have I-O-K that none of the rest of us have."

He screwed up his face. "I-O-K?"

"Intimate operational knowledge," came the multi-voiced re-sponse.

Mongo shrugged. "I just assumed you guys knew my past."

"Don't assume. If you know something we don't, speak up . . . always."

He nodded, and I waited patiently. Mongo stared back at me as if he had no idea why I was waiting.

"Tell us about the rig, Mongo."

"Oh, sure. Well, obviously, it's a semisubmersible—"

"No, that's not obvious. Break it down for us."

"All right. They built that rig in some shipyard, probably in Norway or somewhere over there, and then towed it to the Gulf. That one's a dynamic positioning rig instead of an anchored rig."

I held up a hand. "Wait a minute. Are you telling me that thing isn't anchored to the bottom?"

"Yeah, that's what dynamic positioning means. It holds its position with eight or maybe ten Azipod-type propellers and a high-tech GPS system. The only thing connecting that rig to the bottom is the casing. That one's probably thirty-six inches all the way down to the blowout preventer at the top of the wellhead."

"Hang on," I said. "You're talking over my head. Casing, blowout preventer, wellhead. But we'll get to all of that. What interests me most is that it holds its position via GPS."

Mongo nodded. "Yeah. There's no other way to hold it still."

I stared at the absolutely stationary rig on the monitor. "All of you were there when Meriwether said they'd cut off all communications from the rig, including satellite phones. I'm not a commo genius, but I know basically how GPS works. The unit onboard the vessel—in this case, the oil rig—receives the satellite signal and compares its arrival time to the time the signal left the satellite. The ability to measure that time difference accurately from multiple satellites is the heart of the GPS system. That means the rig is receiving GPS satellite signals. They just can't send any signals from the rig."

Everyone leaned in, so I continued. "Disrupting the Wi-Fi signal would be easy. All they'd have to do is disable the routers, but stopping sat-phone signals wouldn't be so easy. That would take a jamming system and a power source. They've got all the power they could ever need with the generators, but unless they're operating autonomously, they must have some method of communication with a support network feeding them information. That's all I've got. I'm open for ideas, though. Does anyone think I'm wrong?"

Everyone shook their head.

I said, "I don't know why any of that matters, but it's something we didn't know before now."

"I'll tell you why it matters," Clark said. "It gives us a way to receive information when we're on the rig. If Skipper can figure out how to broadcast a signal from the GPS satellites, we can receive the signal. If she can feed us data and watch our reactions in real time, that's a rudimentary form of communication. It's not as good as voice coms, but it's better than nothing."

I pointed at Clark. "Now, that's something I like. What happens if the GPS fails on the rig? Will the rig drift off the drill site? And will that sever the casing, sending millions of gallons of crude oil into the Gulf?"

Everyone turned to Mongo.

The big man said, "That's more than one question. First, if the GPS signal was lost, the rig would initiate an INS."

"Inertial navigation system?" I asked.

"Exactly. It's a gyro-driven system designed to detect rig movement based on highly sensitive gyros made of beryllium and spinning in a vacuum. It's the rigidity-in-space concept. We all learned about that in high school physics, right?"

No one seemed to know what he was talking about, but that didn't slow him down.

"Anyway, the rig would try to hold itself still using the INS. They're obviously not processing crude because no one is moving on deck. The rig is shut down, so crude isn't flowing. The casing would decouple from the rig, but it's connected with tethers so it wouldn't collapse to the seafloor. The rig would hold its position close enough until the GPS signal could be restored, and they could recouple the casing."

"So, no oil would be lost into the Gulf?"

Mongo shook his head. "Maybe a few gallons of residual crude might escape, but it wouldn't be a massive spill."

My wheels were turning as a plan came together in my head. "What sort of systems do you think they have to detect surface traffic?"

"I don't know. I was a roughneck. I moved heavy stuff and stayed filthy. When I was on the rig, the only time I went inside was to sleep."

I pointed at the monitor. "You weren't on *that* rig, were you?"

"No, but I was on one of its sister platforms. It's an old design, but it works."

I smiled. "So, you've been on a rig exactly like this one?"

"Yeah, just like it."

"Again, Mongo . . . you've *got* to tell us this stuff."

"I just did," he said.

Everyone laughed as Penny came through the door. "Uh, why is everyone laughing? I don't think there's anything funny about any of this."

"It's just Mongo," I said. "He forgot to mention, until now, that before he went in the service, he used to be a roughneck on an oil rig just like the Pan America."

Penny turned to the giant. "Mongo, you've *got* to tell us these things."

He held up his manhole-cover-sized hands in surrender. "I just did. Get off my case."

I interrupted their banter. "What did your friend have to say about the audio?"

She reclaimed her seat. "You're never going to believe it. She met and fell in love with a guy at Fort Hood who's a Blackhawk pilot."

"Penny, I need to know about the audio, not her love life."

"Keep your pants on, big boy. I'm getting to that. So, she met the Blackhawk pilot, fell in love, and got married. The Army moved him to Fort Rucker, where he's now an instructor pilot. And this is the good part. Tonya went to work for USAARL."

"What's that?" I asked, losing my patience.

"That's the best part," she said. "It's the U.S. Army Aeromedical Research Laboratory."

In unison, Clark, Hunter, and I said, "She's got a clearance."

Penny smiled. "She's got a clearance."

"How soon can she be here?" I asked.

"As soon as you send that shiny new Citation jet of yours to get her. They live in Dothan, Alabama, and the city just happens to have a nice long runway."

Chapter 6
Maybe America

I dispatched Penny and the Citation and reconvened the planning session. "While we're waiting for Tonya, we need a plan to get the Mark V to the Gulf."

The president, through some mysterious back channels, gave us a Mark V fast patrol boat for a previous mission, and I couldn't think of a better platform from which to launch our assault on the Pan America oil rig. The Mark V was an eighty-foot-long, forty-ton tactical boat designed and built for the Navy SEALs, but thanks to my favorite diesel mechanic and a pair of electronics geeks, my Mark V had been upgraded. She had a raw-water heat exchanging system to shield the two enormous diesel engines, making them far less attractive for infrared and heat-seeking targeting systems. She was covered with a radar-absorbing surface coating similar to the JASSM missile. This made the boat almost invisible to most radar systems. The geeks had designed and installed an additional electronic radar-disrupting system to further cloak her from the prying eyes of radar operators at sea. She had five hardpoints on which a serious selection of firepower could be mounted.

Clark said, "We can always drive it around the Keys. It's about seven hundred miles to Tampa. We could refuel at the yard in Miami and make that in less than twenty-four hours."

"There's another option," Hunter offered. "I know of a company down in Jacksonville. They move oversized loads . . . like Mark V patrol boats. It wouldn't be cheap, but it also wouldn't beat us to death on a twenty-four-hour high-speed boat ride."

Clark said, "That's a much better plan. Get them on the phone."

Hunter made the call while I stared at the ceiling.

Singer interrupted my trance. "What are you thinking, Chase?"

"I don't know," I said. "Something about this feels wrong."

"Everything about it is wrong. Taking an oil rig and holding the workers hostage is the textbook definition of *wrong*."

I shook my head. "No, that's not what I mean. What you're describing is piracy, and America has a checklist for dealing with pirates. We shoot them in the head and put it on the national news. Something about this feels like there's a lot more going on than just some environmental wackos taking over an oil rig."

The team leaned in.

"So, what do you think it is?" Clark asked.

"I can't put my finger on it, but if we go blasting into a situation we don't understand, we're going to find ourselves wading through Hell in gasoline flip-flops, and I don't like it."

Hunter returned with a notepad. "They can move the boat, no problem. In fact, they can move it today, but it ain't cheap."

"How much?"

He ran his finger down the page. "It's fifteen dollars per mile, plus three thousand dollars to load it on the trailer. Then, when they get it to the Gulf side, they'll have to contract a crane or shipyard to put it back in the water. That'll be at least another three grand."

I ran the numbers in my head. "That's less than thirty grand. You three get the boat to Jacksonville. Clark and I'll pick you up in the Caravan."

Singer, Hunter, and Mongo were on their feet before I finished the instructions. Hunter paused at the door. "Where do you want them to take it?"

"United Ship Building in Panama City," I said. "I know a guy there."

Hunter rolled his eyes. "Of course you know a guy."

Anya stood. "I will go with them in boat."

I glanced at my watch. "No. I need you and your missing chromosome here. Penny will be back with the speech pathologist in less than an hour. I want your ears and brain in the room every time that audio is played."

"As you wish," she said.

I shook my head in disbelief. "As I wish? I never expected to hear anything like that from you."

She pulled a small plastic flag from her pocket and waved it between us. "I am American now and on team. Is important I am team player."

"Did Mongo tell you to say that?"

She smiled but didn't answer.

"I thought so. Maybe that big buffalo is exactly what you needed," I said.

She rolled the flag between her fingertips. "Maybe America is what I needed."

* * *

It took fewer than thirty seconds for me to realize why Tonya and Penny were friends.

"Hey, Chase. I'm Tonya. It's so nice to meet you. Penny just won't shut up about you. It's like I know all about you already and we've never met. That's a great airplane. Wow! And this place, oh my gosh. This place is amazing. It's like some sort of antebellum mansion or something. And you're working on some kind of classified project. That's so cool. What I do is so boring, and it's so nice of you to ask me to come help. I can't wait to get started—"

I interrupted. "It's nice to meet you, too, Tonya. Thank you for coming."

The woman continued as if I hadn't spoken. "All of this sounds so exciting. What is it exactly that you need me to do? I'm sure it's going to be nothing like what I usually do. You can't imagine how boring it is. I'm trapped in an office all day long with nobody to talk to, and obviously, you can see I love to talk . . ."

Clark was quivering in some wasted attempt to contain his laughter. I just wanted to come up with a way to get her to stop talking long enough to tell her what we needed.

Penny saved me. "Tonya, shut up!"

Tonya held her hand in front of her mouth and blushed. "Oh my gosh. I'm so sorry. I get to see my old friend, and now I get to be part of whatever this is. It's just so exciting, I can't stand it."

When I met Penny Thomas, she was almost as high energy as Tonya, but she'd mellowed a little. I couldn't imagine what life in their college dorm room must've been like. I'm sure they had no use for a television.

I pulled a file folder from my desk and handed it to Tonya. "This is a non-disclosure agreement. Since you have a security clearance, you know all about NDAs. Anything you see, hear, read, or learn while you're here can never be discussed with anyone outside this room. It's all covered in the paperwork. I'm going to need you to read and initial every paragraph, and sign at the bottom of the second page."

I had my doubts that Tonya would be capable of reading the NDA silently, but she surprised me. After initialing and signing, she handed the file back to me. I signed the witness line and locked the paperwork in the safe with the NDAs for the rest of the team.

"Pull up a chair," I said. "What you're about to hear is an electronic voice issuing a series of threats. As far as you know, this is a training exercise and nothing more. Okay?"

"Sure, okay. A training exercise. Whatever you say."

I played the audio.

"Listen closely. I have taken your environmental disaster of a monstrosity that you call the Pan America. I control every inch of the facility. I have one hundred seventy of your slaves, and production has been halted. It will not restart . . . ever. These are my demands. Notice I did not say terms. Terms are negotiable. Demands are not. You will halt production from all twenty-four of your offshore, planet-killing, greed-feeding factories of filth, and your brother-in-law will declare a moratorium on all offshore oil production within thirty days, or I will sink this rig and all one hundred seventy of your slaves with it. If you make any effort to approach the rig, I will destroy it. If you notify any law enforcement or military entity, I will destroy your rig. If you make any effort to subvert or deny my demands, I will destroy your rig. Thirty days . . . not a minute longer."

Tonya looked up with fear in her eyes. "This isn't a training exercise, is it?"

I bit my lip. "I need to know if that is a computer-generated voice or an altered human voice."

Tonya's chin quivered as she stared at me. "Are you going to save those people? Is that what you do?"

Penny took Tonya's hands in hers. "We need to know what you hear in the audio. Is that a computer or a person?"

She wiped at her eyes, pulled a set of headphones from her bag, then handed me the plug. "Please plug this in and play it again."

I did as she asked, and she closed her eyes as the audio played in her headphones. She listened twice more and slid the headphones from her ears. "It's definitely an electronically altered human voice."

"Can you filter out the distortion and let us hear what his natural voice sounds like?"

"It's not a man's voice. It's a woman's. And yes, I can clean it up, but it will take a couple of hours to do the whole thing. I can get a few seconds cleaned up in about fifteen minutes, if that'll help."

"What do you need?" I asked.

"Just your computer and fifteen minutes of quiet."

We left Tonya alone in the library and made our way to the kitchen.

Clark rummaged through the refrigerator. "I knew we should've kept Maebelle up here. We're going to starve to death."

Maebelle, in addition to being the woman Clark adored more than anyone else on Earth, was the proprietor of *el Juez,* the hottest new restaurant on Miami's South Beach. As much as we all would've loved having her at Bonaventure, the restaurant demanded her attention, and Clark was left behind to fend for himself.

I motioned toward the library with my chin. "She's a handful."

Penny giggled. "Yeah, I used to be just like her, but life with you has taught me to chill out a little. She's high-strung, but she knows more about the sounds that come out of our mouths than anybody I know. It's weird how smart she is."

"That sounds promising," I said. "Do you think she can really filter out the distortion from that audio?"

Penny shrugged. "I've known her for a long time, and she's never lied about anything as far as I know. If she says she can do it, I believe her."

"I hope you're right."

I turned to Clark, who had moved on to scrounging through the cupboards. "Would you mind going to get the guys without me? I'd like to stay here and see what Tonya comes up with."

He spun around with a pack of crackers and a can of tuna in his hand. "Sure, I'll go get 'em."

Fifteen minutes later, Tonya opened the door of the library. "Hey, guys. I've got something for you."

Penny, Anya, and I wasted no time getting back into the library.

"Let's hear it," I said.

"It's not perfect, but I've got it cleaned up enough to hear the real voice behind the audio. I'll work on it some more, but here's what I have so far."

She played the audio, and the voice I heard sent a shiver down my spine. Anya stared at Penny, who looked as if she'd just heard a ghost.

I swallowed hard. "She sounds just like you."

Penny nodded. "Yeah, I know, and I don't like it."

Anya said, "Is not exactly same, but is close."

Tonya spoke up. "Anya's right. It's close. Whoever this woman is learned to talk within a hundred miles of where Penny grew up. She's as North Texas as it's possible to be."

My head suddenly throbbed as if my brain wanted to be anywhere else besides inside my skull. "That's exactly what I was afraid of."

Tonya and Penny sat in silence, waiting for me to continue, but Anya spoke first. "Is not about drilling for oil. This is red herring."

I pointed at the Russian. "Bingo. I don't know what they're hiding yet, or even who is doing the hiding, but I'm going to find out."

Twenty minutes later, I was in the Citation and climbing out of Saint Marys, bound for Austin. I had some questions for Thomas Meriwether, and I needed to look into his eyes when he answered them.

Chapter 7
Interesting Guy

Ignoring the security guards, junior executives, and secretaries who seemed determined to stop me, I burst through Thomas Meriwether's office door with accusation in my eyes and no patience left in my gut.

"Who made the audio, Thomas?"

He bounded from his chair with a long, nickel revolver in his hand. "What the hell do you think you're doing coming in here like this?"

"Go ahead, Thomas. Shoot me if you think I'm a threat, but before you do, you'd better think about who you're messing with. I'm not some two-bit Texas private eye. I've got resources. Did you really think I wouldn't have the audio analyzed? Who's the woman on the audio?"

He lowered the revolver. "What the hell are you talking about? What woman?"

"Don't play games with me, Thomas. I'm in no mood for it, and there's a hundred and seventy people on *your* oil rig who are in at least as bad a mood as me. Tell me who the woman is, or I swear to you, I'll find out what you're doing, and I'll burn you to the ground."

When men are caught in a lie, they do one of three things: they deny it and make counter-accusations, they tell another lie to continue the cover-up, or they break down and confess. Each of those occurrences comes with a unique and easily identifiable look, none of which Thomas Meriwether wore. His was the look of the wrongly accused.

I set my eyes on his. "Look me in the eye, and tell me you have no idea whose voice that is on the audio. If you blink, look away, or stutter, I'm walking away, and I'm keeping every penny of your money."

The man didn't flinch. "Mr. Fulton, I have no idea what you're talking about, and I have no idea whose voice that is on the audio. But what I *do* know is the man I'm paying thirty-five-million dollars to get my people off that rig is wasting precious time accusing me of something I had nothing to do with."

Flinching wasn't something I'd ever do. "Listen closely, Meriwether. Before this is over, I'll know every detail of every lie that was told, and if any of those lies belong to you, I'll take you down. That's what I do."

I slammed his enormous door as I left, and a disheveled secretary screamed, "I've called the police, and they're on their way. You'll be arrested before you step off the sidewalk."

I grinned. "Yeah, I don't think so. You might want to check with ol' Tommy about that call. If I go to jail, I've got a feeling your boss is going to be very unhappy with whoever dialed nine-one-one."

No one arrested me, and I was back at Bonaventure in less than two hours. When I arrived, the whole team was huddled around the kitchen table, devouring two hundred dollars' worth of KFC.

"Meriwether isn't in on whatever's really going on."

Clark looked up and wiped his mouth. "You confronted him by yourself?"

"Yeah, I did, and he didn't blink. He may not believe this is an environmental thing, but he believes his rig—and his employees—are in danger."

Clark dug another leg from the bucket of chicken. "Penny brought us up to speed on the audio, and I agree with you. Something's rotten in the state of Pan America."

"Look at you, quoting Shakespeare," I said. "I'm impressed."

"Just because I didn't go to some fancy college doesn't mean I can't read."

"What's the status of the Mark V?" I asked as I reached for a piece of Original Recipe.

Hunter said, "It's on the truck and will be in the water in Panama City before dark."

"Good," I said. "Let's wrap this up and pack for war. I want a pair of M2s, a 249 SAW, an AR and sidearm for each of us, of course Singer's rifles, and all the ammo we can carry. We'll need night vision, coms, rebreathers, and provisions. Oh, and something sharp for Anya."

Hunter grinned. "We're way ahead of you, boss. The weapons and ammo are locked up on the boat. The provisions and coms are loaded up and waiting to go to the airport. Are we taking the Citation?"

Anya pulled a pair of custom-made fighting knives from her ankles. "I always have something sharp."

The competence of my team was second to none.

"I should've known," I said. "I'll have the crew bring the Citation over tomorrow, but we're going to need the Caravan, too. I like having something amphibious in our arsenal." I'd been dreading the inevitable conversation with Clark, but it couldn't be avoided any longer. "Give Clark and me a couple of minutes, and we'll be ready to go."

The team dispersed as if they wanted nothing to do with the coming chat.

Clark wasted no time. "I know what you're going to say, College Boy, and you're right. I don't have any business assaulting an oil rig."

Although still in great shape, Clark's back injuries left him incapable of full-contact operations and had relegated him to a command and control position.

"I can't risk putting you on that rig when the time comes to hit it, but I want you with us. Hunter still hasn't done his seaplane check ride, so you're the only other qualified Caravan pilot."

He stared down at the tips of his boots as if they held some wisdom he longed to extract from them. "This ain't easy for me, you know. My days of kicking in doors may be over, but I don't have to like it."

"You've kicked in more than your share of doors over the years, and having someone with your experience and mindset as a handler is priceless."

He drove his finger into my chest. "I may sit on the sidelines while you youngsters are out having all the fun, but you'd better know that if you get yourself hung up out there, I'll come busting up in that place like the Kool-Aid Man."

I swatted away his threatening finger. "It wouldn't be the first time. I remember the first time you saved my butt. Anya and I would've been dead in the back room of that strip club in Key West if you hadn't showed up with guns a-blazing."

He chuckled. "We've had some times, haven't we?"

"We certainly have," I said. "But I remember pulling you out of a couple of fires along the way, too."

I could almost see the highlight reel playing in his head. "I guess you have. Those Chinese in Panama had me wrapped up pretty good. If it hadn't been for you and that crazy, little dude. . . . What was his name?"

"Diablo de Agua," I said.

Clark snapped his fingers. "Yep, that's it. That was one wild dude. You guys tore up in there like a pair of tornadoes. That was the only time I've ever seen a live grenade rolling around on the floor."

Clark and I stood in mirrored silence, reliving the missions we'd survived.

Finally, he looked up. "Then there was the Khyber Pass. I owe you my life for that one."

I slapped him on the shoulder. "I'll ask you the same thing the president asked me. Is that what we're doing now? Keeping score?"

"Oh, yeah," he said. "I've got it all written down in a little book I keep under my pillow."

Skipper stormed into the kitchen with a pair of file folders. "Okay, here. These are things you'll need to know. The more I dig, the less I'm buying the ecoterrorist thing."

I took the folders from her hands. "I'm glad to hear you say that. I agree. There's too much wrong with that story. What's all this stuff?"

She pointed toward the blue folder. "This one has your travel arrangements. I've rented a cabin for us on Saint Andrews Bay behind Tyndall Air Force Base. There's a really nice dock where the Mark V and the Caravan will fit perfectly. It also has a boat ramp I believe is wide enough to get the Caravan out of the water if you want. I also rented a pair of Suburbans. They'll be waiting for you at the cabin. Try not to destroy them . . . please."

"That's perfect. How did you find that place?"

She landed a hand on her hip. "It's what I do. I'm the great finder of things."

I laughed. "Yes, you are. What else is in here?"

She pulled the yellow folder from my hand. "This is a dossier on Greg Peterson. He's the OIM on the Pan America."

I thumbed through the bound dossier. "OIM?"

"Offshore installation manager. He's in charge of the rig, and so far, he's the most interesting character in the investigation."

"What makes him so interesting?" I asked, still flipping through the pages.

"He's been married and divorced four times to three women. He likes fast cars, boats, and Brazilian chicks."

"Four times to three women? He married one of them twice? What was he thinking?"

"How should I know? That's not what's so interesting about him. His salary is just under two hundred thousand a year with quarterly bonuses based on things like rig production, safety record, cost-saving policies he enforces, and stuff like that. Last year, including all his bonuses, he made two-fifty-four."

I let out an admiring whistle. "That's a lot of money."

Skipper nodded. "It sure is, but it's not enough to support the lifestyle he lives when he's not on the rig. He pays alimony of almost a hundred grand a year, owns three houses, four really nice boats, and flies chartered private jets to South America several times a year."

"In search of another Brazilian ex-wife, no doubt."

Skipper rolled her eyes. "Who knows what he does down there?"

I grinned. "I bet you're going to tell me what he does down there."

She frowned. "That's the thing. I can't figure it out. When he's there, it's like he disappears. I can't find any evidence of him spending any money, making any money, traveling between countries, or anything. It's like he turns into a ghost the minute he lands in Rio."

"How long are these trips?"

She pointed toward the file. "It's all in there, but they usually last at least two weeks at a time."

"How does he get that much time off from the rig?"

She laughed. "He doesn't stay on the rig all the time, goofy. His schedule isn't exactly like the drillers and roughnecks, but it works out that he spends around three to four weeks on the rig and then two to three weeks at home."

I let the new information wallow around in my head for a few seconds. "Stay on this guy. I want to know more about him—especially what he's doing in Brazil."

"I'll try, but even I have limits."

"We all do. Yours just happen to be a little harder to find than most. Keep on it. Are you staying here or coming with us?"

She shot a look at her watch. "What time are you leaving?"

"Now."

"I want to come, but I can't be ready in less than an hour."

"Then come tomorrow. I'm having the flight crew bring the Citation in the morning. You and Penny can fly over with them."

"Done," she said, and disappeared up the stairs.

Every member of the team brought a unique skill set to the mission. Many of our talents overlapped, but Skipper's were the exception. We could all shoot and fight, though she could do things with a few keystrokes that a hundred thousand bullets could never replicate. Almost no one is irreplaceable, but Skipper came incredibly close.

Having Penny with us on missions such as this represented more than a set of tactical skills. She'd never be an analyst or a trigger puller, but she was my anchor to the world outside of my work—my one tie to the world in which I would never truly belong. I was a warrior, and as something often less than human, capable of violent action humanity need not witness. Penny was the force that made men like me capable of temporary existence in polite society.

Chapter 8
Redneck Riviera

The Caravan, as capable as it was, felt a little crowded and more than a little heavy when I pulled back on the yoke, but the wheels finally left the runway with Clark, Hunter, Mongo, Singer, Anya, and every piece of gear we crammed aboard.

The flight to Panama City took slightly less than ninety minutes with Hunter doing most of the flying. Having a third pilot capable of flying the amphibious Caravan was another invaluable tool in our kit.

As we approached Panama City's Saint Andrews Bay from the northeast, I keyed my mic. "Tyndall Approach, Caravan Eight-Charlie-Fox. We intend to splash down on East Bay, just east of the DuPont Bridge."

The Tyndall Approach controller said, "Roger, Caravan Eight Charlie Fox. Radar service is terminated. Squawk V-F-R and remain clear of the Tyndall Class Delta airspace. Contact Tyndall Tower on one-three-three-point-niner-five for transition into Delta surface area."

"Roger, Eight-Charlie-Fox is squawking V-F-R and off to tower on one-thirty-three-point-niner-five."

Hunter said, "You have the controls. I'm not familiar enough with this area."

"You're doing fine. I've got the radios. You stay on the controls."

"All right," he said. "You're the boss. But don't let me screw this up."

"You won't screw it up," I said. "That's Tyndall Air Force Base at eleven o'clock and about ten miles. See it?"

He leaned forward and peered through the windshield. "Got it."

"Good," I said. "We're going to land on the bay just northwest of the airfield. We'll make left traffic, approach over the bridge, and land to the east."

"Easy enough," he said.

I tuned the tower frequency and keyed up. "Tyndall Tower, this is November two-zero-eight Charlie Foxtrot, an amphibious Cessna Caravan, niner miles northeast. We intend to splash down on East Bay."

The controller replied, "Caravan Eight Charlie Fox, proceed as requested. Use caution for a flight of two F-Twenty-Two Raptors followed by a flight of four F-Fifteen Eagles eight miles west, eastbound landing Tyndall."

I glanced over my shoulder at my team in the back of the plane. "Hey, guys, check this out. There are two F-Twenty-Two Raptors and four F-Fifteen Strike Eagles coming at us from the west."

Everyone except Anya leaned forward, looking for the fighter jets. "They are coming for us?" she asked, her eyes wide with fear.

I fought hard to suppress the laughter I felt rising from my gut. "Relax. They're on our side."

When realization overtook her, she let out a long sigh of Russian relief. "Old habit is hard breaking. This is right phrase in English?"

"Close enough," I said.

Hunter keyed his mic. "Eight Charlie Fox has the fighters in sight. They'll be no factor for us. We'll remain north of the bay and turn base behind them."

The six jets roared past, a half-mile off our left wing. Everyone except Hunter seemed mesmerized by them.

I said, "I guess they're no big deal for you, huh?"

"Actually," he said, "those are the first Raptors I've ever seen. I'm just running through the landing in my head."

"You'll do fine. Just fly it the same as before. It'll be a bit heavier, so carry a little extra speed onto the water, and watch the descent rate."

He nodded and turned the plane to the south. I sat silently in the right seat with my hands in my lap as Hunter turned to the east over the DuPont Bridge. There was only one boat in sight— a small fishing vessel anchored just east of the bridge. Its occupants stared skyward at the unexpected sight of a floatplane descending toward them. We overflew the boat at two hundred feet and continued our approach.

Hunter finessed the floats onto the smooth water of the bay as if he'd done it a thousand times. As we settled into the water, he lowered the water rudders, pulled the power off, and let himself grin. "Now that I've done all the hard work for you, I don't know where we're going. She's all yours."

"I have the controls," I said, and taxied the Caravan toward Callaway Bayou, where our rented cabin and Suburbans waited.

What Skipper called a *cabin* was, in reality, a two-story, four-thousand-square-foot, six-bedroom waterfront vacation dream. The team wasted no time spreading out and claiming rooms, and soon, we were all back in the living room overlooking Callaway Bayou.

"The first order of business," I began, "is to claim our boat. It should be in the water at United Ship Building. It's about five minutes from here on the water, but twenty by land. I want to get the Mark V over here and covered up. That shouldn't take long. Then, I want to get our first look at that rig."

"From the boat?" Hunter asked.

"No, I think we should do a flyby in the Caravan. It looks perfectly harmless. If we show up in the Mark V, they'll likely sink the rig before we get close enough to get a good look."

* * *

The drive to the shipyard wasn't as long as I'd expected. We made it in fifteen minutes. What I didn't expect was to find my boat without a drop of diesel fuel on board.

"What happened to my fuel?" I asked the dockhand.

"Them boys who toted her over here had to empty her out. They can't carry gas of no kind in oversized loads, and this thing's an oversized load if there's ever been one."

I scanned the docks. "Can you fill it back up?"

"Nope," he said. "Ain't got no diesel pumps. But we got some in the truck. We can squirt enough in there so's you can run over t'marina and top it off. They got all the gas you could want over there. Say, what's a boat like this for, anyhow?"

"I'd appreciate you squirtin' enough diesel in there to get me to the marina. How long do you think that'll take?"

He spat a long rope of brown tobacco juice from his lips and then wiped his face with the filthy sleeve of his shirt. "Gimme just a minute or two. I'll be right back." The man ambled up the slope of the boatyard and climbed into a fuel truck. Ten minutes later, the Mark V had fifty gallons in her belly, and my tobacco-chewing friend had five hundred dollars in cash tucked into his greasy pants pocket.

Saint Andrews Marina supported a fleet of two hundred personal vessels and a couple dozen commercial fishing boats, so filling my tanks made a barely noticeable dent in their diesel supply.

We caught the inquisitive glances of the crew of a Coast Guard patrol boat, but they made no effort to intercept us as we powered behind Tyndall Air Force Base toward Callaway Bayou in our favorite waterborne toy.

After securing the Mark V to the dock and thoroughly covering her with canvas tarps to discourage prying eyes, the team climbed back into the Caravan, and we blasted off to the southwest.

"Why's water so green?" Anya asked as we climbed out over Panama City Beach.

"I don't know what makes it green, but because of the color, this whole area has been called the Emerald Coast for a long time. It also has some of the most beautiful beaches in the world. The white powdery sand is like no place else on Earth."

Clark chuckled. "Emerald Coast isn't all they call it. Most folks know it as the Redneck Riviera."

Anya turned to him with confusion in her eyes. "What does this mean?"

He grinned. "Are you asking what a redneck is or what *riviera* means?"

"Both."

"I'm a redneck," he said. "And my brother, Tony, he's an even bigger redneck than me. We're simple people. We don't need much, but we've got skills the rest of the world doesn't have. We can hunt, fish, eat what we catch and kill, and live a long time without going back inside. We work hard, but when it comes time to play . . . well, we do that even harder. We'll drink a beer occasionally, and we'll whip your ass for talking bad about our momma."

Anya smiled. "Then I am also redneck."

I couldn't contain my laughter. "I don't think anyone will ever call you a redneck, but under Clark's definition, I think you're right."

We flew by several rigs on the Gulf.

Singer asked, "What's that fire coming out of the tops of those rigs?"

"That's flaring," Mongo said. "A lot of natural gas comes out of most oil wells, and they've got to do something with it. Flaring it off is the safest way to get rid of it."

Singer scratched his head. "That seems like a big waste."

"Oil companies don't waste anything," Mongo said. "If there was enough natural gas to justify capturing it and bringing it ashore, you can bet they'd do it. But the ones that are flaring are over wells that don't make enough gas to justify the expense of capturing."

"There she is," I said, pointing out the windshield. "That's the Pan America Rig on our nose at five miles."

The team leaned forward to catch a glimpse.

"Man," Singer said, "she sure is big compared to those others we saw."

Clark was doing the flying while I stared at the rig. "Take us down to five hundred feet and pass a half-mile east of the rig."

His answer came in the form of a five-hundred-foot-per-minute descent rate and a ten-degree turn to the left. "All right, guys. Get a good look. We're only doing one pass."

The team peered silently through the right-side windows as the enormous rig loomed to the west.

"Seeing that thing brings back a lot of memories," Mongo said. "I never thought I'd see an offshore rig again."

I asked, "How does it look compared to the rigs you were on?"

"It's identical. They haven't changed a thing."

"So," I said, "if you were on that rig, you'd know your way around, right?"

The big man bit at his lip. "I never spent much time inside. If I was awake, I was on the deck and working. I'd know my way around the deck, but that's about it."

"That's a lot more than any of the rest of us can say. If we have to board her, you're definitely coming with us."

"Do you think there's another way to get that rig back?" Mongo asked.

I scratched my chin. "I can't think of any way other than brute force . . . or at least the threat of force. I'm still not sure what's really happening on that rig, but it's safe to say we'll know soon enough."

Clark said, "I think we should maintain this altitude and keep flying south until we're out of sight of the rig. That way they won't think we were checking on them."

"That's a good idea," I said. "We're going to have to announce our presence at some point, but not yet."

Clark flew us away, slowly turning to the southeast until the rig was out of sight.

I pulled the mic to my lips. "If you were going to sink that rig, how would you do it?"

Clark was first to answer. "I'd blow the columns and let the platform separate from the pontoons. I think you could pull that off with a couple hundred pounds of C-4."

Singer said, "I think I'd blow one pontoon and let the whole thing turtle. That would dramatically lower the amount of C-4 you'd need."

I looked over my shoulder. "Mongo, you're the only one of us who's ever been on board one of those things. How would you sink it?"

"I'd ignite the natural gas stored in the subsurface holding tanks."

Chapter 9
Let's Have a Look

"Hey, Clark. Trade places with Hunter. I'd like for him to get as many landings as possible."

Clark climbed from the left seat and made his way back to the main cabin.

Hunter took his place, pulled on his headset, and secured the shoulder harness. "I have the controls."

I released the yoke. "You have the controls. Now get us home, and put this thing back in the bayou."

"I think I can do that," he said.

He was right. I never touched the controls for the remainder of the flight, and there was no need for any instructions. Hunter eased the lumbering Caravan onto the bay and taxied to the dock like an old pro.

"I believe you're ready for that check ride."

He tried not to smile. "You think?"

Back in the rented house, we ordered pizza and called a pow-wow.

"Let's talk about what we saw out there today," I said.

Clark scratched at his beard. "It sure wasn't what I expected. If I took a rig like that, I'd have a dozen roving patrols and at least four overwatch snipers up high. I'd put at least one heavy boat on perimeter patrol, and I'd have a chopper on deck for egress if things went to crap. I didn't see any of that. Whoever these guys are, they don't believe anyone's coming after that rig."

Mongo cleared his throat. "I agree. If they're showing the force they have, we can take that rig without getting our knuckles scuffed. I couldn't tell for sure, but it didn't look like the guards on deck had anything heavy."

I turned to Anya. "What did you see?"

"I saw soft target, but is what I did not see that is strange."

"What didn't you see?"

"There was no boat and no helicopter. How did terrorists get onto platform? Who delivered them to oil rig, and where is person now?"

Scanning the room, I asked, "Any ideas?"

Singer said, "Maybe they've got a crew boat standing off. Skipper's satellite feeds should be able to answer that question."

"She and Penny will be here tomorrow morning, but I think it's worth getting her on the phone now. Does anyone disagree?"

A room full of shaking heads sent me reaching for my phone.

"Skipper, hey. We're on-site, and you did a bang-up job on this place. The house and location are perfect. The Suburbans are exactly what we needed. Once again, you've outdone yourself."

"Hey, Chase. I'm glad to hear you approve. I'll go ahead and give myself a fifteen percent raise."

"You do that, but first, I need some intel. I want you to find a crew boat, or any boat capable of getting up to two dozen guys off that rig on short notice. It'll probably be within fifteen miles of the rig."

She said, "The Gulf is five thousand feet deep out there, Chase. You can't anchor a crew boat in five thousand feet of water."

"They won't be anchored, but they'll be hovering."

"Okay, I'll look. Give me two minutes."

The line went silent, and I covered the mouthpiece with my palm. "She's looking."

Clark waggled his finger toward the phone. "Put it on speaker."

I pressed the speaker button and placed the phone on the coffee table.

Skipper came back on. "There's nothing like a crew boat anywhere near that rig, but there's a pretty-good-sized freighter steaming from the southwest."

"How far away?" I asked.

"It's about fifty miles, but it's bearing directly toward the rig."

I examined the faces of my team. "What speed is she making, and what's on her decks?"

It'll take a few minutes to calculate her speed. This isn't like radar, you know, but she appears to have a couple dozen land-sea containers on deck. It could be more, but I can't tell. The satellite is directly overhead, so it's tough to see if they're singles or stacked."

"How long will it take you to calculate her speed?"

"I'm working on it now. I'll have an estimate in a minute."

I could see the wheels turning inside the heads of my team. Each of them had a skill set that complemented the others perfectly. I'd built one of the best tactical operations teams on the planet, and there was no group of warriors I'd rather stand beside.

"She's making fifteen to twenty knots. The longer I watch, the more accurate I can get, but that's the best I can do on short notice."

I let my mental calculator do the math. "Replot her course, Skipper. Are you sure she's bearing on the Pan America Rig?"

"Stand by."

Obviously thinking the same thing I was, Hunter pulled the Mark V keys from his pocket.

Skipper said, "Yeah, there's no question. She's going to hit the rig if she doesn't make a turn in the next two-and-a-half hours."

I yanked my phone from the table. "Keep on it, Skipper. We're heading out to meet the freighter."

"Okay. Are you taking the airplane or the boat?"

"The boat. We'll fire up the coms and the satellite link once we're out of the bay."

"Okay. I'll keep it open here and provide overwatch for you. There won't be much I can do other than feed you intel, but it's going to be dark in an hour. I'll be blind after that."

I pressed the speaker button off and put the phone to my ear as we headed for the Mark V. "Yeah, I know, but you'll still be able to see the lights of the freighter and the rig. I want to see what they're doing."

"Be careful, Chase."

"I'm always careful."

"No, you're not, but at least don't hurt anybody on our team."

"I'll promise you that much."

Clark stared at me. "Are we gunning up?"

"Absolutely," I said.

One of the marks of a great team is their ability to move as a single unit. In the minutes that followed, every member of my team armed themselves, mounted the boat, and situated themselves aboard as if they'd trained for nothing else.

Clear of the bayou, I opened the throttles, and the big patrol boat accelerated beneath me. Her size belied her agility as she rose out of the water and pinned the speed indicator solidly on sixty knots. We left Saint Andrews Pass ahead of a pair of shrimp boats and an armada of sunset cruisers heading out to worship the disappearance of another day.

Naval Support Activity Panama City had a pair of fast patrol boats nearly identical to mine—at least on the exterior. They used them to train Naval Special Warfare operators, so the presence of a Mark V cutting through the water at high speed didn't raise an eyebrow from the locals. The tourists may have found us amusing, but the local captains never gave us a second glance. Anonymity was a valuable asset, especially in a tourist town like Panama City, Florida.

Once on the open water of the Gulf of Mexico, I was happy to find the conditions perfect. There was almost no wind, and the seas were less than a foot. The Mark V cut across the water like a rocket ship, and the pneumatic cylinders supporting the crew seating made us feel like we were in the back of a long black limo.

Even viewed at sixty knots, the sunset was breathtaking. I watched for the elusive green flash, but it didn't come. Someday I'd see it, but that wasn't my night.

I glanced over my shoulder. "Somebody get up here and drive."

Anya leapt to her feet and slid between me and the wheel. "I have controls."

"You have *the* controls," I said.

She looked up at me. "Yes, *the* controls. I will learn English articles because I am now American."

I motioned toward the GPS screen in front of the wheel. "There's the rig. Just keep us pointed there, and don't hit anything."

The satellite feed came to life on the multi-function displays, and I fired up the sat-coms with Skipper. "Are you there?"

"I'm here, Chase. Are you running dark?"

"No, we're running lights just like the law says, but we'll douse them before we get in sight of the rig."

"I'm looking for you," she said, "but I'm having trouble picking you out."

I checked our position. "We're sixty-one miles off the Saint Andrews Pass, making sixty knots. We should be the only fast mover in the area."

"There you are," she said. "Satellite surveillance in the dark isn't exactly high-def, but it will be in a few years."

"Where's the freighter?" I asked.

"It's still steaming straight for the rig at nineteen knots. When the sun got low on the horizon, the cargo containers weren't casting much of a shadow, so I think they're single stacks. That doesn't make much sense, but that's what I saw."

I grimaced. "You're right, that is strange. But so far, nothing about this op makes any sense."

Skipper's voice turned ominous. "Hey, while you're just riding, I thought you should know. . . ."

"What is it?"

"Hang on a minute. Let me close the door. Okay. There's something bugging Penny, and I don't know what it is. She's not herself. Is everything okay with you two?"

"Yeah, as far as I know, everything's fine. What's she doing?"

Skipper grunted. "I don't really know, but something's off about her. Maybe it's the fact that you're on an op with Anya, but I get the impression it's something else. I just thought I should tell you."

"Thanks for letting me know, but I can't think of anything that would be bothering her. Anya's with Mongo now. She's no threat, and I'm certainly not interested."

"Yeah, I know that, but you know how we women get sometimes. It's probably nothing, but ever since her friend Tonya got here, she's just seemed a little strange."

"I appreciate the heads-up. Let me know if you figure it out, okay?"

"You know I will. So, back to the mission. It looks like you'll be a tie with the freighter at the rig. Do you need anything else from me?"

"We probably will when we get on-site, but we're good for now. Just let me know if the freighter changes course or speed."

"You've got it. I'll be standing by."

I pulled off my headset and turned to my crew. "Skipper says the freighter is still on course for the rig and we're a dead tie with them, so we'll get to see what they're up to. My gut tells me they'll turn to miss the rig and continue on to Panama City, but it's worth checking out."

Clark yelled over the roar of the engines. "Have you thought about having Skipper check for previous routes for freighters in the area?"

I pointed at my former partner turned handler. "That's why you're in charge."

An hour later, the glow of the Pan America Rig loomed on the distant horizon.

"Okay, let's go dark," I ordered.

Anya doused the lights, and I brought the radar-jamming system online. Two seacocks opened at the flip of a switch, and the heat exchanger system shrouding the engines pumped seawater through a series of copper pipes encasing the massive diesel engines. If the rig had infrared or radar, we would be able to defeat both systems, making us practically invisible in the moonless night.

The upper lights of the rig came into sight, and Anya pulled the throttles back, reducing our speed to thirty knots. "How do you wish for me to approach rig? I mean, *the* rig."

The lights of the freighter on the satellite display showed the ship eight miles southwest of the rig.

"Let's move off one mile west of the rig and watch the show," I said.

Anya brought the throttles back to eighty percent and positioned us perfectly in the calm water just west of the Pan America. Hunter, Mongo, and Singer donned night-vision goggles and lined the bow. I switched one of the MFDs to night vision and let the scene play out on the screen at the helm. Clark sat in the captain's throne, overseeing the whole operation.

I pulled my headset back on. "We're in position one mile west of the rig with the freighter in sight."

"Roger," Skipper said. "I see the lights of the rig and the freighter, but you're dark."

"If you can't see us, maybe they can't, either."

The freighter held her course as she approached the rig, but slowed as she drew nearer. The longer I watched the scene unfolding in front of me, the harder it was to believe. The freighter crept to the windward side of the rig, and four men aimed shotguns from the deck of the ship toward the platform of the massive oil rig. One by one, the shotguns fired, sending messenger lines to the rig. Men aboard the Pan America hauled in the small messenger lines, pulling larger, heavier mooring lines from the freighter to the platform. The operation was clumsy, but in fifteen minutes, the freighter was moored securely alongside the massive oil rig, making the ship look like a child's toy next to the behemoth.

Clark lost his relaxed posture and leaned toward the display. "What the hell are they doing?"

"I don't know," I admitted. "But I know that's no tanker here to take on crude."

Clark leaned closer. "You're right about that, but it doesn't matter what they're *not* doing. I want to know what they *are* doing."

The magnification of the night-vision camera made the image on the screen appear only a few feet away, and we stared at the screen as if our lives depended on us not missing a solitary detail. What happened next left me in utter disbelief but immediately answered the question that had been gnawing at my gut for days. I finally knew the truth of what was really going on aboard the Pan America oil rig.

Chapter 10
Absolutely Anything

Mongo pulled his night-vision goggles from his face and looked across his shoulder. "Are you guys seeing this?"

I didn't take my eyes off the screen. "Yeah, we see it. I guess this isn't about saving the planet after all."

"You got that right," the big man said. "But what do we do about it?"

Instead of answering Mongo's question, I said, "Is anyone counting heads?"

Singer spoke up. "I'm counting."

At that, the only sounds aboard the Mark V were the low rumbles of the idling engines and the humming of fans in the electronics.

"That looks like all of them," Singer said. "I counted a hundred and twelve. About half were little kids."

"I got one-fourteen," Hunter offered. "But Singer's a sniper, so his count is probably better than mine. I agree that half were kids, though."

"The exact count doesn't matter right now," I said. "What matters is that there's over a hundred people being smuggled to somewhere from somewhere, and whoever has control of that rig is running the operation. This thing just turned into a first-class international incident."

Clark clicked his tongue against his teeth. "Like my brother says, if this ain't a mess, it'll sure do 'til one gets here."

I opened the coms with Skipper. "We've got a new situation down here. It's not ecoterrorists. It's a human trafficking operation. Are you saving the historic satellite footage?"

"Yeah, I've got everything from the time we tasked the satellites," she said. "Let me guess. You want me to find out where that freighter came from."

"That's exactly what I want you to do, but that's not all. I also want you to find out where it goes when it leaves here. I don't have the gas to chase them all the way back to Central America."

"I'm on it, but it's not like I have command of every satellite in orbit. I can't guarantee I'll be able to watch it all the way to its destination."

"Do what you can, Skipper. I've got the ship's AIS information. We can always track her that way if all else fails."

I looked back at Clark. "Is there anything else you want to see?"

Without a word, he shook his head, and I turned to Anya. "Take us home, but stay dark until we're across the horizon. There's nothing more we can do here tonight."

Anya followed my command and brought the Mark V about and up onto plane in seconds. We were soon rocketing across the water above sixty knots. The wind had picked up slightly, but the patrol boat didn't seem to care. The ride back to Saint Andrews Bay in two-foot seas was just as smooth as the outbound leg had been.

Anya nudged the boat against the dock, and the team made short work of securing her lines and tarping the conspicuous boat.

Midnight was fast approaching, but I gathered everyone in the living room for an after-action report. "So, the game has obviously changed, and we have a lot of decisions to make. First, we have to decide if we're notifying Customs and Immigration. Any ideas?"

Clark patted his foot against the hardwood floor—a nervous habit he'd taken up since his promotion. "I don't think we have any choice. We have first-hand knowledge of a human trafficking operation. Failure to report it makes us willing accomplices, and I don't think any of us wants that millstone hanging around our neck."

I held up one finger. "I agree, but . . . I don't think the oil rig workers are still on that rig. I think they've been hauled off somewhere."

"Or maybe killed," Mongo said.

I grimaced. "No, I don't think so. Killing that many people, especially people like oil rig workers, would be a monumental task for a handful of wannabe commandos. Besides, disposing of dozens of bodies, even at sea, wouldn't be easy. I suspect they evacuated the workers from the rig, but we need to find out."

"Agreed," Clark said. "The question is, how do we do that?"

Hunter said, "DPVs and rebreathers. We swim in, climb the rig, recon, and swim back out. We can do it tomorrow night from the Mark V. They didn't shoot at us tonight, so there's no reason to think they will tomorrow night."

I let his idea bounce around in my skull. "Diver propulsion vehicle insertion is a great idea, but that would mean a trip back to Saint Marys to get the gear."

"No, it wouldn't," Hunter said. "Skipper and Penny are coming tomorrow in the Citation. Just tell them what to bring."

I shot a look toward Clark. His single nod expressed his agreement. I sent an email to Skipper with an equipment list, and she responded minutes later saying they'd be on deck in Panama City by ten a.m. with all the gear we needed.

I glanced around the living room. "If no one else has any-thing, I think we should get some rest. We'll decide who's climb-ing the oil rig in the morning."

A hearty round of good-nights preceded everyone heading to their rooms.

I settled into my bed and was quickly approaching uncon-sciousness when my door opened and someone slipped through. There was no light in the hallway, so I couldn't see a silhouette to identify my intruder, but based on the nearly silent movement and narrow opening, there was little doubt who it was. I felt her settle onto the edge of my bed, and the scent of her brought floods of memories cascading into my head. It had been a long time since Anya Burinkova had been in my bed, but it appeared that clock had just been reset.

"What are you doing in here, Anya? You know this is not okay."

"Is not what you think. I am here only to talk privately about mission."

I was fully awake, so I reached for the lamp on the night-stand, but she caught my wrist.

"No, Chase. Do not turn on light. Is better this way."

"Okay. What do you want?"

"What I want does not matter. What is important is what is best for team and for mission. You must send me to oil rig to-morrow night. I am smallest, fastest, and quietest. If I must kill someone, I can do it silently. I am best choice. You must know this."

"Listen to me, Anya. I'm not sending Mongo. He's too big. The DPV would lose its mind trying to pull him through the water. Clark's injuries rule him out. He doesn't have the agility or durability for a mission like that. Singer is our sniper. I can't risk losing him, so he's out. That leaves you, me, and Hunter. Skipper and Penny are bringing three sets of gear. Now, get out of my room and go to bed. Penny would shoot both of us if she knew you were in here."

"Is good decision. *Spokoynoy nochi*, Chasechka."

"I thought we talked about you calling me Chasechka," I protested.

"We did," she said. "But if I am in your bed, I can call you this."

I grunted. "You're not *in* my bed. You're *on* my bed. There's a huge difference."

"In Russian is same."

"But you're an American now, so Russian rules of grammar no longer apply. Now, go to bed. *Your* bed."

As silently as she'd entered, she departed, leaving me incapable of sleep. I wondered if I'd ever be able to stop the memories of our past from haunting me.

* * *

It took a little negotiating, but the FBO manager at the Panama City Airport finally agreed to let us drive our rented Suburbans onto the parking ramp to meet the Citation jet. I didn't need prying eyes watching us carry three sets of tactical dive gear across the parking lot. Driving onto the ramp was the only reasonable alternative.

Five minutes after the pilots shut down the engines, we had every piece of luggage and gear loaded into the Suburbans.

I pulled the pilots aside. "Did Skipper arrange a place for you to stay?"

The captain said, "She arranged a pair of rooms on Front Beach for us. Thank you for that, Mr. Fulton. We'll be here when you need us."

"Excellent. Enjoy the beach. We shouldn't have anything on short notice, but keep a phone with you just in case."

The duo pulled cell phones from their pockets and waved them. "In our line of work, we're never far from our phones."

I said, "Thanks for everything, guys. I appreciate what you're doing for us." We shook hands, and I turned to walk away, but paused. "Do either of you have a seaplane license?"

"I do," said the first officer, "but I'm not current. I haven't been in a seaplane in over a year. Why do you ask?"

"I've got a Caravan on floats, and it's always nice to know who can fly when the need arises."

"I'd love to get current again, but for now, I'm no help."

"We'll see what we can do to get you some time in the left seat before all of this is over and you have to go back to work for Meriwether."

He smiled for the first time. "I'd like that."

Back at the house, we serviced the dive gear while Skipper set up her command center. Penny was unusually quiet, and after what Skipper had told me on the phone, that concerned me.

After I was satisfied the dive gear was in top-notch condition, I went in search of my wife and found her sitting on the edge of my bed, staring out the window.

I sat beside her and reached for her hand. "Penny, what's wrong? You're not yourself. I'm worried about you."

She pulled her hand away from mine. "I'm fine."

I swallowed the bitterness on my tongue. "I know you well enough to know that 'I'm fine' never means you're fine. Whatever it is, we can talk about it, or I can simply listen if that's what you need. No matter what it is, it's not too big for us to handle together."

She turned to face me, her eyes glistening with the first indications of coming tears. "Why, Chase?"

I laid my hand on her thigh. "Because I love you, and I want to help with anything that bothers you."

She yanked her leg from beneath my hand. "If you love me so much, how do you explain this?"

She held up two strands of long, blonde hair from one of the pillows on my bed. "Why is Anya's hair on *your* pillow?"

Innocence, like most things in life, is subjective. I was utterly innocent of the transgression Penny was accusing, but Anya *had* been in my bedroom and on my bed. The truth, like innocence, is rarely as simple as it should be.

I locked eyes with Penny. "Anya came into my room last night to convince me to let her—"

She sprang to her feet and stormed toward the door. "Oh, and I bet she can be quite convincing, can't she?"

"Penny, listen to me. I'm not sure what's gotten into you, but there's absolutely nothing going on between Anya and me that isn't one-hundred-percent professional."

"Her hair in your bed, Chase! Is that professional?"

"Penny, she came in here to tell me she wanted to be on the team to board the oil rig. That's it. Nothing more."

She clenched her jaw. "And I'm sure you gave her everything she wanted, didn't you?"

The muscles of my neck tightened as if trying to sever my head from my body. "No, I didn't give her what she wanted."

"Really? So, she's not going to be the one to board the oil rig?"

"No, that's not what I meant. Yes, she's boarding the rig, but not because she. . . ."

She forced a smile. "Yeah, that's what I thought. If she's what you want, Chase, then do it. Just do it. I'm just some rat from Podunk, Texas, anyway."

I stepped toward her as the tears exploded from her eyes and her body shuddered. "Penny, what are you talking about? What's really going on here? This isn't about Anya's hair, is it?"

I gently placed my hand on her bicep, and she gasped. Her first instinct was to pull away, but after an instant, she stepped toward me, allowing me to take her in my arms. Feeling her body jerk and tremble sickened me. The incessant need to talk her into telling me what was truly wrong was almost overpowering, but somehow, I managed to simply hold her as she wrestled with her demon.

Sometimes people don't want help. They just want support from someone who loves them—someone who'll shut up and listen. I wasn't particularly good at that task, but I was devoted to trying.

Penny let me hold her barely long enough to gather her senses, and then she pressed her palm into my chest. "I can't do this right now. It's all too much."

I tried to brush her hair from her face, but she flinched and pulled away. "Penny, I need you to listen to me. I'm in the middle of an operation. It's important that I be able to focus on the mission."

"Oh, I know it is, Chase. Everything you do is always more important. God knows I've figured that out by now."

"What do you want me to do?"

She let out a huff and shook her head. "I shouldn't have to tell you."

I closed my eyes in an effort to refine what I wanted to say into what Penny wanted to hear. "You're right. You're absolutely right. I put the missions ahead of everything else in my life, including us, and I shouldn't do that. I don't know how to explain why without saying things that will only hurt you. And I never want to hurt you."

"Maybe you should've thought about that before you married me. Maybe you should've decided right then what was more important—me, or your job that's going to get you killed. You should've . . ." She threw her hands in the air and stepped back. "It doesn't matter. You're going to keep doing what you do until it kills you, and you obviously don't care."

The words screamed inside my head, burning to escape. I ached to make her understand how important my work was, but there was almost nothing I could do at that moment that would be worse than trying to explain anything. All I could do was make an offering.

"There are over a hundred innocent people on that oil rig, and half of them are children. I'm going to save them. I will keep them alive. After I've done so, I'll then do anything you want. Absolutely anything. No limits."

She froze. "You'll quit?"

"If that's what you want."

She turned for the door. "I'm going back to Saint Marys. If you're sleeping with Anya, don't come home."

Chapter 11
Compartmentalization

Penny slammed the bedroom door, and less than a minute later, my phone chirped.

"Mr. Fulton, this is Jim, your pilot. Mrs. Fulton just called and asked us to fly her back to Saint Marys. I just wanted to check with you."

I growled. "Whatever Mrs. Fulton wants, you will do. Her instructions are my instructions."

I shoved the phone back in my pocket and sat on the edge of my bed, pounding my fist into the pillow where Anya's hair had lain. Keeping a cool head when the world melted down around me was the single greatest skill I possessed, but I'd never had that particular part of my world fall apart before that day. Calm may have been what the world would see, but chaos of the highest order exploded inside my head.

Someone offered a hesitant knock on my door.

"What!" I grunted.

Skipper turned the knob and tentatively stuck her head and shoulders into my room. "Um, Penny asked me to take her to the airport. Is everything okay?"

I held up my palm. "Just do whatever she wants."

To my surprise, Skipper withdrew from the room and eased the door closed, leaving me boiling in broth of my own making.

The Suburban's tires ground against the crushed shell driveway outside my window, and I felt my heart sink into my stomach as the woman I loved was driven farther away with every passing second. Everything inside me wanted to go after her, walk away from the mission, and get on that airplane with my wife, but if I chased her, would the children on the oil rig survive? How many more innocent lives would be lost to whatever was happening in the deep water of the Gulf of Mexico? If I was right and Penny was upset about something other than Anya, she'd still be at Bonaventure when all the mayhem came to an end and we'd stopped the trafficking ring. If I was wrong, and Anya truly was the problem, continuing the mission could be the end of my marriage. I'd made countless decisions affecting thousands of human lives, but the decision that lay before me that day was potentially the most destructive of my life.

Part of me was angry over being accused of a transgression I hadn't committed. Part of me was terrified at the thought of losing the woman I loved. The rest of me was sickened at the thought of being the only person on Earth with the knowledge, expertise, equipment, and team to quickly put an end to an evil lurking barely above the surface just off our shores. All warriors are human, but not every person can be a warrior. A breed of men and women with a core of molten iron in their chests is often the thin, impenetrable line separating mankind from their own destruction. That iron burned inside me and the members of my team, but I dragged a person into a world she was never created to endure. I plunged the woman I loved into a fire she may not have the core to survive. The only decisions left in my life were to shield her from the fire, walk away from the flame, or dive into the heart of the furnace where lesser men would perish.

I stormed through the house and down the steps leading to the dock, ignoring the questioning eyes of my team and their timid silence. Dangling my legs over the edge, I sat on the port-side pontoon of my amphibious Caravan and watched the light dance across the tiny ripples on the water. I don't know how long I'd been sitting there before someone else's weight on the pontoon sent ripples writhing across the surface. Every part of me wanted it to be Penny, but most of all, I wanted it to be anyone other than Anya.

"I'm a sniper, Chase. It's all I've ever been. Do you know what that means?"

Singer's words came as a relief. They weren't Russian-accented, but to my chagrin, they also didn't have a North Texas drawl.

I didn't look up. "Yeah, I think I know what it means to be a sniper."

"There's a lot more to it than just aiming and pulling a trigger," he said. "I watch from a distance and try to form an accurate picture of what's happening in the silence a mile away. When I believe I've done that, I make the decision to change the course of the lives of everyone in my scope with a quarter-inch movement of my right index finger."

I spat into the water, leaving rings of ever-expanding circles radiating from the point of impact. "I'm not really in the mood for word games."

Singer tossed a pebble a few feet away from where I'd spat, and his ripples collided with mine, changing both sets into something neither was before.

I looked up into his face.

He didn't meet my gaze, and he instead stared blankly into the water, just as I'd done for minutes, or perhaps hours, before he arrived. "It's no word game. It's my life. I don't know what happened up there with you and Penny, but I watched from a distance and tried to piece it together. But I couldn't. So, instead of pulling the trigger, I laid down my rifle and came to sit beside my friend who's turning himself inside out."

I picked at the wooden planks of the dock. "She accused me of sleeping with Anya."

"I've only known you a couple of years, but I can't see you doing that."

I let a long sigh escape my lips. "I didn't, but I don't think that's what's really bothering her. I think it's a convenient excuse to start a fight without telling me what's actually on her mind."

He sucked air through his teeth. "Do you have any idea what the real issue might be?"

I stood and walked to the nose of the pontoon. "No, I don't. And that's what makes this so hard."

He drummed his fingers against the aluminum skin of the float. "You're the psychologist, but if you want my advice, I'd recommend doing the hardest thing any of us ever has to do in this job."

"What's that?" I asked without turning around.

"Compartmentalizing. Finding a way to focus on the mission and the lives in your hands without letting outside influences cloud your judgment. When the mission is done, or when the part of the mission that requires your participation is done, you then find a way to shut out the mission and focus on your marriage. Nobody can do both of those things simultaneously. Not even the great Chase Fulton."

The gentle rocking of the pontoon told me he'd stepped to the dock and was walking away. Singer was right. He was always right.

While I was working out a plan to compartmentalize, I methodically removed the cover from the Mark V patrol boat and stowed it away. No plan came together during the mundane task, so I stripped off my boots, socks, and shirt, and dived into Callaway Bayou. Thirty minutes spent swimming at the best pace I could maintain did the trick. I emerged from the water focused, determined, and winded.

"Okay, listen up," I ordered as I came through the door. "Anya, Hunter, and I are the boarding party. Clark is the boat captain, and Singer and Mongo are overwatch from the foredeck."

Everyone stared as if seeing their team leader dripping wet and shirtless was something foreign to them, but no one questioned the plan.

"Skipper," I continued, "you're running the TOC from here. I want every satellite you can beg, borrow, or steal looking down on that rig. Got it?"

She nodded. "Got it."

"We'll power to within four miles of the rig and creep to within a mile and a half as quietly as the boat will run. The swimmers will be in the water at twenty-two hundred. The DPVs will make six knots, so we'll be under the rig in fifteen minutes. We'll split up at the rig, and each of us will climb a different piling as far apart as possible. The search pattern is counterclockwise. We spend exactly twenty minutes on the rig . . . not a second longer. Got it?"

Hunter and Anya both gave the okay sign.

"Zero encounters! We don't engage anyone unless it's in self-defense. I want to get in and out without them knowing we were there. Mongo, how far is it from the main deck to the water?"

He glanced toward the ceiling. "No more than forty-five feet."

I dropped my boots to the floor. "Emergency egress is overboard. Feet first, and protect your eyes. Get back to the gear, and wait for the rest of the team at thirty feet. At twenty-three hundred, we're moving back to the boat."

Everyone except Anya nodded in agreement, so I waited for her comment.

"What if we are caught?"

I grimaced. "They cannot know we were there. The guards are expendable. Deadly force is authorized, but the bodies have to go overboard, and it has to be done silently. Blades and hands only. Sidearms are for worst-case-scenario only. If we start shooting, even suppressed, the gig is up, and we have to take the rig. If I give the order to take the rig, I want the Mark V beneath the platform in under two minutes and Mongo and Singer climbing the pipes. The plan is recon only, though. If this thing turns into a gunfight, there's going to be a lot of blood in the water and a lot of uncomfortable questions to answer."

I scanned the room for questions, but none came. "Okay, cram all the calories you can get into your bodies, and gear up. We've got an op to run."

In my room, I pulled my phone from my boot, unsure if I was hoping to see a missed call from Penny. Thankfully, the screen was empty. I showered, dressed, and had a short talk with God. I'd never asked for things for myself when I prayed, and that evening was no different. I asked for peace for Penny and safety for my team. If I fell under that umbrella as a part of the team, I would be thankful before the stroke of midnight.

* * *

When I stepped aboard the Mark V, the gear was lined up on deck like the Rockettes, and the engines were rumbling beneath the deck. Singer had his Barrett fifty-caliber rifle stowed by the pilothouse hatch and a pair of spotter's scopes at the ready.

Without spoken coordination, every member of the team had dressed identically in all black. The outline of three fighting knives shone through Anya's clothes, while two more were sheathed in plain sight behind each of her hips. Hunter wore a dive knife on his left ankle and a pair of fighting knives on his chest. His sidearm rode tightly against the outside of his right thigh. Mongo looked like an enormous black mountain looming over all of us. His size alone was enough to intimidate most would-be combatants, but unless things turned into a train wreck on the rig, he'd stay on the boat.

There are as many pre-mission personality types as there are operators. Hunter grew quiet and reflective in the minutes before the action. Clark, on the other hand, became everybody's mother as he checked gear relentlessly and ensured everyone was mission-ready. Anya didn't change much. Perhaps she was always ready for a fight. Singer prayed. Mongo ate everything he could find, from peanuts to protein bars. He thrived on calories. A machine the size of Mongo requires a lot of fuel.

Having never served in uniform, I'd never been taught the military mindset, so I was left to my own devices to develop my own pre-combat routine. Positive visualization had been my mainstay since I began my life as a covert operative. I focused entirely on the successful completion of the mission, picturing every step that would lead to ultimate success. However, that night, my positive thoughts were consumed by the terrifying prospect of Penny walking out of my life forever. Anya's hair on my pillow was bad enough to send most women into a rage, but whatever it was that haunted Penny was far more powerful than a couple of strands of blonde hair.

"Hey! Where are you, man?"

I shook off the delirium and opened my eyes to see Clark's face only inches from mine.

He tapped his index finger against my temple. "Whatever you've got going on in there better be mission-related. You've got a boatful of warriors and an oil rig full of hostages depending on you to focus. Will you be able to do that?"

I forced Penny from my head. "Yeah, I'm in the game. Thanks for . . . well, you know."

THE EMERALD CHASE · 97

He slugged my shoulder. "Yeah, I know. Just focus. We need you."

The lights of the rig broke the horizon about eight miles away as the Mark V carried the team toward destiny at fifty knots. At four miles out, Clark reclaimed the helm from Anya and gave me a nod.

I yelled over the roar of the engines and wind. "Gear up! We're four minutes running quiet and twenty minutes from splashing."

Anya, Hunter, and I pulled on our wetsuits, rebreathers, and fins. Singer and Mongo crawled onto the foredeck with rifles and spotter's scopes in tow. At four miles from the rig, Clark pulled the throttles back, allowing the massive patrol boat to come off plane and settle into the calm waters of the Gulf of Mexico. At barely above idle speed, with all lights doused, we crept toward the rig. The night breeze blew from the southwest at five knots, helping to mask the noise of the pair of Herculean diesels rumbling beneath our feet. Arriving undetected aboard the Pan America Rig was paramount to the success of our mission. We had neither the manpower nor the firepower to put up much of a fight if the pirates were prepared to repel boarders.

Commanding a team of highly trained, seasoned operators should've been one of the most stressful endeavors of my young life, but my team anticipated orders before I had to issue them. Instinctually, everyone aboard the boat moved silently, never uttering so much as a whisper. Sound discipline had been drilled into my team's heads until it had become an integral part of their thinking. During drilling operations, the rig generates enough noise to deafen nearly everyone aboard, but when the machinery falls silent, the thunder of a Mark V patrol boat approaching at high speed would sound like a freight train.

At precisely 2200 hours, Clark pulled the transmission into neutral, idled the port engine, and shut down the starboard. He stuck his head from the pilothouse and held up one finger, announcing we'd arrived at our drop point, one mile from the rig. Silently, we donned our full facemasks and took the first breaths from our Draeger LAR V rebreathers.

In sequence, Anya, Hunter, and I performed our communications check.

"One's up. . . ."

"Loud and clear. Two's up. . . ."

"Loud and clear. Three's up. . . ."

"All loud and clear," I declared. "Let's get wet."

Chapter 12
In and Out

Barely leaving a ripple, the three of us slid over the gunwale, following our diver propulsion vehicles into the water, and submerged five feet beneath the surface, we finned away from the metal and electronics of the patrol boat. We surfaced fifty feet from the boat and set our compasses to bear on the Pan America Rig six thousand feet away.

I glanced at Hunter and Anya, whose faces wore the stern looks of seasoned operators focused on the mission. "We'll swim for six minutes at fifteen feet, surface, recheck our bearing, and continue. Any questions?"

Neither spoke, so I gave the thumbs-down descent signal, emptied the air from my buoyancy control device, and slipped beneath the inky surface. At fifteen feet, I added enough air to my BCD to stop my descent and achieve neutral buoyancy. A quick buddy-check revealed Hunter and Anya hovering three feet behind me. I squeezed the trigger on my DPV and felt the fans whir in the housing. Accelerating to six knots, I alternated my attention between my compass, watch, and depth gauge. Neglecting any of the three could lead to catastrophe, and there was no room for that in our mission.

At regular intervals, Hunter and Anya allowed the nose of their DPVs to tap the edges of my fins, reassuring me they were still in trail. The only light came from the small voltage meters on the panels of our DPVs and the luminescence of our compasses and depth gauges, though focusing on the light diminished our night vision. Maintaining a vigilant scan while preserving our night sight was challenging, but the swim would be the least stressful phase of the night's mission.

When five minutes had ticked from my watch, I said, "All stop." We simultaneously released our triggers and drifted to a stop in the warm Gulf water. I held the harness of Hunter's BCD, and he laced his hand through Anya's harness as we swam toward the surface. Just before our heads broke the surface, I said, "No more than fifteen seconds on the surface. Reconfirm your bearing to the rig and re-submerge."

"Roger," came their simultaneous reply.

I broke the surface and gave my eyes five seconds to adjust to the new environment. The rig had doubled in apparent size, and we'd drifted slightly south. I reset my compass to compensate for the current and shot a glance toward where the boat should be. It was invisible in the darkness, but my gut told me Clark, Singer, and Mongo had their eyes glued to the rig, waiting to see us climbing the supports.

We hadn't added air to our BCDs, so the descent back to fifteen feet required only a gentle exhale.

"I adjusted five degrees north to compensate for the current. What did you get?"

Anya said, "Also five degree."

"Same for me," said Hunter.

I pulled the trigger and let the DPV accelerate me toward the waiting rig and whatever awaited us on the platform. Six minutes later, we reached the Pan America and drifted to a stop.

"Okay, it's showtime. Hunter, you take the southern riser, and I'll take the northern ladder. Anya, you climb here when I give the word. Any questions?"

"We will climb on your signal," said Anya, her voice tinny and high-pitched through the communication system.

Hunter and I motored toward our objective, and thirty seconds later, he said, "In position."

I clipped my DPV to the ladder and slipped off my rebreather and BCD. My head broke the surface, and I squinted to see Anya and Hunter slipping from the water a hundred feet away. We climbed in silent unison, each of us checking the progress of the others every few seconds. The climb consumed a full minute, and we reached the platform together.

I peered cautiously across the platform and saw no one on deck other than the four roving guards. Our open channel whisper-com system allowed us to hear even the slightest sound made by any member of the team.

I whispered, "One."

In turn, Hunter, Anya, and the three remaining on the boat sounded off with their preassigned call signs. We had solid coms, and so far, no confrontation. That would soon change.

I started through the hatch. "Let's move."

"Moving," Hunter said.

Staying low, we moved silently in a counter-clockwise search pattern with a hundred feet between us. The deck was littered with dumpster-sized storage sheds and equipment I couldn't identify. The night-vision nods we wore turned the environment into a dystopian industrial landscape that only some warped fiction writer would create.

Our whisper-coms made the distance between us disappear.

"Two," I said, "there's a roving guard at your eleven o'clock and thirty feet."

Hunter said, "Got him. What do you think about taking the rovers home with us?"

His idea had some merit. We had only four choices regarding the roving guards. We could put knives in their necks and send them overboard. I didn't love that plan. We could subdue them and stick them full of ketamine. I liked that plan even less. That would leave the guards on the platform to report our overnight presence to their superiors in the morning. Our original plan to avoid the guards while we searched the rig was falling apart, so that left only one remaining option.

I keyed my mic. "Four, one."

Clark answered. "Go, one."

"I'm calling an audible. We're taking down the four roving guards and bringing them out."

"Roger. Advise ready for us to move in."

There would be no way to swim four unconscious guards back to the Mark V, so extricating them required that our boat approach the rig.

"Roger, four. Will advise."

Anya spoke for the first time. "Are we certain there are only four guards?"

"Certain? No," I said, "but we're *confident* there are only four."

She said, "I can take them down almost silently if you and Hunter will move them."

I whispered, "Okay, but don't kill them. We need to interrogate them when we get them off the rig."

"I will not kill them unless there is no other way."

I said, "Okay, two, form up on three. She'll lead the advance and neutralize the guards, and you and I will stack 'em."

"Roger," came Hunter's only reply.

Anya moved like a cat approaching her prey. The first guard pulled a pack of cigarettes from his shirt pocket, stuck one in his mouth, and fumbled with a failing lighter. Our former Russian assassin took advantage of the man's distracted state and moved like the wind, delivering a crushing blow to the man's neck, followed instantly by a pair of strikes to the temple. She caught his melting body in her right arm and the falling lighter in the palm of her left hand.

Hunter relieved Anya of the burden and hefted the unconscious guard over his shoulder.

If Anya had been wearing a heart monitor, I doubt if her pulse rate would've broken sixty. She pocketed the lighter and crept across the platform, scanning every inch of her environment. Watching her work was a study in tactical precision. She'd been trained to the point of perfection and had become a master of silent dominance.

I trailed her by a dozen feet, taking note of every detail on the platform. Anya shot her hand above her shoulder, signaling me to freeze as we approached the corner of one of the platform structures. A pair of hatches stood six feet from the corner—one marked "Engineering Personnel Only" and the other marked "Hazardous Material Storage."

I focused on the heels of Anya's boots. If she was going to move, her feet would be the earliest and best indication.

Our whisper-coms were open-channel mics between Hunter, Anya, and me, but to communicate with the boat crew, we had to press a PTT button. I hadn't heard Anya speak Russian in some time, so when she whispered, "*Idi ko mne,*" it was clear she'd reverted all her senses back to her training and native language. Our senses run home when we're under stress, intently focused, or frightened. Anya was feeling no fear, and likely no stress, but she was laser-focused on luring the second guard to "Come to me."

Unexpectedly, she moved backward toward me by two silent strides, and bent her knees, lowering her body by several inches. I didn't know what was going to happen when the man rounded the corner, but I was looking forward to the show.

I was not disappointed.

The barrel of the guard's rifle protruded around the corner before anything else, and Anya slid her hand above the barrel. As the man's body followed the weapon around the corner, Anya rose to her full height, directly in front of his face, and seductively said, "Hi, there. You are cute."

His eyes exploded with shock and disbelief. When Anya Burinkova put her lips inches in front of any man's face, it was either going to be a night he'd never forget or the last thing he'd see before his lights went out.

Anya wasn't the only one on deck reverting to her training. The guard gripped his rifle in an attempt to put the muzzle in Anya's chest, but she'd anticipated his reaction and made him pay dearly for it. As he raised the butt of the weapon, she forced the muzzle down and twisted the sling into an ever-diminishing noose as she spun the man around and drew the nylon webbing across his throat. Using the rifle as leverage, she tightened the sling until the guard's brain stopped fighting for oxygen and his body collapsed to the deck.

Impressed and amazed by her skill, I hefted the man across my shoulder, just as Hunter had done with the first guard, and headed back toward the deck hatch leading to the rig supports. I passed Hunter a few strides away, and he continued his return trip to join our resident Russian guard snatcher.

I found the first guard bound and gagged, lying on his side beside a collection of equipment. After adding my man to the pile, I threw his rifle into the water and tucked his radio into my vest.

I keyed my mic. "Four, this is one. Two down and two to go."

"Roger," came Clark's reply.

Moving slowly and as quietly as possible, in an effort to catch up with Anya, I retraced the steps I'd taken before. A little over halfway back to the corner of the structure where she'd strangled the second guard, I saw Hunter moving slowly toward me with a third man over his shoulder.

"She's pretty good at this," he whispered as we passed.

I shook my head. "No, she's just getting lucky."

When I caught up with her, I couldn't believe what I saw. Anya was facedown on the platform, and the fourth guard stood over her with his rifle pressed against the back of her neck. He was reaching for his radio to tell the whole world about the woman he'd captured on deck. I reached for the second guard's radio in my vest and thumbed the push-to-talk button, hoping to jam the transmission Anya's captor was about to make. With any luck, the radio call would come across as nothing more than a squeal and crackle.

Jamming his transmission would only temporarily delay the inevitable train wreck. Everything about the in-and-out zero-contact mission I'd planned had just been blown to hell in the middle of the Gulf of Mexico.

Chapter 13
Best Laid Plans

My low-tech radio-jamming attempt worked, but it was little more than a hiccup in the guard's plan. The veins pressing against the taut skin of his neck displayed the man's stress-laden intensity. The next four seconds of my life could define the entirety of the remainder of Anya's.

"Two, one. Three is down. A guard has her pinned to the deck. I'm thirty feet away."

Hunter's reply thudded in my ear in time with the soles of his boots hitting the platform at a full sprint. "I'm coming!"

A glance over my shoulder revealed no sign of Hunter, so I simultaneously drew my pistol and a long breath. The guard's right index finger was clinched against the trigger of his rifle as my muzzle came to bear on the center of his chest. Further hesitation on my part would cost Anya her life and demolish our mission.

I pressed the trigger of my Heckler & Koch Mark 23. Orange fire would belch from the muzzle of the suppressor, and the only noises would be the pair of forty-five-caliber bullets breaking the sound barrier and the guard's body collapsing to the deck.

The recoil sent my pistol rising in my hand, and I watched in disbelief as the guard's torso exploded into mist. My forty-five would have left thumb-sized entry wounds and soup-can-sized exit holes, but they would never pulverize a human body. While my mind reeled trying to unscramble the puzzle in front of me, my earpiece clicked and the voice of Singer, our Southern Baptist sniper six thousand feet away, belted out, "I'll fly away, oh glory. I'll fly away in the morning."

The thunderous report of the fifty-caliber sniper rifle followed five seconds later, and the whole world knew the gig was up.

I thumbed the coms button and ordered, "Get in here. We need all the help we can get. The mission is now a raid."

Clark's voice filled my ear, along with the roar of the Mark V's diesels. "We're moving!"

Hunter raced past me and jerked Anya to her feet. The three of us ran at full pace toward the largest structure of the rig. The necessity of silence was gone, as was the fourth guard's upper body.

I yelled, "That has to be where they're holding the hostages."

"Do we make entry before the boat gets here?" Hunter asked as we slammed our bodies against the wall near the personnel hatch leading into the structure.

"No," I ordered. "We hold the door and kill anyone who comes through it. We'll breach when everyone's on deck."

In unison, Hunter and Anya replied, "Roger."

We caught our breath and moved to concealment and cover behind an enormous piece of drilling equipment. We had crossing angles of fire on the hatch and enough ammo to keep any forces they had on the other side of the door until Clark, Singer, and Mongo showed up.

I met Anya's gaze. "Are you okay?"

"I am okay, but I should have told you plan. I wanted guard to take me. I wanted to hear his voice. When I let him take me to ground, I locked open bolt on rifle and took from him magazine. I was in no danger."

I turned my face to the dark night sky and sighed. "Yeah, you should've mentioned that."

"I am sorry, but I am not trained to work with team. I was Russian assassin. Is lonely job."

"None of that matters now," I said. "We've got an unknown number of bandits and over a hundred scared hostages. The rest of our night is going to be interesting."

Clark's voice rang in my earpiece. "We're on whisper-coms now and starting our climb. Don't shoot us."

I said, "We're at the southeast corner of the rig behind something that looks like a giant claw from a *Transformers* movie. We're covering the personnel door of the main structure."

"Roger. We'll be there in two minutes."

The next sound I heard both startled and delighted me. It was the radio shoved into my vest.

In crisp Spanish, a voice called, "Miguel, report. Is everything okay?"

"They obviously know we're here," I said.

Hunter nodded but didn't remove his eyes from the hatch. "They obviously *suspect* we're here."

"Good point," I conceded.

The hatch opened a few inches, and the muzzle of a rifle protruded through the opening, followed by the body of young man moving cautiously. He scanned the deck. "Miguel! Miguel! Are you out here?" The man then keyed his radio. "Any guards, report. What is happening out here?"

"I've got an idea," I whispered. "Hunter, I need you to flank him and invite him to join our party. We're going to put on a little show."

Hunter holstered his pistol. "You got it, boss. If I'm not back in five minutes. . . . Well, if I'm not back in five, give me five more. I'll be back."

He slinked off into the darkness as Anya and I kept the new arrival in our sights. Thirty seconds later, Hunter stepped from behind a deck box and tapped the new guard's shoulder. The man flinched, yanked his rifle to his shoulder, and turned to face my partner. Hunter smiled and delivered a colossal right upper-cut to the man's chin. The guard wilted as if his knees had turned to Jell-O, and Hunter shouldered him like a sack of potatoes.

Hunter arrived with his payload at the same time Clark, Singer, and Mongo took a knee beside me.

I surveyed my team. "Welcome aboard, guys. I want Mongo and Singer to hold this position and control that hatch. If they come out one at a time, we can manage them, but if they dis-patch a team, we'll have to cut them down. Got it?"

"Got it," they said.

"Hunter, Clark, Anya, come with me. And bring our new friend." I led them toward the deck hatch where we'd hidden the first three guards. As we approached the stash site, I turned to Clark. "How do you feel about a little game of 'Interrogate the Dead Guy'?"

Clark grinned. "That's one of my favorite games."

"I thought so, but we'll have to do this one in Spanish. Are you okay with that?"

He nodded. "Si."

I motioned toward the unconscious guard in Hunter's arms. "Wake him up. He needs to see this."

Hunter dropped the man to the deck and pulled the small first-aid kit from his vest. He cracked a packet of smelling salts and waved it under the guard's nose. A few slaps to the face had the man's eyes wide open and filled with terror.

I knelt in front of the guard and spoke in Spanish. "Welcome back, amigo." Pointing into the darkness near the edge of the platform, I said, "Watch and listen."

Clark appeared as a shadowy figure holding the form of another man in his grasp. He bellowed, "How many of you are there on this rig?"

The ketamine-induced sleep the victim was experiencing left him oblivious to anything happening around him, but our new amigo didn't know that.

Clark drew his pistol and placed it beside the unconscious man's head. "Answer me or die."

The guard, of course, said nothing, so Clark squeezed off a round, and the guard at my feet jumped as the suppressed hiss of the forty-five wafted through the night air.

Clark hefted the unconscious man's body over the edge of the platform and let him fall. Without hesitation, he grabbed the second sleeping guard and performed the same act with precisely the same results. The question . . . the non-response . . . the pistol shot . . . the body disposed across the rail. Our fully conscious guard watched Clark's show in horror as his dark complexion paled.

After the third unconscious man made his expedition across the rail, Clark stomped toward us, grabbed the terrified man by the collar, and dragged him back into the shadows. The pistol reemerged, and the same question followed. "How many of you are there on this rig?"

"Sixteen guards, three captains, and the *jefe*." The trembling words cascaded from his mouth as the fear for his life consumed him.

Clark tapped the muzzle of the suppressor to the man's temple. "Sixteen, including you and the four dead ones? Or sixteen more?"

"All!" the man cried. "All together, sixteen. But you said four dead ones. You killed only three."

Clark was obviously amused by the man's ability to count while simultaneously wetting his pants. He twisted the guard's arm around his back, lifted him to his tiptoes, and frog-marched him across the platform until they arrived at the lower half of the corpse strewn across the deck. "There's number four, amigo. Any more questions?"

"Who are you?"

"Oh, that one's easy to answer," Clark said. "We're the guys you never expected to see."

Hunter stuck the guard with a syringe of ketamine and dragged him away.

Clark shot a thumb toward the previous captives. "Put him with the others. I think that's a dandy place for him."

"That was my plan," Hunter said as he tossed the limp form across the rail, letting him fall ten feet into the safety nets that lined the platform.

We rejoined Singer and Mongo.

"Any movement?" I asked.

Singer whispered, "Not a peep, but we heard the show Clark put on. Well done. That leaves eleven guards, two captains, and the boss. I like those odds. Don't you?"

"I do," I answered. "If the six of us can't take out fourteen men, we should be selling used cars somewhere instead of saving the world."

Hunter coughed. "Hey, my uncle's a used car salesman, and he does quite well for himself."

"I'm sure he does," I said, "but he doesn't get to do fun stuff like raiding oil rigs in the middle of the night."

He shrugged. "Yeah, you've got a point there. I think he collects stamps for fun."

"Enough," Clark scolded. "We're breaching that door and staying alive. We'll play some other time. Mongo, tell us what's on the other side of the door."

The giant turned toward Clark. "There will be a crew room on the right with showers, sinks, and gear lockers. Most likely, there will be some offices to the left and the crew barracks down the hall to the right. The galley and mess will be on the left at the end of the hall. At least that's how the rigs I worked on were laid out. But that's been a long time ago."

"Okay," Clark said, "that sounds reasonable. I want Hunter and Chase through the door first. If you encounter anyone armed, put him down. Don't hesitate. We're responding to piracy in the interest of rescuing hostages. Does everyone understand?"

We nodded and mumbled our agreement.

"Good. Mongo, you're number three through the door, followed by Anya. Singer can have the rear. The only question we ask is, Where's the boss? *¿Dónde está el jefe?* Got it?"

There were nods of acknowledgment.

Clark continued. "Silence and persistence. We make as little sound as possible, but we never stop moving until we've neutralized every armed man and captured the boss. Let's move!"

I held up my hand. "There's just one more thing. Anya, this is a team op. You do not go off down a rabbit hole. Stay with the team and move as a team. Understand?"

"Yes, Chase, I will stay with team."

We rose as a single unit and moved toward the still-open hatch. The interior light made our night-vision nods unnecessary, so we folded them upward, giving us unrestricted visibility. It took several seconds for my eyes to adjust to the harsh interior lights, but I was thankful to no longer see the world through the colorless lens of my nods.

Mongo was right. The first passageway to the right was a head with showers and lockers. Hunter and I cleared the space in seconds while the remainder of the team held the hallway. Progressing down the long corridor, we cleared several small offices before approaching the entrance to the barracks on the right, and the galley and mess hall on the left.

"Which one first, Clark?"

"Galley first," he said. "There's likely to be fewer folks in there this time of night."

Without a reply, we moved toward the double doors of the mess hall and galley.

I eyed Hunter. "Ready?"

He nodded. "Let's do this!"

We shouldered our way through the doorway and split directions. Hunter went left with Anya and Singer. I led the breach to the right with Mongo and Clark close in trail. Four startled faces shot up in disbelief, and one of the four seated men drew a pistol from a shoulder rig under his left arm. Before he could bring the pistol to bear on any of us, Singer sent a round into the back of the gunman's hand. Blood sprayed in all directions, and the pistol slid harmlessly across the metal tabletop.

An animal cry left the wounded man's mouth as he grabbed at the demolished hand with his left. I remembered the horror of looking down at my destroyed hand after the collision at home plate in the ninety-six College World Series that ended my baseball career. I knew well the shock the man was feeling, but unlike me, he'd likely never regain use of what was left of his hand.

In commanding Spanish, I ordered, "Hands on your heads, and heads on the table. Now!"

I had no expectation of the injured man following my orders, but the others obeyed without hesitation. I motioned toward the bleeding man. "Mongo, get him under control, and stop that bleeding. Singer, you cover and disarm the others. The rest of us will clear the galley."

Mongo and Singer sprang into action, and the remaining four of us moved toward the single swinging door of the galley. I lead the entry, shoving the door to its stops and catching it with my heel to prevent it from swinging back and blocking our ingress.

A single man in the galley wore a white T-shirt and an apron tight around his waist. His reaction did not mirror the men from the mess hall. Instead of showing surprise, his eyes narrowed, and he pulled a butcher's knife from a sheath at his side. With his left hand, he lifted a cleaver from the table behind him and stood in daring defiance to the four armed commandos at his door.

A devious smile came to Anya's lips. "Save bullets. I will handle him."

I couldn't know if it was arrogance or self-entertainment driving her, but I relaxed my trigger finger when she pulled a pair of fighting knives from her sheaths and moved toward the cook. The man had just stolen more chain than he could swim with, and our Eastern Bloc edged-weapons specialist was about to send him to the bottom of the ocean.

Unfazed, he kept moving forward, swinging the blades in front of him with practiced precision. Anya stopped six feet from the aggressor, winked at him, and from her left palm, sent a knife soaring through the air at the man's chest. With the quickness of a cat, he turned his body just enough to allow the flying knife sail past and stick harmlessly in the wall behind him. Renewed confidence overtook his face, and he lunged for Anya, his butcher knife leading the way.

Anya's speed couldn't be measured, but as her right arm ceased its forward motion and her hand released the second knife, the fight was over before the cook knew it had begun. Her knife sank to the hilt in the watery socket of the cook's left eye, and his brain stopped communicating with the rest of his body. He collapsed at her feet, his blood pooling around his head on the greasy deck.

She placed the heel of her left boot on the cook's forehead, pulled her knife from his skull, and wiped it on his white T-shirt. After recovering her first knife from the wall, she sheathed both weapons and turned back with evident satisfaction on her face.

Clark was the first to speak. "Don't let that happen again. A bullet in his brain removes the possibility of any of us getting hurt. We're a small force. Losing one fighter makes our odds dramatically worse. Got it?"

Anya grimaced. "I am sorry. It was foolish. I will not do again."

Clark smiled. "I know you won't, but that was one hell of a performance, comrade. I'm glad you're on our team."

Her smile returned. "I am glad also to be on your team."

Back in the mess hall, Mongo had a tourniquet and pressure bandage in place. The remaining three men were flex-cuffed, and their weapons were on the table, well out of their reach.

Clark said, "Nice work. Put them in the walk-in freezer and secure the hasp."

Mongo, Singer, and Hunter marched the men through the galley and forced them into the freezer.

The one-handed prisoner was showing signs of shock, so I said, "Give him enough morphine to keep him from passing out."

Mongo injected him and shoved him down on a crate of frozen fish. "Keep this elevated, and do not remove the tourniquet. Do you understand?"

The man turned to me in utter confusion, so I repeated the instructions in Spanish.

Mongo shoved the freezer door closed and slid a sharpening steel from a knife block into the lock hole of the hasp.

Clark reached up and killed the power to the freezer. "They'll still be cold, but at least they won't freeze to death."

"Nine down. Seven to go," I said. "It's time to hit the barracks."

Chapter 14
Penthouse

We moved from the mess hall back toward the barracks in a two-column formation, each of us ready to put down anyone who came through the door. Other than the scream following the hand wound, we'd been relatively quiet so far.

Clark asked, "Mongo, what are we going to see in there?"

Mongo pulled down his nods. "Nothing if we don't put our goggles back on. It'll be dark. Most people will be asleep, but there will be at least two guards who should be awake if they're worth whatever they're being paid."

We lowered our nods and eased through the doors. An aggressive entry would only serve to awaken at least a hundred scared humans. We didn't need that kind of chaos.

Mongo was right. Eight feet inside the door were a pair of guards, each leaning back in their chairs. One was sound asleep, but the other blinked in the dim red light from the overhead bulb. He was slow pulling his pistol, but fast enough to trigger Clark's reaction. Two forty-five caliber rounds permanently put out the man's lights.

I stepped into the second guard, who was rapidly waking from his dreams and plummeting into an eyes-wide-open night-mare. I shoved my knee beneath the front edge of his chair, preventing him from getting his feet back on the floor, and chopped at the wrist of his right hand as he pulled his sidearm clear of its leather holster. The weapon clattered to the deck, and I shoved the muzzle of my pistol beneath his chin. "*¿Dónde está el jefe?*"

His mouth didn't move, but his eyes shot to the overhead. "Oh, so he's upstairs, huh?"

"*¿Quién eres tú?*"

"Why does everyone keep asking me who I am tonight? I'm starting to get a complex. As far as you're concerned, hombre, I'm the sandman. Now, go to sleep." The butt of my pistol to his temple sent him crumpling from the chair and onto the deck. I rolled the man onto his side. "Put him in the freezer with the others."

Mongo hefted him from the deck and headed for the galley with Singer providing cover.

A flash of movement caught my attention, and I spun, sticking my pistol into the face of a bright-eyed little boy of perhaps five years old.

"*¿Qué está hacienda, señor?*"

Quickly lowering my gun, I asked, "What's *your* name?"

"I'm Roberto."

"Where are you from, Roberto?"

"Are you going to hurt me, señor?"

"No, Roberto. I'm not going to hurt you. I'm here to help you. We're the good guys. Tell me where you're from."

The boy said, "I live near Rio Hondo. No, I *used* to live near Rio Hondo. I don't know where I live now."

"Rio Hondo in Guatemala?" I asked in disbelief.

"Si, Guatemala."

I looked over my shoulder. "They're Guatemalan."

Clark sighed. "Okay, that answers one question. Now, how are you going to keep that kid quiet while we find the bosses?"

I turned back to the boy and lifted him into the chair where the guard had been sleeping. "I need you to do me a favor. Can you do that?"

"Si."

"I need you to sit right here in this chair and watch over your friends and make sure they're safe. I'll be back to get you and your friends out of here in a few minutes, okay?"

"Okay, señor. I can do that."

We moved quietly from the barracks and back into the hallway just as Singer and Mongo stepped from the mess hall.

"Okay, Mongo," Clark said. "It's time for you to play tour guide again. The bosses are apparently upstairs. What are we going to find up there?"

"It's the engineer's quarters. Those guys didn't sleep in open bays like the roughnecks."

"Will the doors be locked?" I asked.

Mongo shrugged. "I don't know, but when has a locked door ever stopped us?"

Clark turned on his heel. "Let's go. Mongo, you're the point man. Take us to the penthouse."

We climbed the metal stairs leading to the upper deck of the main structure as quietly as possible. Boots on metal grate stairs aren't exactly stealthy.

Reaching the second deck, Mongo pulled the door open an inch and peered down the hall. "It's clear, and there's light."

Clark ordered, "Clear the rooms as we come to them. Same teams as downstairs. Go!"

We reached the first door on the right. Anya set up left of the door, Hunter squared up in front, and I knelt to the right with the doorknob in my palm. Hunter gave the nod, and I gave a twist. The knob turned easily, and Hunter led the entry, flipping on the overhead light as we entered. He moved straight into the space while Anya and I broke right and left on entry.

The room contained an empty bed, cluttered desk, and a pile of filthy clothes in the corner, but no humans, *jefe* or otherwise. Clark and his team made the same discovery in the first room on the left, and we continued down the hallway, alternating entries while the other team covered the hall. The first four rooms revealed nearly identical results, leaving only two doors remaining in the hallway.

Clark whispered, "Let's hit these two simultaneously, and do it hard."

We lined up in a three-man assault formation with Hunter and Mongo poised to kick the doors in. There would be nothing subtle about our next entry. Anya and I stood ready to follow Hunter while Singer and Clark did the same behind Mongo.

Clark gave the order. "Hit 'em!"

Hunter's boot heel landed as precisely as one of Singer's fifty-cal rounds and sent the door shuddering inward. Although I didn't look over my shoulder, it sounded as if Mongo had kicked the other door completely from its hinges. We poured into the two spaces with weapons at the ready.

I yelled, "Hands up! Hands up! Hands up! Do it now!"

I heard Clark yelling, "Get on the ground!"

Fully prepared to engage at least two armed combatants, I scanned every inch of the vacant space. The room contained nothing, not even a pile of dirty laundry. I called, "Clear."

With no gunfire from the other room, I assumed Clark's entry team had found the same as mine, but instead of the disappointing declaration of "Clear," Singer yelled, "Grenade!"

Anya reacted instantly and threw a sidekick to the metal door, sending it back against its jamb. The three of us dived to the deck of the empty room, just as we'd been trained with our ass to the blast, covering our heads with our hands and arms, and opening our mouths in anticipation of the shock wave from the grenade.

The next sound I heard was even more terrifying than the initial grenade call.

Clark roared, "Mongo! No!"

Seconds ticked by like hours as I imagined the giant diving onto the rolling grenade without a thought of his own safety as he sacrificed his three-hundred-pound body and hundred-ton heart to save the lives of his teammates. I'd heard a few hundred grenades explode in my life, but when the blast came, it was a muted, sickening thud, obviously smothered and contained by a massive body . . . a body like Mongo's.

Anya leapt to her feet, screaming, "No!" and ran from the room. I lunged to catch her, but she evaded my grasp. The carnage awaiting her in the next room would be enough to send her into a rage beyond comprehension.

I pictured the big man's body riddled by shrapnel and explosive concussion. He would be all but unrecognizable when Anya saw what remained of the man she loved. With my gut roiling with anxiety, hatred, and disbelief, I gave chase, hoping to catch her before she had to witness the gruesome scene. My ears were still ringing from the blast when I heard the sound of distant pistol fire. I tried to brace myself for shock, and I burst into the room where Mongo had made the ultimate sacrifice.

The scene unfolded in front of me in irrational flashes of light and muted sounds. Clark and Singer lay on their backs, pistols held in outstretched arms, firing wildly into the ceiling. As if in slow motion, I watched the two men empty their weapons, reload, and continue pouring lead into the overhead.

Forcing myself to accept the reality of the horrific events of the past few seconds, I refocused my sight on Anya as she buried her shoulder beneath Mongo's supine form. His lifeless body must have felt like an elephant's bulk as she struggled to roll him onto his side. Her boots dug at the deck, trying to find purchase, but slipping with every thrust.

I reached down and grasped her shoulder, pulling her away from Mongo. "You don't want to turn him over. It's no use."

She yanked free of my grip and yelled up at me. "*Pomogi mne, pozhaluysta!*"

Her cries for my help in her native Russian sounded as distant as the pistol shots. Soon, another set of shots joined the first, and I turned to see Hunter pumping forty-five-caliber rounds into the ceiling alongside Clark and Singer. Nothing about the scene made sense to me.

Anya bellowed, "Chase! Help me!"

She would not be denied, and there was nothing I could do to pull her away from the body of my friend and the man she loved, so I surrendered and knelt to join her efforts to reveal the devastation the grenade had wrought.

With combined effort, we rolled Mongo onto his side, and the momentum of the movement continued his motion until he lay faceup, eyes wide in a lifeless stare at the ceiling where my three remaining teammates continued to punish whatever existed in the space.

To my astonishment, Mongo's chest wasn't blown open. There was no blood, no entrails, and no scorched, shredded flesh. His clothing was burnt, and the gear in his load-bearing vest was blown to unrecognizable debris, but against all reason, his body was intact.

I reached for his neck, but my hand landed on top of Anya's above his carotid artery.

"He's alive!" she yelled, but it sounded as if she were at the bottom of a well.

"Keep him alive," I shouted as I jumped to my feet, the reason for my partners' seemingly irrational behavior now clear. Shoving my head between Hunter's legs from behind, I hoisted his weight onto my shoulders and stood to my full height. Hunter gave no resistance and tore at the ceiling tiles with reckless abandon, sending shards of metal, asbestos panels, and light fixtures flying in every direction.

With his pistol held horizontally over his head, he emptied the magazine into the overhead space, dropped the weapon, and reached down for mine. I shoved the butt of my pistol into his grip and reloaded the one he'd dropped into my left hand. Hunter squirmed like a writhing beast until he planted a boot on my shoulder and thrust himself into the ceiling.

"Get me up there, too!" Singer yelled, and I cupped my hands into a stirrup. He stepped into my grip and hurled himself upward. Clark stood, reloaded, and stepped toward me, but I shoved my palm into his chest. "No! You stay here and help Anya with Mongo. He's alive. I'm going up."

Although his scowl said he wanted to step on my head and join Hunter and Singer, he conceded and cupped his hands for me. I took the leg-up and scurried into the overhead.

Reaching to pull my night-vision nods into place, I discovered they were no longer on top of my head. They'd been lost sometime during the entry and explosion, so into the darkness I crawled, determined to find the bastard who'd dropped the grenade on my team.

Chapter 15
Your Momma's Cornbread

Chasing Singer's and Hunter's silhouettes in the confines of the overhead, I scampered like a rat through the space, determined to catch, capture, or kill the cowards running from us. Although I couldn't tell who, one of my partners slinked through an opening and vanished from sight. Seconds later, the other disappeared just as quickly. Pistol in hand, I dived through the same hole the others had used and rolled to my feet in a poorly lit corridor.

I bolted into a sprint in an effort to catch Hunter and Singer. They shouldered their way through a hatch onto an upper deck of the rig, and I gained a little ground on them. I ducked through the hatch, into the darkness, and paused, hoping my eyes would adjust in time to join the fight.

Before I could bring the world into focus, Hunter shoved me away from the still-open hatch just as a shot rang out and a bullet ricocheted off the metal frame behind me.

"You can't silhouette yourself in front of a hatch like that," Hunter said.

His admonition shouldn't have been necessary, as I'd been trained to avoid suicidal mistakes. But his reaction saved my life.

We sent a wall of lead across the deck and into the abyss of night sky, but had little hope of actually hitting anyone.

I grabbed Hunter's LBV. "Where's Singer?"

"He's getting some altitude. He's still got his nods."

I shot a glance overhead but couldn't find our sniper in the steel structure spiderweb. "We've got to find some cover."

He shoved me toward a massive wall of equipment, and I slid behind a heavy steel panel. Hunter leapt in beside me and pulled a latch on the panel. The wall opened, revealing a collection of tools, including several flashlights.

I thrust my hands into the box. "Grab all the lights you can. I've got an idea."

We loaded our arms and crept our way to the limits of our cover. I flipped on the first flashlight and hurled it across the deck, sending a beam dancing and twisting through the night. Hunter got the picture and followed suit, throwing his lights flying and rolling in every direction.

My hearing was beginning to return to normal after the explosion of the grenade, but the sounds of the flashlights hitting the metallic deck were still slightly muffled. What wasn't muffled were the bullets skipping across every surface around us.

"How many of them are there?" I asked.

Hunter peered around the end of the bank of equipment. "I saw three, but I think there's only two shooting at us."

"I agree. Give me a boost up. I may be able to get a shot from on top of whatever this thing is."

He bent and caught my foot, lifting me toward the top of the equipment stack. I scampered up the irregular surface and found a nook behind a column just as my eyes regained some of their night vision. Two more shots rang out, and I caught a glimpse of the muzzle flash belching from a weapon. I put six or seven rounds directly on the position of the flash and heard a body collapse to the deck.

The sound of footsteps thundering up a ladder echoed through the air as I leapt from the stack and scooped up one of the lights. I accelerated toward the sound with the beam piercing the veil in front of me. Three shots rang out from my left, and I returned fire on the run. The report of Hunter's pistol reverberated from behind me until the other weapon was silenced.

"I'm on your six moving to eight," Hunter yelled as he raced across the deck behind me. The footsteps on the ladder grew fainter but left little doubt where I was headed. The only ladder in sight was encaged inside a metal structure leading skyward and into the belly of the night. I had full faith Hunter would keep the shooter pinned down as I scampered up the ladder.

Ascending into the darkness, I felt something tapping at my neck beneath my left ear, so I swatted at whatever it was. To my delight, I discovered my dangling earpiece from my whisper-coms and shoved it back in place. "Singer, how do you hear?"

"Loud and clear, boss. I've got eyes on you on the ladder, and I can see Hunter putting the gunman down beneath you."

Hearing his voice gave me a sense of relief I'd not expected. "Do you see the guy above me?"

Singer said, "No, but I saw him move away from the ladder to the right. You're clear all the way to the top."

I increased my pace up the ladder, reenergized by Singer's overwatch. "I need your eyes, Singer. I lost my nods, so talk to me."

"I'm moving and scanning," he said. "I'll find him."

I looked at the pistol in my hand as I climbed ever faster. "How much ammo do you have left?"

Singer said, "I'm down to one magazine plus four. How about you?"

"I've got whatever's left in my pistol. That's it."

He let out a laugh. "Then I guess it's a good thing we're running out of bad guys."

I paused to catch my breath before taking the final steps to the platform. "Good point, but with these three, that still leaves two more unaccounted for."

"Nope," he said. "They bled out in the ceiling above Mongo. I saw their bodies when we turned into tunnel rats back there."

I pulled myself from the ladder and landed on the platform in a crouch. From that lofty elevation, I saw the lights of at least one more oil rig in the distance. Knowing we were so close to hundreds of roughnecks who'd kill to be crawling all over the Pan America to rescue their colleagues somehow made me feel better about our operation.

"Talk to me, Singer."

"Keep moving to the right. He's behind the big round thing that looks like the top of an iceberg."

"Iceberg? That's what you see?"

He chuckled. "That the first thing that came to mind. Maybe it looks like a volcano."

"That's better," I said. "I'm moving toward your iceberg volcano. If anything moves in front of me, I need to know."

"Still scanning," he whispered.

I moved as quietly as possible, listening for any movement in front of me. Two steps . . . pause . . . listen . . . two more steps.

Out of the silent darkness came a thud, and the world before me exploded with brilliant white light. I threw up my hand to shield my eyes and shoved my pistol toward the center of the light.

In confident Spanish, a voice bellowed, "I wouldn't pull that trigger if I were you."

I peered through my fingers until my eyes adjusted to the light. Slowly, the outline of a figure emerged, and I squinted in a mostly futile effort to focus.

"*¿Por qué no?*" I asked.

"You'll soon see why not," the voice returned.

Singer's voice rang in my ear. "He's got a dead man's switch, Chase."

My heart sank. "Tell me about the switch, amigo."

"Ah, now you understand why you shouldn't shoot me. This whole rig is wired with enough plastic explosive to send us to the moon, so I suggest you put down your gun and order your man down there to release my soldier."

"Did you hear that?" I whispered.

Singer said, "Yeah, he thinks it's just you and Hunter. Do what he says and get him to move to the left about three feet."

"Okay," I said, a lot louder than necessary. "I'm laying down my gun." In sloth-like movements, I stretched out my left arm and placed my pistol on the deck.

"Good. Now kick it away."

I gave the pistol a swift shot with the toe of my boot and sent it sliding away until it came to rest six feet to the man's right. "There. You've got my gun. Now, let's talk about that switch. Are you really willing to die for whatever this is?"

He laughed. "Oh, amigo. You've not figured it out yet, have you?"

"Enlighten me," I said as I moved toward him in short strides.

"Who sent you? Who do you work for?" he demanded.

"I work for the man who owns this rig. I'm here to do a job—just like you. Only, my job doesn't have to end with you dying. All my boss wants is to get his rig back. You can walk away."

He waved the dead man's switch in front of his face. "Stop! If you come any closer, I'll release the switch."

I took another step toward him and shot my eyes to my pistol on the deck.

Instinctively, he followed my gaze to the weapon and let out a smile. "Oh, you want your gun back. Is that it?"

I took another step. "No. I want you to disable that switch and get in your boat or call in your helicopter—whatever you've got planned for egress—and I want you to disappear. No one else needs to die tonight, especially not any of those innocent people downstairs."

The man took two sliding sidesteps toward my pistol and held the switch above his head. "Go ahead, gringo. Keep walking, and I'll kill us all. I don't care about any of those people down there. They're just refugees desperate to get to America any way they can."

"So, that's it," I said. "You're a trafficker."

Singer whispered, "Get him to take one more step, Chase."

The man laughed. "You can call me whatever you'd like, but I'm a man who moves people and things that need to be someplace else. And I get paid very well to do it."

I held up my hands in front of me as if surrendering and took a half-step forward. "I understand. We're the same, you and me. We're just doing a job. It's my job to get this rig back, and it's your job to get those people to America. I get it." I took another step.

He waved the switch like a torch in front of his face. "No, gringo. We're not the same. I've got five hundred pounds of plastic explosive under my thumb, and you've got nothing."

I stared at my pistol and smiled. "I've got that gun."

He looked down at my Heckler and Koch, took two more steps, and tapped it with his toe. "Do you mean *this* gun?"

Singer whispered, "Move your head, Chase."

"No, not that gun. . . ." I turned and pointed behind me. "That one."

With accuracy few men could match, Singer sent a forty-five round through the dead man's switch, splintering the metal and plastic housing, and leaving the man crashing to the deck, his left hand gushing blood.

I closed the distance between us and landed my boot inside his right elbow. The bones of the joint crumbled beneath my weight as his now useless hand clawed for my pistol. Lifting my boot from his arm, I planted it beneath his chin. With his right arm broken and his left hand practically gone, I recovered my pistol from the deck, giving it a satisfied look. "On second thought . . . maybe I *was* talking about this gun." I holstered the weapon and nodded toward my sniper. "Nice shot, Singer. Now how about helping me get this guy down from here? He's in no condition to negotiate a ladder by himself."

"I'm on my way, boss."

Singer arrived on the platform whistling "How Great Thou Art." Our prisoner whimpered like a pitiful child as Singer not-so-gently helped him down the ladder. Hunter met us at the bottom with a prisoner of his own, trussed up like a rodeo steer. His hands were flex-cuffed behind his back and his bootlaces were tied together in a knot that was never coming loose. The man was wearing a black vest that looked like something a photographer would sport. A pair of flashbang grenades protruded from a pouch on the front of the vest, but in the man's bound condition, the grenades were no threat to us.

"Hey, Clark. How do you hear?"

"Broken but readable," came his crackling reply.

"We're on our way back down. We got 'em all."

"Roger. Mongo is . . ."

The transmission broke up before I could hear his status report.

We led our prisoners back through the maze of the structure of the rig. Hunter dragged his man most of the way, and Singer repeatedly scolded the other man for bleeding on him.

We entered what I'd begun calling the grenade room and found Mongo still unconscious and Anya wiping his face with a wet cloth.

Hunter's prisoner looked down at him and laughed. He spat at Mongo and growled, "You may have won, but we killed your giant."

Clark thundered toward the man and caught him just above the Adam's apple, driving him into the wall with his tied feet hovering an inch above the ground. Through clenched teeth, Clark growled, "Boy, you'd rather shit in your momma's cornbread than ever spit at any one of us again. You got that?"

Anya rose with her narrowed eyes driving Russian daggers through the man in Clark's grasp. Following two deliberate strides, she sent her knee exploding into the man's crotch. "Did you drop grenade from ceiling?"

A defiant and pain-filled grin crossed the man's face, and Anya pushed Clark's hand from his throat. In one swift motion, almost too quick to see, she snatched the pin from one of the grenades protruding from the vest, spun the man around, and shoved him to the ground, facedown on top of the grenade. Before he could react, the second muted explosion of the night sent the man's body bucking into the air. Blood poured from his mouth and nose. Being less than half Mongo's size, his body couldn't withstand the blow, and Anya had sent another soul to meet its maker.

Chapter 16
Payday

Mongo let out a dinosaur noise, and Anya fell to his side. He slowly opened his eyes one at a time and took in the scene around him. "Well, I know this ain't Hell, 'cause Singer's here, but it don't look much like Heaven either, so I must've survived. Please tell me you got the rest of the bad guys."

Anya leaned down and kissed the big man's cheek. "Yes, we have all of them, and I killed the man who threw grenade at you."

He looked up at the beautiful Russian and tried to smile. "Of course you did."

I took a knee beside him. "It's good to have you back, big man. You had us worried."

He looked down at his burnt torso. "I'm not gonna lie. It feels like somebody dropped me off a building, but that must've been a flashbang and not a frag grenade."

"Yeah, it was just a flashbang, but you didn't know that when you jumped on it, did you?"

He pressed his fingertips to his abdomen and groaned. "Ah, sure I did. I don't like any of you guys enough to fall on a real grenade for you, and that's all we ever need to say about it, okay?"

Humility and self-sacrifice are the hallmarks of my team, and those are character traits that cannot be taught. I considered myself fortunate to have a family such as that. I only hoped, should the day ever come when duty demanded the ultimate sacrifice from me, I'd have the courage the men and women around me deserved.

Hunter glared at me with raised eyebrows. "So, what do we do now, boss?"

"That's a good question. Let's start by getting *el jefe*'s bleeding stopped and that hand wrapped up. He's probably going to need a splint on his right elbow, too. He had a little accident upstairs."

Singer laughed. "I guess, since I started the bleeding, it's the least I can do to get it patched up."

I took the man by his broken elbow. "Before you give him any relief, I have a few questions. I think he'll be more willing to answer before you load him up with morphine."

"That's a good idea," Singer said.

"Let's start with something simple, like your name. Let's have it."

His dark eyes drilled into mine.

I squeezed my eyelids closed and pinched the bridge of my nose. "If you're going to be this defiant about your name, this is going to be the longest night of your life." I threw a front kick to his right hip, spinning him ninety degrees, then shoved him into the corner of the room. The collision with the corner sent his body crashing into his broken arm, and he let out an animal yell that would've sickened a man with less resolve than me. Blood dripped from what remained of his left hand as I drew my pistol, knelt in front of him, and pressed the muzzle to the top of his booted foot. "Let's try this again. Maybe you didn't understand how this whole American interrogation thing works. I ask you a question, and you immediately answer with the truth, the whole truth, and nothing but the truth. If you don't, I get to put a bullet through your foot. *¿Comprende, amigo?* Now, what is your name?"

"*Mi nombre es Ricardo.*"

"Very good, Ricky-boy. Very good. Now we're getting somewhere. Tell me where the crew of the rig is."

"They're dead," he growled.

I squeezed the trigger, and my forty-five hissed as the round escaped the muzzle of the suppressor and the sole of Ricardo's foot became a gaping exit wound. He collapsed to the deck, anguish consuming his face and blood pouring from his foot.

"I'm going to run out of extremities, and you're going to run out of blood if you don't start playing by my rules, Rikki-Tikki-Tavi. Now, where is the crew?"

"You can't do this to me. I have rights in America."

"Oh, is that what you have? Rights? Okay, Dick. America is two hundred miles *that* way." I pointed in the direction I assumed was north. "Enjoy the swim." I hopped to my feet and holstered my pistol. "Throw him in the water. He has no value to us anymore."

Hunter grabbed Ricardo's only healthy remaining limb and dragged him out the door. The trail of blood he left in his wake told me the man wouldn't be conscious by the time Hunter got him to the rail, but the shock and horror he was experiencing robbed the pirate of any sense of logic.

"Okay, okay! The crew is downstairs in the provisions hold."

I turned to my giant. "Is that a real thing, Mongo?"

He grunted. "Yeah, it's where they store food and supplies. It's probably big enough to hold the crew."

I motioned toward Ricardo. "Get that bleeding stopped, but don't let him pass out. I'm going to find the crew. If they're not there, or if any of them are hurt, hungry, or uncomfortable, *he's* going in the water as shark bait."

Clark jumped to his feet. "I'm going with you."

When Clark and I reached the hatch to the provisions hold, we discovered the hatch was welded closed. I ran my hand down the bead of weld. "I'd give a thousand dollars to have Earl with us right now. She'd have them cut out of there in no time."

"If they're in there at all," Clark said.

"Good point." I grabbed a metal pipe from the deck and beat on the hatch like a lumberjack felling a tree.

A few seconds later, someone started yelling from inside.

"Can you hear me?" I yelled back.

"Yeah, we can hear you. Who are you?" came the muffled reply.

"We're Americans, and we've regained control of the rig. We're going to get you out, but the hatch is welded. Where can we find a torch?"

A new voice sounded from inside. "You'll see flammable stickers on lockers. There will be a torch in any locker with that sticker."

"Okay. Hang tight, and stay away from the hatch. We'll have you out soon."

The voice was right. The first locker we found with a flammable placard had a pair of torches and a tool that looked like a chainsaw with a huge metal-cutting wheel.

Clark hefted the saw. "I think this'll do just fine."

Sparks flew, and the cutting wheel made short work of the weld. I spun the wheel, and the mechanism securing the hatch withdrew. Nearly two hundred hungry, dirty, pissed-off oil rig workers poured out of the hold. Questions roared, and several of the workers embraced us while others cursed and demanded their shot at the men who'd taken over their rig.

We finally got the hoard calmed down enough to explain what was going on.

"Listen up!" I said. "We have control of the rig, and the people who shut you up in there are either dead or in custody upstairs. We'll have a crew boat here shortly get you back ashore. Is there anyone who needs immediate medical attention?"

We sorted through the injured workers, triaging to the best of our ability. Everyone had been fit and healthy when they went into the hold, so no one was in life-threatening condition.

"I'm sure you work in departments, so I'd like for department heads to take a roll call and account for your people. Report to whoever is in charge, and get me an accurate head count. I need you to stay out of the barracks for now, but if you want to make use of the galley, feel free to do so. But be careful . . . There's quite a bit of blood on the deck up there."

That garnered a round of cheers, and I took advantage of the opportunity to get Clark out of there and back to the rest of the team.

Mongo was in a lot of pain, but he'd made it from the deck and onto a bed in one of the abandoned rooms.

"We found them, and they're free," I reported.

Singer pointed toward Ricardo. "Does that mean I can save that guy's life now?"

"Yeah, that's what that means," I said. "But we still have one huge problem. The barracks are full of people who think they're being taken to America. They aren't going to be particularly happy about being"—I made air quotes—"rescued."

"Ooh, that's a good point," Hunter said. "What are we going to do about that?"

I held up one finger. "I've been thinking about it, and I've come to the conclusion that those people are not technically our problem. Our job was to liberate the rig and save the crew, if possible. We've done that. What Thomas Meriwether wants to do with two hundred Guatemalans on his oil rig is up to him, but that's not our only problem."

Clark spoke up. "Yeah, we've got to do something with these pirates. We've still got five of them—mostly alive. I'm not so sure about Ricardo, but the others are going to make it."

I grimaced. "Again, that's not *technically* our problem."

"It may not *technically* be our problem, but there's no question it's practically ours. We made the mess, and somebody's gonna have to clean it up."

"I think it's time to wake up Mr. Meriwether and let him know we'll be cashing his check."

It rang nine times, but that could've had more to do with the satellite connection than Thomas Meriwether's hesitance to answer his phone in the middle of the night. His sleep-laden voice finally came on the line. "Yeah?"

"Mr. Meriwether, Chase Fulton here. I have some good news. Let me know when you're awake enough to hear it."

Sounds of movement came through the phone, and he cleared his throat. "Yeah, yeah, go ahead, Mr. Fulton."

"My team and I have regained control of your rig. Your crew is generally unhurt and all alive. I can't say the same for the pirates. Your rig was being used as a staging area for a human trafficking ring. There are approximately a hundred fifty Guatemalan refugees aboard the rig now. We have four surviving pirates, including their captain. He's badly injured, but he'll survive. The Pan America Rig is, once again, yours. You may send your helicopters and crew boats whenever you'd like."

"You can't be serious," he belted. "You mean you have the rig back already?"

"Yes, Mr. Meriwether. Your rig is back under your control. I'm going to surrender command of the platform back to your installation manager as soon as we hang up."

He took a swallow of something. "But what about the Guatemalans? That's what you said they were, right? Guatemalans?"

"Yes, at least some of them are Guatemalan. I can't be certain of the rest, but they're all secure in the barracks."

"Okay, but what are you going to do with them?" he asked.

"I'm not going to do anything with them. I was hired to recapture your rig and return it to your command without involving law enforcement or federal government agencies. I've done that, and the escrow account has been liquidated."

"But what am I supposed to do now?"

I clicked my tongue against my teeth. "I'm not in the business of dealing with refugees, Mr. Meriwether, but I'd recommend calling the Coast Guard and Immigrations and Customs Enforcement. They're trained and equipped to deal with situations like this."

He stammered, "But what about the pirates, as you called them?"

I sighed. "As far as I know, your crew escaped, overpowered the bad guys, and took your rig back. Those roughnecks aren't easy people to keep down. Regardless of what you decide, I'm glad we could help."

He stuttered and began offering more arguments, but I closed the connection.

Clark held up his hands as if impatiently awaiting my report. "How'd it go?"

"He's not exactly thrilled about the dead bodies and barracks full of refugees, but he didn't grunt when I told him we'd emptied the escrow account. Now we need to find Greg Peterson. He's the offshore installation manager. I want to surrender this ship back to its captain and get out of here."

"I'm on it," he said, obviously as anxious to disappear as I was.

* * *

A man of perhaps sixty with a shortage of hair and an excess of belly stuck out his hand. "I'm Greg Peterson."

"It's nice to finally meet you, Mr. Peterson. I'm Chase. My team and I—"

"Oh, I know very well what you and your team did tonight, and we owe you our lives for it."

I shook his offered hand. "You don't owe us anything. We're glad we could help, and your boss paid us very well to do it. There are, however, a few things you and I need to discuss. Is there someplace we can talk privately?"

"Sure. Follow me." He turned and headed for another hatch in the main structure of the rig, leading me to a cramped office.

I wasted no time. "Mr. Peterson, I understand you're the offshore installation manager on the Pan America. Is that correct?"

"It is," he said somewhat hesitantly. "This is starting to sound like an interrogation, though."

"It's no interrogation. It's just a matter of maritime law. Essentially, you were the captain of this vessel, and even though it's nominally attached to the ocean floor, it's still a seagoing vessel in the eyes of the Coast Guard. I'm sure none of this is news to you."

He nodded. "Yes, well, I'm not a salty sailor—I'm an oil driller. But I understand your point."

"Good. Due to the nature of how your vessel was commandeered and held, it became necessary for deadly force to be used to liberate and reclaim your ship from the pirates who attacked and imprisoned your crew. Do you understand the necessity and importance of the word *pirate*?"

He let out a long sigh. "I do now."

"Your boss, Thomas Meriwether, wanted to make sure you and your crew were safe, and of course, he wanted his rig back in service. It would appear to me that a resourceful group of roughnecks under your command escaped from the imprisonment imposed on them by the pirates, and overpowered those pirates. In doing so, those brave men saved the lives of every innocent man and woman aboard. Is that how you perceive the events of the last twelve hours, Mr. Peterson?"

He closed his eyes and sucked the ends of his mustache into his mouth. "So, you were never here, right?"

I leaned forward. "Mr. Peterson, I don't even exist."

"I understand," he mumbled.

"There are a few things you need to know. First, there are approximately one hundred fifty Guatemalan refugees in your barracks."

He shook his head and blinked repeatedly. "What?"

"The rig was being used as a staging point for a human trafficking operation. The head honcho is nursing some pretty nasty wounds, but he'll live. I suspect the authorities would enjoy having a chat with him. A few of his men survived when 'your brave employees' took back your rig, but some didn't."

He seemed to refuse to open his eyes. "This is all a little overwhelming for me. I never imagined something like this happening."

"Most people never imagine things like this, Mr. Peterson. That's why people like my team and me are necessary, but none of that matters now. Right now, I need you to look at me and listen closely."

He finally opened his eyes, although he wore a look of anxiety. "Okay. I'm listening."

"Your vessel was overtaken by pirates. I liberated your vessel. In doing so, I temporarily assumed responsibility for your ship and all aboard. Now that both you and your vessel are free, I'm relinquishing responsibility and command of the vessel back to you, her rightful captain. I need you to acknowledge and accept that responsibility."

He stood and again offered his hand. "Thank you for liberating my ship, and I accept responsibility for her and every soul aboard."

The handshake was my ticket off the rig, and I was thankful to receive it.

"Oh, there's just one more thing," I said. "Your brave crew also restored your communications, so you should probably call your wife and let her know you're okay."

For the first time, the man smiled and didn't close his eyes. "My brave crew sounds pretty impressive."

I chuckled. "Oh, they are."

* * *

With the help of a crane aboard the Pan America Rig, we lowered Mongo's three hundred pounds back to the deck of our Mark V patrol boat. He was in no shape to descend a ladder under his own power, and none of us could carry him.

Clark took the helm, and the forty-ton boat was soon cutting across the wave tops at fifty knots. Singer slept, Anya fawned over Mongo, and Hunter and I strapped into a pair of articulating seats behind the pilothouse.

After fifteen minutes of silent contemplation over what we'd done, Hunter finally spoke. "Not a bad result, all in all."

I stared into the night sky as the first lights of civilization bloomed on the northern horizon. "It's not over."

Hunter sighed. "Yeah, I know."

Chapter 17
Breakfast of Champions

Everyone reacts differently when an intense mission comes to an end. Tier-one operators tend to perceive such missions as part of normal life and treat the hours following the action much the same as they'd treat unpacking groceries from a shopping trip. My team cleaned weapons, repaired damaged gear, and went to bed. The exception was Mongo. He skipped the cleaning and repairing portions and headed straight to sleep.

Two hours after sunrise the following morning, I called the Citation crew. "Good morning. I have some good news. Your sentence has been commuted, and you're free to take your airplane and go home."

"We enjoyed working with you, Mr. Fulton. My first officer will be disappointed he didn't get a chance to fly your Two-Oh-Eight on floats, but I'll break the news gently. If you ever need us again, don't hesitate to call."

We delivered the boat back to the shipyard and made arrangements to have it hauled to Saint Marys. In spite of the expense, it was far easier than running around the Florida Keys and back up the East Coast. That trip aboard *Aegis* would be leisurely and more vacation than occupation, but running the Mark V that distance on the open ocean would be grueling. I was more than happy to write the check.

The next call was the one I both dreaded and longed to make. Penny's phone rang five times and went to voicemail. "Hey, it's me. The mission's over. Everyone's okay except Mongo. He's hurt, but not critical. I'll be home this afternoon."

Clark caught my look. "Maybe she's still sleeping."

I checked my watch. "It's almost ten o'clock on the East Coast. Penny's never slept past seven since I've known her."

He shrugged. "Well, maybe she's busy."

"Or maybe she's dodging my call."

Clark played with the toothpick in his mouth. "Are you thinking what I'm thinking?"

I didn't look up. "If you're thinking the Pan America was just the tip of the iceberg and this thing isn't over, then yeah, I'm thinking what you're thinking."

"It's best to take the money and walk away," he said.

"Yeah, that's probably what's best, but I suck at that walking away part. Remember the nun in Saint Augustine?"

He laughed. "Yeah, I remember, but do me a favor this time. Give it twenty-four hours. Go home, talk to Penny, and find out what's going on there before you stick your nose into a human trafficking ring. Can you do that . . . for me?"

"Are you coming back to Saint Marys with us?"

He consulted his watch. "I need to get back to Miami. I'm sure the restaurant is falling apart without me."

"Maybe you should call Maebelle and find out. If she needs you, I'm sure she'll let you know."

"That woman would never admit to needing anybody."

"We have some business to take care of tomorrow morning at Bonaventure, and I'd really like for you to be there."

"What kind of business?" he asked.

I stood. "The life-changing kind."

* * *

Skipper had the Tactical Operations Center torn down and loaded aboard the Caravan before noon. The bulk of our gear was packed aboard the Mark V and would be trucked back across the state. Weaponry and ammo are heavy, and even though the Caravan was more than capable, I liked leaving off unnecessary weight.

We made a nest for Mongo in the back of the plane. His insistence on waiting until we returned to coastal Georgia to see a doctor didn't make any sense to me, but I wasn't going to waste the energy or time required to argue with him. In the end, it was his decision.

The flight home with Hunter at the controls was uneventful, exactly as flights should be, and we touched down just after three o'clock. Back at Bonaventure Plantation, everything was in order. *Aegis* rested peacefully tied to the dock in the North River. The horses—as badly as I hated them—munched on the green grass of the pasture. And the old house stood majestically, just as she had for over a hundred years. Everything was exactly where I'd left it . . . except my wife.

My team was a family, so everyone knew there was trouble in paradise, but no one brought it up. As much as I loved the antebellum house that had been in my family for generations, I would always feel most at home aboard my catamaran, *Aegis*. With Penny missing and ignoring my calls, I briefed the team to meet me at Bonaventure for breakfast the next day, and I went home.

I tossed off the lines and motored away from the Bonaventure dock. A boat is far more than a means of transportation. To anyone who's never owned and loved a boat, they are merely chunks of floating fiberglass and metal. Those of us who've spent parts of our lives aboard boats know they have hearts and souls. They become faithful companions and even frustrating tormentors at times, but through it all, we love our boats, and we find it almost impossible to believe they're incapable of loving us in return.

Aegis felt empty as I unfurled the genoa and silenced the diesels. We cut across Cumberland Sound and out the Saint Marys inlet to the North Atlantic. She performed exactly as she'd been designed and built to do, but she did so coldly, with no passion. Although I loved the sun on my face and the elegance of harnessing the wind, doing it alone felt foreign and empty. It occurred to me I'd never sailed *Aegis* alone. The day she became mine, Anya stepped aboard before me. When I believed Anya was dead, Skipper or Clark was always with me on the boat. And after I met Penny, she'd been a fixture in my life and aboard *Aegis*. It was perfectly rational the experience should feel abnormal. Part of me wanted to savor the moment and take in the beauty of the afternoon, but I couldn't shake the sickening feeling in my gut. I missed Penny's wild hair dancing in the wind, her infectious smile, and feeling her near me. I missed simply knowing she was aboard. It wasn't the same without her, and I had to repair the damage between us, no matter what it took.

My anchor found purchase in the muddy bottom of the mouth of Egans Creek at the southwestern corner of Fort Clinch. Cooking was not on my list of things I wanted to do, so I settled on a sandwich and my first old-fashioned of the night. As I sat alone on the upper deck, it was easy to believe I was the only person left on Earth. Three old-fashioned cocktails later, I was dozing off and reaching for the woman who should've been in my bed.

* * *

Dawn broke over Amelia Island, and I stretched awake, still alone. I called the bed-and-breakfast a few blocks from Bonaventure and asked them to deliver breakfast for eight. The young man promised to make the delivery by eight thirty.

The morning was dead calm, so the eight-mile trip back to the Bonaventure dock would be done entirely under diesel power, which added environmental insult to my psychological injury. I was without Penny and wind, leaving far more than just my sails empty that morning.

Skipper met me on the dock and tossed the lines aboard. "Hey. Are you okay?"

I tied off the lines to the deck cleats and hopped down. "No, I'm not. I'm worried about Penny. She won't answer the phone, and I have no idea where she is."

Skipper raised her eyebrows. "Hello? It'll take me less than ten minutes to find her."

I gave her a hug. "I've been thinking about that, but I think she wants to be left alone."

She frowned. "This is your first real fight, isn't it?"

"Yeah, it's the first *big* one, for sure."

She took my arm and turned for the house. "Then you don't really know what she wants, do you?"

"I don't even know what she's mad about."

* * *

Breakfast arrived right on time, and the team filed into the kitchen. There was a perfectly good dining room at Bonaventure, but everyone seemed to prefer the kitchen table. Eight beautifully prepared grand Southern breakfast plates were arranged perfectly around the table, and just like most families, everyone knew exactly where to sit. When I realized there were only seven of us, my heart sank. Anya was the first to notice my disappointment. Without a word, she took Penny's plate from the table and slid it into the refrigerator.

Singer prayed, and we dug in. As with every meal from the B and B, breakfast was magnificent, but there was hardly a word spoken. I didn't like how that felt.

"So, I guess it's time to talk about the eight-hundred-pound gorilla in the room." Anya furrowed her brow, so I said, "That's an American phrase meaning something everyone notices, but no one talks about."

"I think this is dumb phrase."

For the first time that morning, we shared a much-needed laugh. "You're right. It is pretty dumb, but the point is, all of you know something is going on with Penny and me. I wish I knew what it was, but I don't. She's angry with me for some reason, and I'm going to find out why. When I do, I'll find a way to fix it."

Anya's frown returned. "She ran from you and did not tell you why?"

I pushed a pile of roasted potatoes with my fork. "She found your hair in my bed in Panama City."

Mongo groaned, "What?"

I held up both hands in surrender. "No, it's not what you think. And I don't think that's really what Penny's upset about. It was just a convenient excuse to start a fight. Anya came into my room for two minutes to ask me to include her on the boarding party for the oil rig assault. That's it."

Mongo turned his stare to Anya.

"This is true, Marvin. I was only there to ask to be on mission."

The wounded giant relaxed and reached for her hand.

I continued. "I honestly don't know what the problem is, but I'm going to take care of it. She's too important to me to just let her go. I'll get to the bottom of—"

The doorbell interrupted my speech.

Skipper hopped to her feet. "I'll get it."

I motioned for her to stay. "No, keep your seat. I've been expecting it, and I'll have to sign for it anyway."

When I returned with the package, the conversation around the table ceased, and every eye turned to me.

Skipper was the first to speak, of course. "Are you gonna tell us what you got?"

I tore open the package and withdrew six thin leather wallets, each containing a personalized black card. "What we did together over the past week was nothing short of remarkable. Every one of you excelled. You risked your lives to save people you didn't know, and you accomplished something fewer than a thousand people on Earth could've done. You are an elite group of warriors. I've never been prouder to work with anyone."

I passed out the wallets, and one by one, everyone pulled out their cards and stared back at me.

I cleared my throat. "We were paid exceptionally well for what we accomplished. Most of you have spent your careers working for a daily rate of less than a thousand bucks. Those days are over. Men and women like you are not day workers. You are professionals of the highest order with unmatched skill sets you've developed over years of training, experience, and pain. It's time those years paid off. Each of those cards is linked to your own personal account in the Cayman Islands and contains a balance of five million dollars."

A cacophony of sighs and disbelief arose from the table, but I held up my hands. "Stop. The money is yours. You earned it. That's enough money for you to never have to pick up another weapon or disappear into the night, unsure if you'll make it home. We didn't do this one for our country. This one was mercenary, and mercenaries get paid."

Clark stared down at the card and then tossed it across the table, where it landed like a feather in front of Mongo. Singer's card was only a second behind Clark's.

The big man looked up, obviously in pain, but also riddled with confusion. "What are you doing?"

Clark said, "If that had been a frag grenade instead of a flash-bang, you wouldn't be here eating breakfast with us. You're the one who deserves that money . . . not me."

"Exactly," Singer said. "Besides, what am I going to do with five million dollars? I've got the church downtown, the monks up in South Carolina, and I've got you guys. What else could I ask for?"

The giant's eyes filled with tears, but he managed to choke back the emotion. He threw the cards back. "If either one of you can look me in the eye and honestly say you wouldn't have done the same thing if you'd seen that grenade first, then I'll take your money. Otherwise, put those in your pockets."

Anya ran her fingers through Mongo's unruly beard. "This is why I love being American girl."

Skipper sat, fixated on the card in her delicate hands as if it had her hypnotized. I threw a napkin at her. "Are you okay, Skipper?"

She looked up, pale-faced and wide-eyed. "Is this for real? Are you really telling me I've got five million dollars?"

"Yes, all of you do. That's how this works. Thirty-five million dollars divided by seven is five million."

"But I didn't do anything. I was just the analyst."

I nodded. "Okay, then we'll take a vote. Since Skipper was just the analyst, who thinks she doesn't deserve an equal share?"

Hunter slapped the table. "That's just ridiculous. If anything, you deserve more than us. You could learn to do what we do, but none of us is smart enough to do what you do. We couldn't do any of this without you, and nobody at this table will disagree."

He sat back in his chair, took a long swallow of the coffee that was growing cold in his mug, then smiled. "You know something? You're the only millionaire I know named Skipper. Come to think of it, *all* the millionaires I know are sitting at this table."

I found myself staring at the empty chair where Penny should've been, and Clark slapped my arm. "Come on. Let's go for a walk."

Let's go for a walk had become Clark's way of saying, "We need to talk." And *we need to talk* usually meant I had screwed up.

Chapter 18
You and Us

As usual, our walk ended up with us sitting in a pair of Adirondack chairs in the gazebo overlooking the North River.

Clark drummed his fingers against the arm of his chair. "What are you doing, Chase?"

Yep, I screwed something up.

I stared in his direction, but he wouldn't look up at me. "What do you mean?"

He closed his eyes, took a long, deep breath, and finally locked eyes with me. "You just destroyed the best tactical team I've ever been a part of, and I think you did it on purpose."

"What are you saying?"

He spat through the planking of the deck between his boots. "Don't do this, Chase. I've known you too long, and I've watched that head of yours outthink everybody and everything around you too many times for you to play that crap with me. What are those people in that house supposed to do now? Huh?"

I slid to the edge of my seat, narrowed my eyes, and pointed toward the house. "Those people can now do whatever they want. They can—"

He jabbed his finger through the air in my direction. "Those people *were* doing what they wanted. They were kicking down doors and knockin' heads. That's what they do. It's who they are. And you just yanked that away from every single one of them."

"What are you talking about? I put together an op and nego- tiated a contract that made you and every one of them richer than they ever dreamed of being."

He scowled. "You're damned right, you did. You made them richer than they ever dreamed because none of them ever dreamed of being rich. None of them! Every single one of them, including me, dreamed of saving the world one bullet at a time. That's the difference between you and all of them . . . and me. You're different than us, Chase. You went to college, you played baseball, and you dreamed of playing in the big leagues and get- ting rich doing something you love."

He kicked the stool away from his chair and leaned toward me. "Nobody in that kitchen did any of that. Every one of them . . . no, every one of *us* did what we had to do to get through high school because we couldn't wait to run as fast as we could into that recruiter's office with our diploma in hand and sign up to wear a uniform. But it wasn't a uniform like you had in mind. Ours didn't have a number on the back and a baseball team name on the front. Oh, ours had a team name on the front, but they all started with the words *United States*. See the differ- ence?"

I slid back into my seat and let his admonition sink in. He was right. I wasn't like him and Hunter and Mongo.

In a desperate attempt to justify my actions, I asked, "What about Skipper? She never ran into any recruiter's office."

He painted on the smile that meant someone had just walked into the trap he laid. "Really?"

I knew he had me, but I didn't know exactly how. "Yes, really. She never served."

His smile broadened. "How quickly we forget. Let me remind you of a certain breakfast you, me, and Skipper had in the dining room at the Jekyll Island Club one morning. I seem to remember her begging you and me to be her recruiters and get her into The Ranch. Does any of that ring a bell for you, College Boy?"

As usual, Clark was right. That's precisely what Skipper had done, and we talked her out of it.

He watched the realization fall over me. "So, what do you expect them to do now that you've taken away their identities, their sense of purpose, and the only thing they've ever had—a team?"

I swallowed the lump in my throat. "They don't have to stop operating just because they've got a little money."

He laughed. "A little money? See, there it is again. That's the difference between you and us. Five million dollars isn't a little money to us, Chase. It's all the money in the world. We've lived our lives in three-figure daily rates. Eight hundred bucks a day is a fortune for us. That's what you don't understand. When you hit those home runs and gunned down those baserunners trying to steal second, you were laying the foundation for a career that would pay you ten million bucks a year." He paused and shook his head. "When we were digging foxholes at Fort Bragg and jumping out of airplanes at Fort Benning, we were laying the groundwork for base pay of two grand a month, and maybe, just maybe, if we survived long enough, we might make three or four hundred bucks a day as a civilian security contractor. See the difference?"

I stared at the river. "I'd never thought of it that way."

He let out a sound of disgust. "Don't lie to me. We're beyond that. We've known each other too long, and we've been through too much. But more than that, don't lie to yourself."

He beat on the arm of his chair. "Look at me. Look in my eyes and tell me you didn't tear this team apart on purpose."

I met his stare. "Why would I do that?"

He frowned. "Are you asking me, or are you asking yourself?"

"Maybe both," I admitted.

"Okay, I'll go first," he said. "You did it because you picked sides."

"What?"

"You picked sides. When Penny stormed out, that was an ultimatum. It was her telling you that it was time to fish or cut bait. You could keep running all over the world and solving everybody else's problems, or you could be her husband, but not both. And I think you decided to buy your way out by handing out those little black cards."

"That's not what—"

He interrupted by blowing air through his lips in a strawberry. "Come on, man. I thought you were a psychologist. What did they teach you at that fancy school? How to overlook the obvious? It's staring you right in the face. Open your eyes."

"So, what am I supposed to do?"

"If you want out, walk out. You've always had that option. You're not under any contracts. You don't have to play another season to earn free-agent status. You can walk away anytime you want, but you didn't have to destroy the team to do it. Yeah, we need each other. That's what being a team is all about, but no one person is irreplaceable. You could walk away, and there's plenty of work for those people in that house."

I watched a pelican dive on a school of baitfish and come up with his gullet full of salt water and breakfast. "So, what am I supposed to do now? It's not like I can undo it. I can't walk in there and say, 'Never mind. I was just kidding. I'm going to need those cards back.'"

"No, you're right. The damage is done. I just hope you're prepared for the fallout."

"What do you mean? What's the fallout going to be?"

He stuck his toe beneath the lip of a footstool he'd kicked away and pulled back in front of his chair. "I'll break it down for you, College Boy, and we'll start with me. I'm going back to Miami to a girlfriend who doesn't want or need me getting in her way at the restaurant. The money means I don't care if the restaurant fails. If it does, I can throw money at it, or we can walk away from it. That means I stop caring about the biggest dream she has ever had, and when we don't care about our partner's dreams, what's left to care about?"

"But I think—"

He held up a hand. "I'm not finished, and I don't care what you think. Let's talk about Singer now. He's going to give it all away. The church will get a new building. Those monks will get new robes or whatever. I don't understand that whole thing anyway, but that's beside the point. He'll give every penny away and then start looking for work again. How long do you think it takes to give away five million bucks?"

I shook my head.

"I don't know, either, but it'll take a while, and when a sniper is out of the game for a while, there's nothing left for him when he tries to come back. The younger, faster, sharper guys have come up, and there's no room for the old dinosaur anymore."

"But it doesn't have to be that way," I said.

He held up a finger. "Let me finish. How 'bout Hunter? He'll invest the money because he's smart, but he'll buy a little cabin in Idaho or maybe Alaska, and he'll fly-fish for trout and hunt bears. And do you know what that will give him time to do? Think. That gives him twenty-four hours a day to think about what happened to him overseas and how the Air Force didn't need him anymore. Then he'll think about how much he loved being your partner and being part of your team, and then he'll remember those things are gone, too. Do you remember what Ernest Hemingway—your hero—did in the mountains of Idaho when he realized the world he loved didn't need him anymore? He put a gun in his mouth. And how about Anya? What do you think she's going to do with the money? I'll tell you. She's going to get bored because all she knows is espionage and playing with knives. Is that a personality you want running around free in the world with limitless financial resources and no way to entertain herself?"

His points were valid, regardless of how badly I wanted to argue against them.

He licked his lips. "I could go on, and we could run down the whole list, but let's fast-forward to you. What are you going to do with the eleven million bucks you've already got in the bank, plus the five million you made on this op? I'll tell you what you're going to do. You're going to find that pretty wife of yours, and you're going to apologize for something you don't even know you did. She's gonna cry, and you're gonna cry, and it'll all be forgotten. Then, you'll get on your boat and set off to parts of the world none of the rest of us can pronounce, much less spell, and you're going to live the life you always dreamed baseball would give you. But one day, you'll be on the French Riviera, sipping whatever the hell they drink in France, and you'll read an article in the newspaper about a beautiful former Russian spy turned American operative who stuck a throwing knife in the vice president's neck or something crazy like that, and you'll start asking yourself about the rest of your former team—the team who sat at your feet and agreed to follow you into the pits of Hell for three hundred bucks a day. And you'll find Hunter's obituary, and my divorce decree, and an article about some small-town sheriff's deputy who took a bullet in the back while singing some gospel hymn."

He stopped talking and stared out over the marsh while his words filtered their way into my soul. Clark finally stood and put his hand on my shoulder. "I don't want you to answer me. I just want you to think about the first thing that comes into your head when I ask you one simple question. Can you do that?"

I looked up at him. "Sure."

He nodded. "What's the one thing you care about most in the world? Don't answer me. Just think about it. Then, when you've given it plenty of time to marinate, I want you to ask yourself how every member of your team would answer that question. And that answer, my friend, will be the difference between you and us."

Chapter 19
What I Know

Until that moment, I'd never drawn a line between myself and my team. I'd always believed we viewed the world through the same lens, but I was wrong. I was wrong about a great many things, and I still had so much to learn. I let my new reality percolate as I watched six more pelicans join the first one who'd discovered the buffet. Nature is a brilliant teacher if we're patient and smart enough to watch, listen, and learn.

There was no way to undo the damage I'd caused among my team, but perhaps it could be mitigated. As my thoughts moved from chaos to somewhat organized ideas, I stood to return to the house.

Hunter startled me by stepping into the gazebo the instant I left my chair. "Hey, Chase. Have you got a minute to talk?"

My heart leapt in my chest, but I tried to hide my surprise. "Sure. I always have time for you."

I motioned toward the chair Clark had previously occupied, and Hunter slid into the sloping seat.

"What's on your mind?" I asked, fearing I already knew the answer.

"It's the money," he began. "It's great and all, but what am I supposed to do with it? Is there some kind of retirement account or somewhere I can put it so I'll have it if I live long enough to retire?"

As usual, Clark was right.

"You have plenty of options," I said. "Of course there are retirement funds, and that's not a bad idea if you want to keep working—" His look of confusion stopped me mid-sentence. "What is it?"

"What do you mean, *if* I want to keep working? Working is what people do until they die, get hurt too bad to keep at it, or retire. I hope I'm a long way from any of those. Besides, you need me. I'm your partner now that Clark got shot up and promoted. What are you gonna do for a partner if I quit?"

That's when I let out the last words I ever imagined would come out of my mouth. "What if I'm done?"

Hunter roared with laughter. "What does *that* mean? You're never gonna be done. You're just like the rest of us. You're a shooter, and you'll always be a shooter 'til they put you in a box and drop your trigger-pullin' butt in the cold ground."

How could Clark and Hunter have such diametrically opposed views of who and what I am?

"Haven't you ever played that game of trying to decide what you'd do if you won the lottery?"

He propped up his feet. "Yeah, sure I have. Everybody plays that game, but I've never bought a lottery ticket in my life. But if I did, and if I won, I always figured I'd buy a nice truck. I've never had a brand-new truck. And then I'd tip pretty waitresses really good for the rest of my life."

"But you never thought about quitting?" I asked.

He stared into the rafters of my gazebo. "Yeah, I thought about it when the Air Force told me I was medically unfit to serve. I knew that was BS, but what could I do? Then I got the job with the Navy at Kings Bay, and that was a pretty good gig. I didn't have to worry about making rent or scrounging for food. I sorta figured I had it made 'til you came along."

"What do you mean, 'til I came along?"

He picked at a splinter of wood on the arm of the Adirondack. "Ah, you know. I figured I'd just get old and die over there at the submarine base, playing with the sea lions and watching the subs come and go. Then, out of the blue, you popped up right next door with my dream job. You know how it is, Chase. Guys like you and me . . . we'd rather die in the weeds, full of bullet holes, with a gun in each hand and grenade pin in our teeth, than rot away behind some desk somewhere."

"Those aren't the only two options, you know. We made a lot of money. We can do almost anything we want for the rest of our lives."

He adjusted himself in the chair. "Yeah, I know. That's exactly what I'm talking about. We want to do the stuff that makes a difference for people who can't do it for themselves. Now, it doesn't matter if it pays or not. We can go do it anyway."

A warrior to the core, I thought.

"What about traveling, seeing the world—without getting shot at—and doing the things you've always dreamed of doing?" I asked.

He stared up at the ceiling of the gazebo. "Well, I guess I could buy me a little cabin on a creek somewhere in Montana where's there's plenty of trout. I hear there's elk out there the size of dump trucks. I wouldn't mind bagging one or two of those big boys for the freezer."

I had a newspaper clipping aboard my boat from July 3, 1961, the day after Ernest Hemingway took his life in Ketchum, Idaho. I could quote the article word-for-word from memory, but in my mind for the first time, the face in the accompanying picture wasn't Hemingway's.

I tapped my boots together. "Maybe you're right. Maybe cabins in the woods aren't for guys like us."

The splinter from the arm of the chair finally surrendered to his picking, and he used it as a makeshift toothpick. "Yeah, that's how I see it, but I'm not the boss."

I stood and reached for his hand. He grabbed mine, and I yanked him from the chair. "I'll get you the number of a guy in the Caymans who does a nice job of turning a little bit of money into a lot of money. I'm sure he'd be happy to set up some sort of retirement plan for you."

* * *

Skipper met me at the kitchen door. "Do you want me to find her?"

I closed my eyes and sighed. "Of course I want you to find her, but I'm not sure she wants to be found. I think she probably wants some time to work out whatever this is."

Obviously ignoring everything after *of course*, she said, "Okay, good, 'cause I already did. She's in Plainview, Texas."

I took her by both shoulders. "Look at me, Skipper. You weren't listening. I said—"

She pulled away. "Oh, I *heard* what you said, but I *did* what you meant."

My hands fell to my side. "What's in Plainview, Texas? And maybe more importantly, *where* is Plainview, Texas?"

She motioned for me to follow her to the library. "Come on. I'll show you. I've got it pulled up on the computer in here."

I let her lead me down the hall and into my favorite room of the house. Thousands of books lined the floor-to-ceiling shelves, and it smelled exactly how libraries should smell.

"Plainview is a little town of just over fifteen thousand people about fifty miles north of Lubbock on Interstate twenty-seven.

There's not much there, but, interesting fact, James Clark, the founder of Netscape, is from there."

"What is Netscape?"

"Never mind," she said. "But Jimmy Dean was also from there."

"Oh, the sausage guy?"

"Yeah, the sausage guy . . . among other things. Anyway, I don't know why she's there, but I'm tracking her new cell phone, and that's where it is."

"Wait a minute. Did you say *new* cell phone?"

She nodded excitedly. "Yeah, her old one is still here at the house somewhere. I've not looked for it, but it's definitely here. She bought a new one in Jacksonville with her credit card and took out ten thousand dollars in cash. She also bought an airplane ticket to Atlanta, but that's the last time she's used the card."

I squeezed my eyelids closed. "So, all you know for sure is that she bought a cell phone and an airplane ticket, and that the cell phone is now in Plainview, Texas. Right?"

"Well, no. I know she took out ten grand in cash, but it sounds like you think she's not with the cell phone she bought."

I tried not to smile. "Penny's smart. She's far too smart to think she can just buy a new cell phone and disappear. You can only live so long on ten grand, and she knew you'd be able to find any trail she left."

Her shoulders slumped. "Yeah, you're right. The phone in Plainview is probably a red herring."

"Don't get discouraged," I said. "She doesn't know all your tricks—just the basic ones. See if you can find out if there's any reason she'd be in Plainview. Do you have a way to check airline manifests to see who was on which flights?"

She scratched her forehead. "Yeah, I can do that, but it's not easy. And it takes a while."

"Just see if she was on the flight to Atlanta, and then look for flights to Lubbock or someplace close to Plainview with an airport that left after she would've arrived in Atlanta. Oh, and see if you can figure out how she got to Jacksonville. The BMW and the VW are still here."

She slid into the seat behind the desk. "I'm on it."

I turned to leave the library and give her some privacy, but when I reached the door, I spun on my heel. "One more thing. Do you know where Anya is?"

Skipper raised her eyebrows. "Are you sure you want to run to Anya for advice on this?"

"No, it's not like that. I just need to talk to her."

"Chase, isn't she the reason Penny's so upset?"

I swallowed hard. "I don't think so. I think it's something else. We just have to figure out what."

"Talking to Anya is probably a bad idea, but if I had to guess, she's upstairs with Mongo."

I took the stairs three at a time and knocked on the door to the room Mongo typically used, primarily because of the enormous bed. No answer came, so I cracked the door. Mongo's and Anya's gear was in the corner, but neither of them was anywhere to be found.

"They're gone to the hospital," announced a voice from behind me.

I spun to see Singer coming down the upstairs hall. "You've got to stop sneaking up on me, or I'm going to hang a bell around your neck. How do you do that?"

"Silent but deadly, baby. Silent but deadly."

"Okay, whatever. How long have they been gone?"

He looked at his watch. "Since just after breakfast when you went outside with Clark. Mongo's hurting pretty bad."

"I'm sure he is, but he's a tough old goat. He'll be okay."

Singer shot his eyes toward the ceiling. "I'm praying you're right about that."

I licked my lips. "Um, would you mind if we had a talk?"

"Sure. What's on your mind, boss?"

I led him toward the sitting area at the end of the hall, where a pair of wingback chairs framed a two-hundred-year-old mahogany table. A copy of Hemingway's *For Whom the Bell Tolls* rested on the antique table.

"This isn't a boss kind of conversation," I began as I settled into the chair. "This is one of those spiritual advisor things."

"Oh, one of those. I thought we might be having one of those sometime soon. Let's hear it."

I wasn't sure where to begin, so I started with the most awkward opening possible. "I didn't sleep with Anya."

He suppressed a smile. "Yes, you did, but maybe not lately."

His attempt at humor worked, and I relaxed a little. "Okay, you're right. I did, but not in a very long time, and definitely not since I've known Penny."

He folded his hands on his lap. "First, you need to know and understand that you're not always going to be the man God expects you to be. You're not even going to be the man you expect yourself to be every time. But the thing you need to remember is this . . . Just like God, the people who love you are always going to stand beside you, even when you don't live up to your potential."

I bit my lip. "I appreciate that, Singer, and I'm lucky to have you on my side. But honestly, I didn't sleep with her."

He made an abbreviated nodding motion with his head. "Okay, I believe you, but you don't think Penny believes you, right?"

"No, that's not it. I think she knows I haven't slept with Anya . . . lately. I think it's something deeper than that, but I don't exactly know what it is yet. Skipper is searching for her, even though I'm not sure that's the best thing. What do you think?"

He scratched his chin. "What do I think about what, the fact that searching for her isn't the best thing, or that she's upset about something other than Anya?"

I let his question linger for a moment. "Well, both."

He crossed his legs and put on that knowing look of his. "I agree with you that Penny probably knows you've not slept with Anya . . . lately . . . but there's more to it than that. Try to look at it from her perspective. You put your life in Anya's hands, and you trust her when the bullets start flying."

"Yeah, but in a tactical environment—"

He put his hand on my arm. "How much time has Penny spent in tactical environments?"

I let out a long sigh. "Okay, point taken. To her, it looks like I enjoy running off with Anya into the night, and she has no idea what we're doing out there . . . bullets or no bullets."

He grinned. "You're catching on. So, with that in mind, think of how that makes her feel. I'm not saying she's insecure enough about Anya to make it an issue that could hurt your marriage. I'm just saying it's an underlying factor, like a burr under a saddle. It seems like a small thing, but to the horse, it gets worse and worse the longer the trail drags on."

I picked at my fingernails. "I can see that."

He locked eyes with me. "Now, I need to ask you a question. When did you first notice Penny getting out of sorts?"

"To be honest, I've been so focused on the operation that I—"

He replaced his hand on my arm. "No, that's a cop-out. When was the last time you remember her being perfectly normal?"

I stared out the second-story window across the pasture where the horses picked at the green summer grass. "She was all right when we got back from Austin."

He said, "That's when things started heating up for the op."

"That's right. It started getting intense when we all listened to the audio about the oil rig."

He stared upward as if he were replaying the moments in his head. "I seem to remember her acting strange right after her friend Tonya got here and started working on the audio."

It was my turn to replay the scene. "I think you're right. It spooked her when the voice on the tape sounded so much like hers. I remember the look on her face. It was a little unnerving."

"Does she have a TS clearance?" he asked.

The toes of my boots came in and out of focus. "No, not officially."

"So, she's never had a background check?"

I was uncertain of his implication, but I tried to remember what precautions I'd taken when she came into my life. "Dominic ran a background check, but nothing major popped up. A speeding ticket and a night in jail for a bag of weed that wasn't hers. That was a long time ago, though."

"How about her family? What do you know about them? Have you met her folks?"

My heart sank. "No, I don't even know their names. I know her father was in the liquor business, but honestly, I don't know if he's still alive."

Singer cocked his head. "You mean you married her without knowing anything about her family or background?"

"I know about her background. She learned to fly with her dad when she was a teenager. She graduated from Baylor with a degree in sociology, and she's a great sailor. And she. . . ."

He sat in silence, awaiting my list of things I knew about my wife.

My anger rose alongside my embarrassment as I ran out of things I knew about the woman who shared my bed and my last name.

Chapter 20
Second Chances

"Find her! Whatever you have to do, find her!"

Skipper jumped as I burst through the door into the library. "Don't do that to me. You nearly scared me to death. Are you okay?"

I pulled up a chair beside her. "No, I'm not okay. Have you found her yet?"

She took my face in her hands. "Chase, look at me. Calm down. What's going on with you? What did Anya say to you to get you this fired up?"

I pointed toward her computer. "Anya's gone with Mongo to the hospital. I talked to Singer, but I'm not fired up. I'm just determined. We have to find her, and we've got to do it now."

"Okay. I'll find her. Just chill. What did Singer say to get you so . . . *not* fired up?"

"It's not what he said. It's what he made me realize. I don't really know anything about Penny's past, her family, or anything before we met. I don't know what I was thinking, but there's something going on, and I have to figure out what it is. That starts with finding her."

She rolled her chair back to the desk and pulled the keyboard close. "Okay, I'm on it, but if you keep bursting in here like that, I'm going to have a heart attack, and then you'll be on your own."

A knot formed in my throat. "I'm afraid I'm already on my own."

She spun in her chair and put her hands on my knees. "No, you're not. You've got all of us, and we're going to find her. We'll get to the bottom of this, no matter what it takes."

She stared at the floor for a moment and then looked up. "Before this goes any further, though, I need to know the truth. Did you?"

"Did I *what?*"

She rolled her eyes. "Did you sleep with Anya again?"

I set my eyes intently on hers. "I did not, and I will not, but I think you know that's not what this is about."

She turned back to her keyboard. "I'm glad you didn't, but I want you to know that even if you had, I'd still help you find her because I'm on your side—even when you're wrong."

I grabbed the remarkable woman I'd watched grow from a clumsy girl into one of the best intelligence analysts in the game, and I hugged her like the little sister I'd always perceive her to be.

She returned the hug and then shoved me away. "Now get out of here and let me work. I'll come find you when I have something worth sharing."

I kissed her on the forehead. "You do that, but hurry."

She pointed toward the door. "Out!"

* * *

I met Hunter coming through the kitchen with a cell phone in his hand.

He said, "I think I found Penny's phone."

I took it from his hand and pressed the power button, but nothing happened.

"I already tried that," he said. "It's dead."

I plugged it in by the coffee maker. "Where did you find it?"

He motioned toward the door with his chin. "I went out to check on the horses because I knew you weren't going to do it. Why do you hate them so much?"

"Hunter, focus. Where did you find Penny's phone?"

"It was in the bottom of the trash can in the barn. I took the bag out, and it broke. I cleaned up the mess and found the phone."

I stared at the phone as the red charging light came on. "I wonder why she'd throw it in there instead of the river."

He shrugged. "Who knows why women do anything they do?"

"Good point," I conceded, "but Penny rarely does anything unintentionally. I think it's the writer in her. She plans things out long before she does anything."

"I don't know, man, but I'm here to help if you need me."

My phone chirped before I could answer him. "Chase here."

"Please hold for the president."

I stammered. "Yes . . . yes, of course." Hunter furrowed his brow, and I waved him off. "It's the White House," I said.

Hunter chuckled. "Of course it is. Who else would it be?"

"Chase, how are you?"

"I'm fine, Mr. President. How are you?"

"Oh, I'm tied in a dozen directions and being pulled in two dozen more, but that's just business as usual. Listen, I was calling to thank you for that thing you did. That's some damned fine work, and my family and I won't soon forget it."

"I wouldn't have any idea what you're talking about, sir, but if I'd done anything, and if I knew what you were taking about, I'm sure I'd say you're welcome."

He laughed. "Ha! That's it, my boy. Say, are you really going to take Tommy's money for that job?"

"What money, Mr. President?"

"Yep, that's what I thought you'd say. Well, suffice it to say we owe you one, Chase."

"Just one, sir?"

"Goodbye, Chase, and thanks again."

The line went dead, and Hunter stared with anticipation in his eyes. "Well, what did he say? Are we all getting the Presidential Medal of Dirty Deeds Done Dirt Cheap?"

"Actually, he wanted to know if we were really going to take Thomas Meriwether's money."

Hunter grinned. "Oh, really?"

"Yep, really, and I asked him, what money? That was the end of it, but he did say thanks."

He shook his head. "That still freaks me out."

"What?"

"The fact that the president calls you on your cell phone."

I laughed. "He's a heck of a shot on the skeet field, too. Next time you're at Camp David, you should challenge him to a round."

He rolled his eyes. "Yeah, I'll do that . . . next time I'm at Camp David."

I shot another glance at Penny's phone, hoping it had enough charge to come to life. "Seriously, I'm going after Penny. I've got to find her."

He checked his watch. "What time do we leave?"

Clark stuck his head through the kitchen door from the back gallery. "Did somebody say we're leaving? If it's a mission, I'm in. For that matter, I'm in even if it's not a mission."

The enthusiasm of my team to follow me into the abyss with a dive knife in their teeth without asking why would never cease to amaze me. Every one of them was a more qualified leader than I'd ever be, yet I never doubted each of them would step in front of a bullet for me. I just didn't understand why.

"Well, I'm leaving," I said, "but it's not a team mission. I'm going after Penny."

He stepped through the door. "Do you know where she is?"

"Skipper's working on that now. It looks like she's in Texas, but I don't know yet. That may be a bit of misdirection to throw me off the real trail. She's smart and crafty. I just wish I knew why she's running."

"Are you sure it's not the Anya thing?" he asked.

"There is no *Anya thing*. It has to be something else. As much as I don't want to believe it, I think it has something to do with the oil rig job."

In his typical style, Clark pulled open the refrigerator and began grazing. Between bites, he looked up. "So, when are we leaving?"

From down the hallway, Skipper yelled, "Chase! Get in here! I'm pretty sure I found something worth sharing."

Clark slammed the refrigerator door and passed me on the way to the library. Hunter was only a second behind. The three of us huddled behind Skipper at the computer screen.

"What is it?" I asked. "What did you find?"

She pointed to a grainy image on the screen. "It's Penny's birth certificate. I found it in the scanned archives of the Hale County Courthouse. Her parents are Mitchell and Carla Thomas, but I'm sure you already knew that."

I sighed. "Actually, I didn't know either of their names."

She shot a look over her shoulder. "Hmm. Well, anyway, that's not why I called you in here. I did some more digging and came up with Mitchell's pilot's license and his liquor license. The last time the liquor license was renewed was in August of nineteen ninety, and the FAA doesn't have any record of him after the next January. Sometime in ninety-one, it's like he drops off the face of the Earth."

I leaned in. "What are you talking about? Did he die?"

"That's the weird thing," she said. "There's no death certificate, but he's just gone."

"What about Carla?" I asked.

Skipper's fingers danced across the keys. "I was just starting to look for her. I have some searches running in the background."

Clark, Hunter, and I stood in silence, watching Skipper work. Her fingers played across the keyboard like machine-gun fire until she suddenly froze.

"What is it?" I demanded.

"Uh, Chase, your mother-in-law is in prison."

In perfect unison, the three of us said, "What?"

Skipper stroked the keys for a few more seconds. "She was convicted in nineteen ninety-one of narcotics trafficking, tax evasion, and racketeering, plus a bunch of other things, but those are the biggies."

My heart sank into my gut. "But that can't be right. There must be another Carla Thomas. That's a pretty common name, right? Are you sure that's Penny's mother?"

Skipper plowed back into the keyboard as I stood on trembling knees, praying it was a mistake.

Skipper paused again as a newspaper article filled the screen.

In one of the most massive federal trials in Texas history, the Honorable Judge Samuel Ray Cummings handed down the first of what promises to be dozens if not hundreds of federal convictions in the Jimenez Cartel case. Carla Phillips Thomas received the first sentence of the case, in which nearly two dozen defendants will stand trial throughout the year. Thomas received an astonishing forty-seven-year sentence for her role in the international narcotics operations of the Jimenez Cartel. In total, the Jimenez Cartel is accused of importing hundreds of tons of cocaine, heroin, and other narcotics from Central and South America. Attorneys for Thomas say they will appeal, but the damning testimony of Thomas's husband, Mitchell Wade Thomas, seemed to seal her fate and ultimately result in her conviction. Thomas will serve her sentence, at least initially, at Federal Prison Camp Bryan just outside of College Station.

Hunter was the first to speak. "Well, I guess now we know why Mitch Thomas dropped off the face of the planet after the trial."

My mouth felt like a bowl of cotton as I choked on the words. "He's in witness protection."

Clark put his hand on my shoulder. "If he's still alive."

Motioning frantically toward the computer monitor, I said, "Find him."

I expected Skipper to plug in some secret analyst code or something, and the Federal Witness Security Program files would magically appear on the screen. I should've known better.

She didn't move. "Chase, I can find out what the chairman of the Joint Chiefs had for breakfast, but even I can't crack into WITSEC files."

"There has to be a way," I roared.

Skipper put her hand in the center of my chest. "Chill out. I'm working on it."

I took a knee and tried to gather my wits. Hunter pulled a chair from the corner and slid it behind me. The seat felt like a thousand daggers piercing my flesh. "Why wouldn't she tell me?"

Hunter laid his hand on my shoulder. "This ain't the kind of thing you bring up at the breakfast table, Chase. I'm sure she meant to tell you a thousand times. She probably even tried but could never get it out."

"It wouldn't have changed anything for me," I groaned, barely above a whisper.

Hunter said, "Yeah, but she didn't know that."

Skipper spun in her chair and took my hands in hers. "Chase, look at me. The day you two got married, it all happened so fast. The Judge just kinda sprang it on you. It wasn't like you had time to pull each other aside and spill your guts. I'm sure Penny—"

I squeezed her hands. "None of us can be sure of anything when it comes to Penny anymore. We have to find her."

Skipper's eyes were full of sadness and sympathy. "Why don't you go have a drink with Clark and Hunter? I'll keep digging, and I promise to let you know as soon as I find anything."

* * *

Hunter parked me in a rocking chair on the gallery while Clark poured drinks. When he delivered the cocktails, I took mine from his hand. "Thanks. I know this isn't the answer, but it'll do for now."

Clark perched himself on the railing and stared through the honey-colored whiskey in his tumbler. "I've chased bad guys on every continent except that frozen one down there at the bottom. I never can remember if that's Arctica or Antarctica, but the point is, I've never done anything like what we're about to do."

I took a long swallow and let the smooth whiskey coat my parched throat. "This one isn't your fight. This one's personal. It's my mess that I created, and I can't ask any of you to jump in it with me."

Hunter lifted his glass, holding it up between Clark and me. We took the hint and touched the rim of his glass.

"That's the beauty of it," Hunter said. "You ain't asking. We're volunteering, and I think I speak for all of us. Well, except maybe Anya. She's probably gonna have her head stuck up Mongo's butt for a while."

For the first time in an hour, I smiled. "Yeah, I don't think I want Anya on this one anyway."

That garnered a little laughter until Skipper came through the door with a sheet of paper in her hand.

"What's that?" I asked, almost afraid to hear the answer.

She handed me the paper. It was a printout of another newspaper article dated February 19, 2003.

In an effort to relieve federal prison overcrowding, one hundred fifty-seven non-violent federal prisoners were released yesterday on a program the Federal Bureau of Prisons is calling the "Second Chance Act." One of the most notable prisoners released under the Second Chance program is Carla Phillips Thomas, who has served less than twelve years of her forty-seven-year sentence for narcotics trafficking, tax evasion, and various other offenses. A prison spokesperson told The Bryan-College Station Eagle that Carla Thomas plans to return to her hometown of Plainview, where she will be required to submit to weekly drug testing by her parole officer. Thomas is the only female federal prisoner in Texas released from incarceration on this program.

Chapter 21
My Secretary

I stared up from the paper. "I was right. None of this has anything to do with Anya. Penny's gone to find her mother."

Clark set his tumbler on the gallery rail. "Looks like we're going to Texas."

Skipper stood motionless, a condition I'd rarely seen. "Um, I'm a little out of my league here. I don't really know what to do next, but if you'll tell me what you need, I'll figure it out."

My tumbler joined Clark's on the rail as I stood from my rocker. "I know you will, Skipper. Start with her phone. It's charging beside the coffee maker. I need you to trace every call she made or received for the past ten days. I need to know who was on the other end and where they were. Can you do that?"

Skipper bit at the nail of her index finger. "Yeah, probably, but it'll take some time."

"Then get on it. We've got to have some place to start."

Hunter asked, "You don't need me to fly, do you?"

I shook my head, and he downed his glass of whiskey.

Pausing in the kitchen, I turned to Clark. "I want to be reasonable about this. If we charge into Plainview like a freight train on Main Street, like you're so fond of saying, we'll spook the whole town, and we'll never find Penny. I think this one needs to be on the down-low."

He ran his hand through his hair. "I'm not good at down-low, but I think you're right. If we start poking around and asking questions in a town that small, we're going to stand out like a rhinoceros at a bunny farm."

Hunter laughed. "I've heard of the Bunny Ranch outside of Vegas, but never a bunny farm."

Clark said, "A rhinoceros would stand out there, too."

"Come on, guys. Get your heads in the game," I said. "We don't need Mongo. He's a rhinoceros everywhere he goes, and Anya would be a flashing neon sign in Plainview. I can't imagine having any need for a sniper, so that rules out Singer. I know both of you want to go, but think about it. Do either of you really think we need three sets of boots on the ground out there?"

Clark stepped back through the door and then returned with our tumblers from the gallery. "I guess these are both mine now. I'll work with Skipper to run the ops center. How do you plan to get there? It has to be over a thousand miles, and that's a long ride in the Caravan."

I grinned. "But not in the Mustang."

He threw up his hands. "Talk about a rhinoceros . . . If you put the Mustang on the ramp in Plainview, you might as well march in there with a Ranger battalion."

"Not a problem," I said. "We'll fly into Lubbock, rent a car, and drive to Plainview."

"Works for me," Hunter said. "What are we packing?"

I considered his question. "Clothes for a week, sidearms, a thousand rounds, and commo gear."

He disappeared up the stairs just as Mongo and Anya came through the front door. Anya was carrying a drug store bag in one hand and holding Mongo's arm with the other.

"Hey, guys. Welcome back. What did the doc have to say?"

Mongo wrinkled his nose. "Ah, it's just some bruising. I'm good."

Anya glared up at the giant. "He has three broken ribs, second-degree burns, and he must have surgery when swelling from broken ribs goes away."

"Surgery?" I asked. "What for?"

Mongo started to speak, but Anya cut in. "Is much like hernia in muscles of abdomen. And he must have rest in bed for three weeks."

"So, how do you feel, big man?" I asked in an effort to let Mongo speak.

"The ribs are a little tender. You know how it is. And the burns itch a little, but it's not all that bad. What's been going on here? Have you found Penny?"

I glanced toward the library, unsure how much to tell him. "We think we've found her."

Anya's eyes widened, but she didn't interrupt me.

"I was right. What's going on with her has nothing to do with any of us, especially not you, Anya. It's some family drama in Texas."

"Have you talked to her yet?" Mongo asked.

"No, not exactly. It's a little complicated, but Hunter and I are flying out there tomorrow morning. We can tell you about it later, but it looks like you need some rest."

He looked down at his enormous body. "Yeah, I'll get some rest, but I'll be ready to go with you and Hunter in the morning."

Anya twisted the big man's thumb as if she were trying to remove it from his hand. "You will rest for three weeks, just as doctor says, and then you will have surgery."

Mongo frowned at me. "Can you handle it without me?"

I laughed. "I think we'll manage. You're welcome to stay here as long as you want."

"Thanks, but I think we're going to head back to Athens unless you need Anya on this one."

"Hunter and I have it under control. You just take care of yourself, and good luck with that evil nurse of yours."

Anya narrowed her eyes and leaned toward my face. "Is scar still on tongue? If is not, I can make another."

Almost six years earlier, Anya had split my tongue in half with one of her beloved fighting knives when I wouldn't answer her questions. That was before we were on the same team, but she enjoyed reminding me of that day as often as possible.

I locked eyes with her. "Feel free to try anytime you're ready to lose another toe."

* * *

I raised the hangar door about ninety minutes before sunrise the following day. As the hangar lights came to life, my North American P-51D Mustang glistened under their glow, and her new name, *Penny's Secret*, suddenly took on more meaning than ever before. The warbird had been the prized possession of my mentor and father figure, Dr. Robert Richter. He'd named her *Katerina's Heart* after the woman he'd loved during the Cold War, who just happened to be Anya's mother. After getting the beauti- ful flying machine shot to hell by a Russian spy ship off the Georgia coast, I rechristened her *Penny's Secret* because of the beautiful smile my wife almost always wore as if she knew a se- cret the rest of the world would never hear.

Hunter broke my trance. "Every time I see her, she's more beautiful."

"What?"

"The airplane. She's gorgeous. I still can't believe you own a Mustang."

I slid my hand across the fuselage and the painting of my wife on the nose of the sixty-year-old airplane, sitting with her legs crossed. "Yeah, I feel the same way."

We conducted the preflight inspection in the hangar to take advantage of the light and then pushed the five-ton airplane onto the ramp with the John Deere tractor modified specifically for the job. With the old girl full of fuel and anxious to climb into the western sky, I ran through the startup checklist and listened to the massive Rolls-Royce Merlin engine rumble to life. With a flip of the avionics master switch, our headsets came to life, and I could hear Hunter's tinny voice. "Man, that sure is sexy."

"Yes, it is, my friend. There's no other sound in the world like a Merlin. You have the controls. We'll take off on runway three-one."

"I have the controls," he returned.

We taxied to the runway and conducted the run-up and be-fore-takeoff checklist.

"Okay, just keep her on the centerline," I said. "I'll be close on the controls with you. Remember to use plenty of right rudder when the nose comes up. She'll want to turn left pretty hard."

I held the controls loosely as Hunter accelerated down the runway and *Penny's Secret* took to the air. Twenty-five minutes later, we were breathing pure oxygen through our masks and cruising westward at twenty-two thousand feet, making almost four hundred knots across the ground.

As the autopilot managed the flight with very little input from either of us, I said, "Imagine hand-flying one of these things escorting bombers for eight hours over England and Germany in nineteen-forty-five. Those guys had to be exhausted when and *if* they made it home."

Hunter said, "Warfare sure has come a long way since then. I can only imagine what our grandkids will use to kill each other a hundred years from now."

"Have you ever thought about having kids?" I asked.

"Sure. I just haven't met the right woman yet. I think I'd like to settle down a little. Believe it or not, I lay awake last night thinking about that exact thing. With the money you gave us . . ."

"I didn't give you anything. You earned that money."

He chuckled. "Whatever. Anyway, I was thinking maybe I could spend a little time in Miami with Clark. You know I've got a weakness for dark-haired Latin girls."

"You've got a weakness for all girls," I said, "regardless of their hair color or country of origin."

"That may be true," he admitted, "but I'm especially fond of Cuban girls."

The one-thousand-forty-mile flight from Saint Marys to Lubbock took less than three hours, and thanks to the autopilot that Cotton, the mechanic, had installed, we arrived unfatigued and ready to hit the ground running.

The Mustang garnered attention everywhere I took her, and Lubbock was no exception. Linemen, pilots, and even the FBO staff all wanted to get a close-up look at *Penny's Secret*.

I pulled the FBO manager aside. "If you could find a little hangar space for my Mustang, I'd really appreciate it. I don't want to leave her on the ramp if I don't have to."

He scratched his cheek. "I'll see what I can do, but we're pretty full."

"It's worth a hundred fifty bucks a night to me if you could get her inside. I could probably even throw in a ride for you in the front seat if you could help me out."

A smile replaced his contemplative scowl. "I think I know just the place for her."

I handed him my credit card and headed for the rental car counter. "Good morning. I'm Chase Fulton."

The young lady behind the counter laid a stack of paperwork on the Formica surface. "Yes, sir. Your secretary called, and everything is taken care of. I just need your signature at the bottom and a copy of your driver's license."

I turned to Hunter. "My secretary called. I can't wait to tell Skipper about her new job title."

"She'll put a bullet in your skull," he warned.

I signed the paperwork, passed over my license, and collected the keys.

The FBO manager met me at the door to the rental office with my credit card and his business card. "My cell number is on the back. Call anytime if you need anything. We'll take good care of your Mustang."

I glanced down at his card that said "Michael G. Thomas, Lubbock Aero General Manager" and stuck out my hand. "Thank you for your help, Mr. Thomas. You wouldn't by any chance be related to any Thomases up in Plainview, would you?"

He shook my offered hand. "I'm sure I am. There's about a million of us in Texas, but I don't know anybody up there. I'm from Galveston originally. I moved out here to take this job."

We found our rental car at the curb, a relatively new Toyota Camry.

Hunter said, "Your secretary made a nice choice. Nobody's going to remember us in this thing."

I shook my finger at him. "That's a dangerous game you're playing. I won't be the only one she kills if Skipper catches you calling her that."

He laughed. "I actually think it's got a nice ring to it."

We turned from North Cedar Avenue onto the Interstate 27 service road and accelerated up the ramp.

On the forty-minute drive to Plainview, I said, "We should check in with Skipper."

Hunter held up his phone. "I'm way ahead of you."

He punched the speaker button just as she answered. "Hey, guys. How was the flight?"

"Uneventful," I said, "and my *secretary* had the perfect rental car waiting for us when we landed."

"Secretary? Uh, I don't think so," she spouted with a lot more attitude than necessary.

"I'm just repeating what the lady at the rental counter said. I didn't know I had a secretary, but I must admit, I like it."

"You can like it all you want when you actually get one, but I'm an analyst. I don't take dictation."

"Maybe not," I said, "but you do a great job of reserving rental cars."

She said, "I'm hanging up now. Good luck without me."

"No, no, wait! I'm just messing with you. Do you have any news for us?"

She cleared her throat. "If you're finished wasting time, I'll tell you what I've got. The first thing is a list of names and phone numbers from Penny's phone. Second, guess how many federal parole officers there are in Plainview, Texas."

"I have no clue," I said.

"None. That's how many, but I found out there's one who travels from Lubbock to Plainview every Thursday for meetings and drug tests with the three federal parolees in Hale County."

"I wish you were here," I said. "You deserve a huge forehead kiss and bonus."

"Okay, for the record, the forehead kissing thing is disgusting, but I'll take the bonus . . . especially if it's like the last one you handed out."

"That one's going to be hard to top, but I'll see what I can do."

"Okay, enough with the foolishness. Let's get back to work. The parole officer's name is Tina Ramirez. She meets her parolees in the municipal court complex at the corner of Ninth and Broadway on Thursdays between ten and noon. It's right next door to the police department."

"Great work, Skipper. Did you happen to get the names of her parolees?"

"Of course I did. What do you think I am, some kind of secretary? The first one is Ronaldo Berringer, a forty-four-year-old white male convicted of wire fraud. The second is Jason McAllister, a thirty-five-year-old white male convicted of some kind of interstate commerce crap I don't understand, but the third is one Carla Phillips Thomas."

I checked my watch. "Would you look at that? My watch says it's Wednesday. That means our favorite federal parole officer is due in town tomorrow morning."

Chapter 22
We've Got a Problem?

Hunter and I learned my "secretary" had booked more than just our inconspicuous Toyota. She also made reservations at one of Plainview's most incognito hotels, although perhaps calling it a hotel is too flattering for the Prairie View Inn. There was no prairie, no view, and although I can't say I know the technical definition of the word *Inn*, it was safe to declare the whole name a lie.

What the Prairie View Inn did have was plenty of available rooms with almost no possibility of being kept awake by noisy next-door neighbors. Everything smelled like stale cigarette smoke, and the beds had plastic wrappers on what they called "mattresses." It was going to be like trying to sleep while someone crumpled a plastic grocery store bag beside my ear.

Hunter and I took adjoining rooms, but not the typical adjoining rooms with a pair of back-to-back lockable doors. Our rooms adjoined because the sheetrock crew hadn't finished repairing the damage from the assault some previous tenant had committed on what had been the wall.

The city of Plainview is a quaint little Northwest Texas town with low buildings, long, straight city streets, and populated by some of the friendliest people in the world. The problem with friendly people is their curiosity, and Shirl, the sixtyish, bulbous waitress at the Lone Star Café was the perfect example.

"Good evening, boys. I don't reckon I know you two. You ain't rodeo cowboys 'cause your britches ain't tight enough, and them ain't cowboy boots. You ain't big-city oilmen 'cause you ain't wearin' clean hats. Big-city oilmen never get their hats dirty. And you ain't roughnecks 'cause your fingernails is clean. That only leaves one thing you could be."

I sat in the cracked, plastic-covered booth seat, staring up at the waitress and hanging on every word, anxious to hear that one thing Hunter and I could be. If the next words out of her mouth were, "You boys must be spies," Shirl was getting a thousand-dollar tip.

"What can I get you to drink, sugar?"

We sat in silent disbelief of Shirl's conversation shift.

Hunter stammered, "Just water for me."

"Just water for me, too," I said.

Shirl leaned in. "Boys, if money's tight, I'll throw in a couple sweet teas, and I won't put 'em on the bill. You don't have to just drink water."

I laughed and placed my hand on the woman's round, freckled forearm. "Thank you, Ms. Shirl, but we like water."

"Suit yourself," she said, and disappeared through a pair of metallic, saloon-style swinging doors.

Hunter slapped the table with both hands. "Did I miss something? If we ain't cowboys, big-city oilmen, or roughnecks, what are we?"

I couldn't stifle my laughter. "I don't know, but I can't wait to find out."

"Do you think she'll tell us?"

I shrugged as our water arrived, and Shirl pulled out an order pad and yellow pencil. "What'll you have, baby?" Neither of us spoke, so Shirl bumped me with her ample hip. "That's you, baby. You're baby. He's sugar."

It was getting better by the minute. "I think I'll have the country fried steak, mashed potatoes, and green beans."

She put her hand on my shoulder. "Hang a minute, baby." Then she turned toward the swinging doors and yelled, "Hey, Bobby. Is them green beans scalded or are they good?"

A voice that could've belonged to a dump truck echoed from the kitchen. "Tell 'em they don't want the beans."

Shirl looked down. "The beans ain't good, baby. You're gonna want the fried okra, and do you want gravy on the mashed taters or just on the steak?"

"Fried okra sounds good, and I'd love gravy on everything," I said, trying not to snicker.

"You got it, baby. Gravy on everything. Dagnabbit, my pencil's broke again. Hang on a minute, sugar."

She laid the pad on the edge of the table, withdrew a pocketknife from her apron, and sharpened her pencil, allowing the shavings to fall on the floor. She wiped the blade of her knife on her apron, closed it, and returned it to the pocket. "Okay, sugar, I'm sorry 'bout that. What can I get you?"

Hunter pointed toward the laminated menu. "That world-famous cheeseburger sounds good."

Shirl rolled her eyes. "Sugar, ain't nobody outside of Hale County ever heard of that cheeseburger. It ain't a bit more world-famous than I am, but it is good. Bobby's uncle runs a cattle ranch . . . Well, he don't run it no more after that trouble with the law he got into. I'm sure you boys heard about that. But he still works out there. That's where we get all our meat . . . Well, except the chicken and fish and shrimps. But all the meat comes from out there, and it's some of the best there is. You want fries or onion rings? The onion rings are better 'cause Bobby's niece raises the onions. She went off to Tech and got some kind of big fancy degree over there, and she raises the best onions I've ever had." She patted her stomach and exhaled in an exaggerated motion. "And you can tell from my belly and my breath I eat plenty o' onions."

Hunter grinned. "Onion rings it is, then."

Shirl left again without telling us that one thing we must be.

Hunter leaned across the table with a conspiratorial look on his face. "Did you ever watch the show *Alice* when you were a kid?"

"I don't think so."

He pointed toward the kitchen. "This place reminds me of Mel's Diner from that show."

"Oh, yeah, I do remember that. And you're right, that's hilarious."

Our dinner arrived, and mine looked like a plate of gravy. I stared up at Shirl.

"You told me you wanted gravy on everything."

I took the plate from her. "Yes, ma'am, I did. Thank you."

I suddenly coveted Hunter's cheeseburger, but one bite into my country fried steak changed my mind. We ate in relative silence for ten minutes until we'd earned our place in the clean-plate club.

Shirl showed up with a pitcher of water and refilled our glasses. "You boys want some chocolate pie? I made it, of course, 'cause Bobby don't bake on account of he's colorblind, you know."

I stared at Hunter, hoping he could explain to me what color-blindness has to do with the ability to bake. He bit his lip in an effort to control the laughter he clearly wanted to let out.

I said, "Yes, ma'am. We'd love some pie."

Out came the pencil and pad again. "Two slices of pie and ice cream. You do want ice cream, right? What kind of ice cream do you like?"

"I like chocolate," I said.

Hunter looked up. "I like every kind of ice cream, so whatever you have is fine with me."

Shirl scribbled on the pad. "Okay, good, 'cause all we got is vanilla. I'll be right back."

"This place is the best," I whispered as Shirl walked away.

Hunter chuckled. "You can't make this stuff up. You're gonna have to write a book about all the crazy messes we get into some-day."

"Aww, Penny's the writer. We'll let her do it."

He forced a smile. "We *are* going to find her."

"I know. It's like we told Thomas Meriwether . . . We don't fail."

He offered up his fist for a bump. "Dang right, we don't."

The pie and ice cream arrived, and it melted in our mouths.

With his mouth full, Hunter mumbled, "This is incredible pie."

When we'd earned our second gold star for cleaning our plates, Shirl arrived with the check. "It'll be eleven eighty-four."

I reached for my wallet. "No, put them both together. I've got it."

Shirl looked at the ticket. "Put both of what together?"

"The bills," I said. "I'll pay for both."

"Baby, it's eleven eighty-four for both of 'em."

I handed her a twenty.

She said, "I'll be right back with your change."

I held up a hand. "No, Ms. Shirl, just keep it. Everything was perfect . . . especially the service."

Her eyes turned to saucers. "Are you sure, sugar?"

"Yes, ma'am."

She gave us both a hug as we left. She smelled a lot like our rooms at the Prairie View Inn.

Back in the car, Hunter said, "I'm not sure leaving her a tip like that was such a great idea. She's going to remember us now."

"It was eight bucks," I argued.

"Yeah, but it was eight bucks on a twelve-dollar ticket."

"We should've had the sweet tea."

Our drive through town didn't take long. The municipal court building at the corner of Broadway and Ninth was easy enough to find. Just as Skipper had said, it was right beside the police department. Except for the size of the building, nothing about it surprised me. Skipper had called it a *complex*, but the squat, single-story building could've been a bank or a small-town post office. Nothing about it qualified as a complex.

Diagonally across the intersection of Broadway and Ninth was the tree-lined parking lot of the Plainview Daily Herald. The trees provided excellent concealment, and the proximity to the municipal court building made it the perfect spot to surveil the parking lot for the arrival of the federal parole officer and her parolees. With any luck, the guest of honor would arrive, and we could have a little chat with my ex-con mother-in-law.

The building directly across Ninth from the court building was a vacant, two-story brick structure with oversized rain gutters and downspouts.

Hunter motioned toward the building. "Those downspouts would be easy enough to climb, and the top of that place would make a great observation post."

I turned from the brick-paved surface of Broadway onto Ninth and circled the block to get a look at the back side of the vacant building. We found ourselves on Ash, in front of Ash High School, and I wondered if Penny had walked across the stage and collected her diploma from behind those walls. Maybe I'd get to ask her.

Our tour of the city continued until we were comfortable with the south side of Plainview.

"Okay, so here's the plan," I began. "I'll wait in the car in the parking lot of the newspaper building, and you'll monkey yourself up onto the roof of the building. We'll watch for Carla to show up, ID her car, and follow her when she leaves."

Hunter nodded. "I like it, but what if she hits the interstate when she leaves and heads for Canada?"

I reached into my backpack behind the seat and pulled out a three-inch square black box and tossed it to my partner. "That's our little what-if gizmo."

Hunter inspected the non-descript device. "What is it?"

"It's a GPS tracker. Skipper gave me two of them. We just stick that thing on the frame of Carla's vehicle, and Skipper can track her anywhere she goes as long as the batteries hold up."

"And how long's that?"

"Skipper said seven days, more or less."

He frowned. "I like the more part, but how much less?"

"Who knows, but hopefully it won't take us a week to track her down."

* * *

I was right about the wrap on the mattress. It sounded just like someone fighting with a plastic bag. Between Hunter snoring in the other room of our luxury two-room suite and the rustling bag, I may have gotten seven or eight solid minutes of quality sleep.

The hot water worked in Hunter's room, and the cold water worked in mine, so our showers were a chorus of cold-water gasps and cries of scalding agony.

"Well, that was an adventure," Hunter said.

I pulled on my boots. "Yeah, mine, too. I think the only way to recover is breakfast at Mel's Diner."

"You're on," he said, "but this time, go easy on the tip."

We walked across the street and discovered how the Lone Star Café stayed in business. We were the only customers for dinner the night before, but there was a line of people waiting for seats at seven-thirty.

Hunter groaned. "I don't want to stand in that line. Do you?"

"Nope, I surely don't. I spotted a Carl's Jr. out by the interstate. I think that's the same thing as Hardees. I say we hit them up for breakfast and be in place at the court building by nine."

Hunter nodded. "Sounds good, but I would like to do breakfast with Shirl before we skip town. If it's good enough for that many people to stand in line, we definitely need to try it out."

"It's a date," I said, and we walked back to our car in the motel parking lot.

Breakfast at Carl's Jr. was dependably good, and we didn't have to stand in line. We stocked up on bottled water and snacks for our stakeout. There's something about surveillance that makes me hungry, and empty plastic bottles come in handy when you can't leave your post to go to the head.

We circled the block around the municipal court building and police department before pulling into the parking lot of the Plainview Daily Herald. There were more cars in the lot than I'd expected, but they provided additional concealment as long as no one got nosey about the guy from out of town sitting in his car and staring at the court building. Hunter stuck two candy bars and bottles of water in his cargo pants and headed for the vacant building.

A few pedestrians were strolling along Broadway and nonchalantly enjoying the world around them; however, a guy climbing a downspout would be difficult for anyone to ignore. Our whisper-coms made communication barely more than a thought. Anything either of us said would be instantly broadcast to the other without the need for pressing a push-to-talk button. The open-mic system ate batteries like candy, but they were a godsend in tactical operations.

I watched the pedestrians milling about. "Hunter, I think it'd be best to go around back so no one gets suspicious about the monkey climbing the building."

"Great minds think alike. I'm headed around back now."

Traffic on the street was light, but the sun was already turning the morning air into an oven. I'd chosen wisely when I made the decision to send Hunter to the rooftop while I sat in the air-conditioned comfort of the Camry.

Hunter's voice came alive in my earpiece. "You're never going to believe this, but there's a ladder propped up against the back of the building."

"A ladder?"

"Yeah, a ladder. It's on top of the portico, and I'm certain it wasn't there last night."

"That's interesting," I said.

"It sure is. Do you want me to go up?"

I thought for a minute. "Yes, we need you on that rooftop, but if there's an inspector or something up there, just play it off like you're interested in buying the building and wanted to see the roof."

"You got it, boss. Up I go. Hey, come to think of it, I could buy this building if I wanted . . . as long as it's less than five million dollars."

"That's exactly what you need," I said. "A vacant building in Plainview, Texas."

He didn't respond, but I could hear the sounds of him climbing the portico column and then his footsteps on the ladder rungs.

I scanned the street and checked my watch. It was just past nine, and Skipper had said the parole officer works from ten until noon. I figured she would arrive a little early to set up for the meetings, but what did I know about how federal parole officers work?

Hunter's footsteps silenced and were replaced with the sounds of his breathing. I couldn't see him from my position in the parking lot, but it was clear that he'd reached the top of the ladder and stopped. I was suddenly concerned, and his next transmission did nothing to reassure me.

"Uh, Houston, we've got a problem."

Chapter 23
Hello, Lady

Hunter's definition of a problem was significantly different than mine. If he'd encountered half a dozen armed men determined to prevent him from claiming the rooftop, he would've simply dispatched them one by one and mentioned it afterwards, so whatever the problem was, deserved my attention.

"What's the problem?" I asked.

"I've solved the mystery of the ladder. There's a guy, appears to be in his fifties, fit, salt-and-pepper hair, maybe six feet tall and one ninety. He's set up an observation point exactly where I was planning to park. He's got a spotter's scope, but it's a civilian model. Nothing special."

"Did he see you?"

"If he'd seen me, I wouldn't be huddling at the top of the ladder, whispering sweet nothings in your ear. I'd be kicking his ass. Now, what do you want me to do?"

No battle plan survives first contact with the enemy. I should've known things were going far too well. I had no way to anticipate anyone else doing the same thing Hunter and I were doing, but it was well past time for something to go wrong.

"Come back down and find a position where you can see both the court building and the other spotter when he comes down the ladder."

"Roger. I'm moving."

I listened intently, but Hunter's descent was virtually silent until his boots hit the ground beside the portico. It sounded as if he'd leapt from several feet above the hard-packed ground and conducted a parachute landing fall. Back on his feet, I could hear him jogging.

When the jogging stopped, he said, "I'm not having any luck finding a new O.P., but I think I found our mystery man's truck."

"Do tell," I said.

"It's a white F-One-Fifty with a ladder rack. There's a pair of elastic straps hanging from the rack where a ladder just like the one on the building would be."

"Do you see any other ladders in use in any direction?" I asked, praying his answer would be what I wanted.

"Nothing. And it looks like someone tried to hide this truck. It's parked behind what's left of a run-down lean-to under a tree. The engine is still warm, so it's been driven very recently."

I shoved my hand into my ruck and withdrew one of Skipper's GPS tracking devices. "I'm coming your way. I'll be there in thirty seconds."

Shooting a glance toward the top of the vacant building, I ran to the west and turned south down the alley. Hunter was waiting at the corner of a dilapidated building and looking skyward. "Keep coming. You're good."

I rounded the corner and followed my partner beneath the tree and behind the lean-to. "This has to be his truck."

"Yeah, I agree. You attach the tracker, and I'll watch for our spotter."

I crawled beneath the truck, stuck the tracker to the frame, and powered it up. I scampered back to my feet. "Who do you suppose that guy is?"

Hunter shrugged. "I don't know yet, but based on the fact he left his ladder exposed on the back of that building, he's either supremely confident no one will see or question him, or he's careless and stupid. Right now, I'm coming down on the careless and stupid side, but I reserve the right to change my mind."

"I tend to agree, but I'd sure like to know who he is."

Hunter pointed to the spot where a license plate should've been on the truck. "That's an interesting touch."

I knelt behind the bumper and examined the screw holes for the tag. "They're clean. He must've taken the plate off recently."

Hunter drummed his fingertips together. "Hmm. Now, I'm starting to doubt my careless and stupid diagnosis."

"Maybe Skipper can run the VIN number."

"It's worth a shot," he said.

I used my shirttail to wipe the dust and grime from the lower-left corner of the windshield and reveal the metal vehicle identification number plate as I pushed the speed dial button.

"Hey, Chase. Is everything all right?"

"Yeah, it's all good, but we have an unexpected visitor, and I need you to run a VIN number and tell me who owns a truck."

She scrambled to find a pad and pen. "Okay, go ahead. I'm ready."

I read the number slowly, making sure to pronounce each letter and number carefully.

Skipper read it back. "By the way," she said, "it's just a VIN. The N means number, so please stop calling it a VIN number. Do you want me to run it while we're on the phone?"

"OCD much?" I asked.

She huffed. "I'll tell you what you can do with your OCD and your *secretary* if you don't straighten up. Do you want me to run the number or not?"

"If you can, that would be great."

"Okay, give me just a second."

I placed my hand over the phone. "My secretary's running it now."

Hunter shook his head in disapproval and jogged back to the corner of the building to have another look at our mystery man's position.

Skipper came back on the line. "Are you sure you read the VIN correctly?"

I peered back through the glass. "Read back what I gave you, and I'll double-check."

She read the number, and I compared it, digit for digit. "That's exactly what's on the plate."

She sighed. "Hmm. Let me try again."

Her keystrokes were deliberate and rapid. "There's something really weird going on here."

"What is it?"

"I'm not sure yet, but I need you to find the CVI number on the truck."

"What's a CVI number?"

Her exasperation was growing. "It's a confidential vehicle identification number. It's going to be very similar to the number on the VIN plate, but it'll be stamped somewhere on the frame."

"Okay, hang on. I'll see what I can find."

I crawled back under the truck and shone my penlight on the frame. After several minutes of studying every inch of the metal, I finally found it and pulled my phone back to my ear. "Okay, I've got it."

"Send it," she said.

I gave her the number, and again, her fingers went to work.

"Uh, Chase, that vehicle doesn't exist."

"I assure you it exists. I'm looking at the rusty undercarriage as we speak."

She clicked her tongue against her teeth. "Did you say rusty?"

"Yeah, the frame, suspension, and exhaust are pretty rusty."

"There's a lot going on there. Since there's no record of the truck existing, that probably means it's built from more than one wrecked truck, or it belongs to some branch of the federal government. The rust could mean it's been driven near salt water for an extended period of time, or it's been driven where they get a lot of snow. The salt and chemicals they use to keep the roads from freezing can cause cars to rust pretty quickly."

"We're a long way from any beach," I said, "but you don't have to go very far to get into the Rockies from here."

"Then it's probably from someplace where it snows a lot. I'm sorry I couldn't be any more help."

"No, you've done enough, but I just activated one of your trackers. It's on this vehicle. It's a white F-One-Fifty pickup with a ladder rack."

"Okay," she said, "I'll keep it in sight. Oh, by the way, there just happens to be a National Weather Service satellite twiddling its thumbs about twenty miles overhead if you'd like for me to borrow it. It may have a decent camera."

I grinned. "Add one more forehead kiss to the list. Yes, yes, and yes. Grab the satellite. There's a guy on top of the building we were going to use as an observation point. I think this is his truck. If you can put eyes on him, that would be fantastic."

The keystrokes returned. "I'm on it. I'll know in less than five minutes if I can nab it."

"Keep me posted," I said as I ended the call. Back on my feet, I peered across Hunter's shoulder. "Any movement?"

He shook his head, "No. The dude is settled in. What do you think about stealing his ladder and trapping him on the building?"

I checked my watch. "It's nine thirty-five. We need eyes on the court building."

Hunter glanced back at the rooftop. "I don't think there's any place I can see both the court building and the ladder. You're gonna have to decide which one is more important."

Those were the decisions I hated most. If we let the spotter get away and the tracker didn't work, we'd never know who or what he was, but if we missed Penny's mother, we'd have to wait another week for the check-in and drug test.

"Let's focus on the court building. We've got the tracker on the truck, and Skipper's lining up a satellite overhead. We can catch up with whoever that guy is later. Right now, we need to grab Carla Thomas."

Hunter glanced back at the truck. "Say, did you happen to see a spare tire while you were playing around under that truck?"

"Yeah, there's one under there, why?"

He pulled his switchblade from his pocket and produced the spring-loaded blade in an instant. "It'd be a shame if our friend up there had to change a flat tire before he skedaddled back off to wherever he came from."

"I like the way you think. Right front would be particularly unfortunate for him."

Hunter smiled. "Say no more, boss. I'm on it."

After leaving his mark on the right front Michelin of the Ford, Hunter met me back at the car. A plain white sedan with federal government plates pulled up to the curb at the court building, and we put our binoculars to our eyes.

"I bet that's our girl," Hunter said.

"Could be. We'll see when she gets out."

The driver of the sedan opened the left front door, slid her black high heels to the scorching asphalt of the parking lot, and stood. I don't know what federal parole officers are supposed to look like, but this one could've walked off the cover of *Vogue Magazine*. She wore a navy-blue pencil skirt and a thin white top.

Hunter let out a low whistle. "Hello there, lady parole officer."

She closed the door, took three steps toward the rear of the car, and opened the back door. When she bent over to retrieve something from the back seat, Hunter stopped breathing. She reemerged, holding a medium-sized file box and a jacket to match the skirt. Her glossy black ponytail played against her collar, and her olive complexion screamed Brazil or Colombia.

Hunter reached for the door handle. "I think our lady parole officer needs somebody to get the door for her."

Before I could stop him, he jogged diagonally across Broadway and headed straight for the mirrored, double glass doors of the municipal court building. As Tina Ramirez approached the door, Hunter stumbled and slammed into her, knocking her box from her arms and sending its contents splaying across the sidewalk. My partner was a genius.

I watched him kneel at her feet and hastily pick up and reorganize the box's contents. Once everything was back in its place, he held the door for Ms. Ramirez and followed her inside. Less than a minute later, my partner emerged from the backside of the building and ran across Ninth. Shortly thereafter, he was back in the seat beside me with stars in his eyes.

"Man, she's gorgeous, and she smells as good as she looks."

"Nicely done, Romeo. Did you think to inventory the box while you were drooling over the parole officer?"

He held up his palms. "What do I look like, a secretary? Of course I checked out the box. It contains four urine sample cups and three files. Two of the files are really thick, and the other one looks like it may have a dozen sheets of paper in it. The two thick ones belong to Ronaldo Berringer and Jason McAllister. The other has Carla Thomas's name on it."

Chapter 24
Clark's Clichés

"I suppose that's one way to confirm we're at the right place. All that's left is to wait until Carla shows up."

Hunter scanned the street. "It may be a little late to ask this question, but what do you plan to do with Carla Thomas when she shows up? Are we going to grab her, follow her, or what?"

I scratched my chin. "To be honest, I was hoping you had a plan for that part."

He didn't look away from the street. "Nope. That's why you're in charge. You get paid to make the tough decisions."

I grimaced. "Finding Carla isn't my goal. It's just a step toward finding Penny. I think she's here to see her mother. Why else would she be all the way out here?"

He abandoned his scanning and turned to face me. "You don't know that she *is* here. You only know that a cell phone she bought is, or was, here."

"You're right," I admitted, "but the only way to find out is to follow her mother and see if she leads us to her. I have a suspicion Penny may be with her mother for today's meeting with the parole officer."

Hunter made a face. "I hadn't considered that, but it's a possibility. And an interesting one, at that."

My phone chirped. "Chase here."

"Hey, it's me," Skipper said. "I'm having trouble with the satellite. It's a National Weather Service bird that's really good at looking down at clouds, but there's no detail at all for the surface. It's like looking at a pixelated mess. We're not going to get anything useful from it. I'm sorry."

"Don't be sorry," I said. "You're doing your best. Are there any other satellite options?"

"Ugh. No. There's nothing I can grab in the area for forty-eight hours. I hate it. We really need our own satellite."

"I'm afraid we can't even pool our cash and afford a satellite, but I love your enthusiasm."

"Maybe someday," she said. "Oh, I've been going through the list of numbers Penny called and who called her. So far, it's all benign. She made and received one call from her friend, Tonya, the speech-language pathologist. There was one call to buy the airline ticket and a bunch to and from you, but there was one that stood out."

She had my attention. "Oh? Let's hear it."

"It was a call to Anya that lasted six and a half minutes."

"What!"

"You heard me," she said.

Hunter punched my arm and pointed toward the court building. "There's a car pulling in."

"Hang on just a minute, Skipper. I'll be right back."

I didn't give her a chance to answer. Hunter and I pulled our binoculars to our eyes and focused on the car. The driver's door opened, and outstepped a balding, chubby, used-car-salesman-looking dude in a cheap suit.

I lowered my binos. "If that's Penny's mom, the sex-change operation was a terrible decision."

Hunter dropped his binoculars to his lap. "Nope, that's our boy, Ronaldo Berringer. I caught a glimpse of his picture in the file I conveniently and clumsily knocked to the ground."

"All right. That's one of the three. I guess we're back to waiting."

He looked toward the vacant two-story building. "Yeah, it's back to waiting for us, but I wonder about our friend on the rooftop."

"Good point," I said. "I just assumed he was here for the same reason we are, but that may not be the case."

"You know what they say about assumptions. They're the mother of invention—or something like that."

"Have you been learning clichés from Clark?"

My phone chirped again. "Oh, crap. I forgot about Skipper."

I pulled the phone back to my ear. "I'm sorry."

"Don't be sorry. Be better," she said. "You laid down your phone and started playing word games with Hunter, so I hung up and called back."

"I'm sorry. It won't happen again. But we saw our first parolee show up."

She cleared her throat. "What do you want me to do about the call with Anya?"

I closed my eyes and let a million scenarios play through my mind. "Is she still there?"

"No, she and Mongo went back to Athens."

I sighed. "What do you think I should do?"

"I think you should call her and find out what that phone call was about. That's what I think you should do, and if you don't want to do it, I will."

"No, I don't want you to do it, but I don't need the distraction right now. When we're finished with this stakeout, I'll call her."

"Okay, but if you chicken out, I'll be glad to call her."

"Thanks, Skipper, but I don't think I'll be chickening out when it comes to finding out what's happened to my wife."

"Okay, well, that's all I have for you, but I need you to call me when Penny's mom shows up. Oh, and get a picture. I have to see how she looks 'cause that's how Penny's gonna look in twenty-five years."

I chuckled. "Something tells me in twenty-five years, Penny won't have the wear and tear of a dozen years in a federal prison."

"Maybe you're right about that, but get a picture anyway. See ya."

I laid the phone on the seat. "You're never going to believe who Penny called for six and a half minutes."

Hunter looked curious. "Who?"

"Anya."

He frowned. "Anya? Why would she call Anya?"

"I can think of a few possibilities. The first one starts with 'What the hell were you doing in bed with *my* husband?'"

He chuckled. "Yeah, that's a possibility, but I don't think a call like that would last six and a half minutes."

"You're probably right. Maybe she called Anya to tell her she was leaving me."

He took in a long slow breath and let it out. "She's not leaving you, man. This is something else. I've been left, and this ain't it."

"What do you think it is, then?"

He played with his beard. "I'm not willing to say, yet, because I don't want it floating around in your head if I'm wrong."

"Really? You think I'm going to let you get away with that?"

He shrugged. "You can't make me tell you . . . yet. You need me for now. I'll tell you when it's all over, but I'll confess—I hope I'm wrong."

I shook my head. "Me, too."

I pointed down the street. "There goes Ronaldo."

Hunter pulled his binoculars into place. "That didn't take long."

"I guess a drug test and checking in is pretty quick. I've never been on parole, so I wouldn't know."

"Who do you think will be next?" he asked.

"It's a fifty-fifty shot."

"Is that some of that fancy math they taught you in school, College Boy?"

I raised my eyebrows. "You have been spending too much time with Clark."

"Maybe so, but for now, I think I'll go see if Zacchaeus comes down out of that sycamore tree."

"Nicely done," I said. "Singer would be proud."

Hunter stepped from the car. "Yep, that's what I do . . . I live my life to make Singer proud."

Ronaldo drove away in the same direction he'd come, and I made a note of his license plate number just in case.

Hunter was back in less than five minutes. "The ladder and truck haven't moved."

"That must mean our Peeping Tom wasn't here for Ronaldo."

Several minutes passed without another car pulling into the municipal court building parking lot, so I declared it to be snack time. We had a bottle of water and split a candy bar. I was shoving the wrapper into the empty water bottle when a white Ford Focus pulled into the parking spot Ronaldo had vacated.

Hunter and I repositioned our binoculars simultaneously.

"It's definitely a woman," he said.

I stared intently, counting the seconds until the door opened. When it finally did, a tall brunette in a floral-print dress stepped from the car and scanned the street. When she turned toward the entrance to the court building, I felt my heart sink.

Hunter whispered, "What are you thinking, Cowboy?"

"I think it's her. She's the right age, height, and with a little imagination, she could've looked like Penny thirty years ago."

"I agree," he said. "Name the game. What are we doing?"

A thousand options ran through my head, but I quickly settled on one. "I'm going in. You get the tracker on the car."

"What about our spotter upstairs?" he asked.

"No matter who he is, it doesn't matter if he sees you. There's nothing he can do about it."

I didn't wait for an argument from him. I jumped from the car and headed across the street. As my boot hit the sidewalk on the opposite side of Broadway, I reflexively looked up toward the roof of the vacant building across the street. I didn't see the watcher, but the morning sun in the eastern sky glistened off the lens of his spotter's scope. It was definitely focused on the front of the municipal court building.

I'd forgotten I was still wearing my whisper-coms until Hunter's voice blasted in my ear. "Nice job, Captain Obvious. Did you get a good look at him?"

I couldn't suppress a grin. "Oh, yeah, we waved and exchanged pleasantries. He seems like a nice guy. No, I didn't get a good look at him, but I saw the lens of his scope."

"I'm sure he got a look at you," he said.

I ignored him. "I'm going in. Get that tracker in place."

I yanked the door open and stepped from the ninety-degree air of the sidewalk and into the coolness of the building. There was a double-door to the right that opened into a long corridor. The hallway was vacant except for a black sign on a metallic pole standing about twenty feet away. The door beyond the sign was propped open, but every other door in the hall appeared to be closed.

An island reception area stood straight ahead, but there was no one behind the counter. I could hear voices coming from beyond the island, but they were muffled and distant. At least one of the voices definitely belonged to a female, but I couldn't be sure about the other. I paused to let my heart rate diminish and then headed past the island. The foyer led to another corridor in the back of the building. As I made the turn, the corridor opened into a wide waiting area with at least a dozen chairs. Carla Thomas stood with her back to me as she conducted a transaction with someone behind a bank of glassed enclosures.

Instinctively, I patted my hip for reassurance I was still armed. My SIG Sauer P226 was exactly where it belonged beneath my shirttail, so I continued toward the woman. From behind, she could be my beautiful wife with thirty extra pounds. The gray in her brown hair shone as I approached. I could feel my heart thundering in my chest, and through my earpiece, I could hear Hunter crawling beneath the car.

The man behind the glass came into sight, and our eyes met. He offered a friendly smile and a brief nod. "I'll be with you in a minute, sir."

I ignored him and focused on the woman who'd shot a glance across her shoulder at me and then returned her attention to the man inside the window.

He slid something through a curved metal tray beneath the bottom of the thick glass screen. "Will there be anything else, Ms. Thomas?"

"No, Walter, that's it. And you know better than calling me Ms. Thomas. It makes me feel old."

My heart stopped, and my breath came in raspy jerks. The world moved in slow motion, and my mind whirred as I tried to decide what to do next.

They say, in the moments of highest stress, a well-trained operator reverts to the lessons he's had drilled into his head in his years of training and experience. That's precisely what happened once the instant of panic passed.

Eliminate the witness. Block avenues of escape. Assess the target's ability to resist. Determine an egress route. Remain in command of the scenario.

Carla Thomas turned toward me, and Penny's bright eyes shone in her face. Her thin nose mirrored my wife's, and her determined stride was unmistakable.

I offered a brief nod and stepped aside, allowing her to pass. "Good morning, ma'am," I said.

Her acknowledgment came in the form of a questioning look and a quick nod, and I turned my back to the man behind the glass as Carla passed me. In five strides, we'd be out of sight of the man, and I would've eliminated the witness.

Double-glass doors stood to the right, and the corridor narrowed as it led back to the entry foyer. I positioned myself between Carla and the doors behind me, effectively blocking the closest avenue of escape.

Her dress hung loosely on her hips, showing no sign of a concealed firearm, and her purse hung from a long strap across her right shoulder. She clutched the strap near the clip that held the bag. I studied the worn leather purse. It was certainly large enough to conceal a weapon, but there was no outline of a gun silhouetted against the leather, and it bounced in time with her strides as if it were light and unburdened by the weight of a loaded gun. I believed she was unarmed. Her fingernails were short and neat, so they weren't a considerable threat to my eyes or flesh. Her open-toed high heels were strapped tightly to her ankles, making them difficult to remove quickly. That meant she couldn't run or kick with any degree of force.

I had assessed her ability to resist.

The front doors of the building were thirty-five feet away, straight ahead, and the back doors were half that distance behind me. The long hall to the left of the front doors led to a single exit door at its end.

I'd determined my avenues of egress.

All that remained was for me to command the scenario.

I whispered into the coms. "I've got her. Block the front door."

Hunter's one-word reply reassured me we were definitely in command of the situation. "Roger."

My partner stepped in front of the doors and pressed his boot against the bottom, where both doors met at the threshold. That was my cue to move.

I increased my pace and stepped to Carla's right, placing my hand on top of her purse to prevent her from drawing a weapon in case I'd missed it. "Ms. Thomas!"

She stepped toward the wall and clutched her purse to her stomach. Her eyes widened in obvious fear. She wasn't reaching for a gun; she was protecting her cash. She took two trembling steps backward until her back was against the wall and the fear in her eyes doubled. "Who are you, and what do you want?"

"My name is Chase Fulton, Ms. Thomas, and we need to have a talk."

Chapter 25
Coconspirators

The woman clutched her purse ever more tightly, and her eyes darted about the space as if she were looking for a rescuer. I hadn't expected her to be timid. I'd pictured her to be more like her daughter . . . a fighter.

I stayed close enough to remain in control of the scenario, but I relaxed my posture, hoping to reduce her blood pressure. "I'm not going to hurt you. I mean you no harm at all. I simply want to find Penny. Where is she, Carla?"

The woman's brow furrowed, her eyes narrowed, and her shoulders visibly relaxed. "What did you say your name is?"

"I'm Chase Fulton. I'm Penny's husband. I suspect she's at least told you she's married by now."

The woman made a face as if I were speaking a language she'd never heard, and the sound of a door opening to my right caught her attention. Reflex sent my head turning toward the sound as a relatively fit man in his early forties came through the front door of the court building with a briefcase in one hand. I could still see Carla Thomas through my peripheral vision, and she wasn't moving. The man turned to his right and disappeared down the corridor by the front doors without giving us so much as a glance.

When I turned back to Carla, her look of confusion had become relief. She reached for my hand and smiled in the way only a mother can. "Mr. Fulton, I'm sorry, but I'm not who you think I am. I don't have a daughter named Penny. My only daughter is Jessica, and she's married to a Marine in Okinawa."

"But you're Carla Thomas, right?"

She leaned toward me. "No, sweetie. I'm Barbara Jean Thomas. The only Carla I know is Carla Jeffries, but she doesn't have a daughter at all. I'm afraid you've got the wrong Ms. Thomas. But shame on you for marrying a girl without her momma knowing."

"But if you're not Carla Thomas, what are you doing here?"

The woman looked back toward the glass cage. "I was paying a speeding ticket that my no-count son got so they wouldn't take his license. His daddy needs him on the ranch, and he needs him to drive."

I felt embarrassed for what I was about to do, but I had to be sure the woman was telling the truth. "I know this is going to sound strange, but would you mind if I saw your ID? Carla Thomas is an ex-convict, and she's probably crafty enough to come up with a story like yours on the spot. I'm sorry for asking, but I'm sure you understand."

She unzipped her purse and began to finger through the contents. "That is an odd request, but I'll show you my license because I know some Thomases from out east of here, and like you said, they're crafty."

Barbara Jean produced a driver's license with a picture and full name. She was clearly not Penny's mother, and I felt like a fool.

I handed the license back. "Ms. Thomas, I'm so very sorry. I can't tell you how embarrassed I am. I hope I didn't frighten you."

She took the license from my fingertips. "I hope you find this Penny of yours. It sure seems like you're going to a lot of trouble."

"You have no idea, ma'am. Again, I'm really sorry."

She pulled her hand from mine and headed for the exit. I trotted ahead of her and held the door open. Hunter's eyes darted between the woman and me. Instead of saying anything to make the situation more awkward, I simply shook my head.

Back in the car, Hunter said, "I bet that was awkward."

"You think?"

"Who was she?"

"This is the part you'll never believe. Her last name is Thomas, but she's Barbara Jean, not Carla. I checked her license."

"You checked her license? Are you serious?"

"I'm dead serious. That's *why* I checked her license."

He let out a single chuckle. "Amazing. Anyway, the guy who came in while you were checking the wrong Ms. Thomas's license was the other parolee, Jason McAllister."

I glanced up to see Barbara Jean driving north on Broadway. She didn't see me, but if she had, I believe she would've waved.

Hunter slapped his forehead.

"What is it?" I asked.

He pointed northward at the white sedan. "There goes our last GPS tracker."

I let my head fall back onto the headrest, and I let out a moan.

"We could always follow her and get it back," Hunter said.

"We can't follow her. We have to stay here for when the right Ms. Thomas shows up."

He clicked his teeth. "You said you saw her license. Do you remember her address?"

"I wasn't looking for an address. I was checking her name."

He motioned down the street. "There goes Jason McAllister. Two down. One to go."

I watched him drive away, and I glanced at the vacant building. "Do you think we should check on our rooftop friend?"

Hunter opened his door. "I'm on it."

He was back in less than five minutes. "Truck's still there, and the ladder hasn't moved."

My watch reported it to be ten minutes after eleven. "What are we going to do if she doesn't show?"

Hunter drummed his fingers on his thigh. "I've been thinking about that. Since our boy on the roof didn't leave, that means he's here for the same reason we are. If she doesn't show, we pin him down and make him tell us who he is and what he's doing. Somehow, he's wrapped up in this, and we need to know how."

The sun continued its climb into the North Texas sky, and the world seemed to wilt in the burgeoning heat. The Toyota's temperature needle rose with the sun. It never reached the red line, but I considered shutting it down and taking up a spot beneath a shade tree.

We checked our watches incessantly.

"It's eleven forty-five," Hunter said. "She's not coming. I say we pay Ms. Ramirez a little visit."

"What about our buddy on the roof?"

"He's not going anywhere fast. He still has a tire to change."

"Okay, let's do it," I said as I turned the key, giving the nearly overheated car the break it so badly wanted.

Inside the front doors of the court building, we turned right and headed down the corridor. The sign and open door I'd seen earlier turned out to be Tina Ramirez's Thursday morning office. Hunter led the way.

Ms. Ramirez looked up as we walked in. The look on her face and subtle smile said she remembered one of us. "Well, if it isn't the infamous sidewalk assailant."

Hunter put on the closest thing he had to an innocent face. "Yes, ma'am, it's me. Listen, I came in here to apologize again for bumping into you out there."

She lowered her chin. "Bullshit. Why are you really here?"

Hunter shot a look at me, then back to the parole officer. "I should've known I couldn't pull a fast one on you, Ms. Ramirez."

She continued her lowered chin stare. "Many have tried, and most have failed. I've been doing this a long time. What can I do for you Mr . . . ?"

"Hunter," he said.

"What can I do for you, Mr. Hunter?"

"No, not Mr. Hunter, ma'am. Just Hunter, and you're not old enough to have been doing this very long." Hunter glanced at me and then back at the woman. "It's not what you can do for us, ma'am. It's what we can do for you."

She blushed. "Oh, I'm older than you think, but what is it you *think* you can do for me? Let me guess. You two are bounty hunters, and you want to drum up a little business from the federal government."

My partner stifled a laugh and looked at me. "Is that what we are? Bounty hunters?"

I shook my head.

"My partner says we ain't bounty hunters, Ms. Ramirez, and the truth is we got all the work we need, but I still think we can help you."

She leaned back in her chair and checked her watch. "Okay, I'll play along, Mr. Hunter. Excuse me . . . just Hunter. What is it you think I need help with, and what makes you think you're the man, or men, for the job?"

"Well, I . . . I mean, we . . . just happened to notice you had three files in that box of yours, and only two visitors. It looks to us like one Carla Phillips Thomas stood you up."

She self-consciously straightened the files on her desk. "Yes, well, we have an entire U.S. Marshals Service Fugitive Task Force at our disposal to find our lost sheep, so I can't imagine what you think you can do that the Marshals can't."

Hunter pulled up a chair and sat down in front of the desk. He pressed his left thumb against Carla Thomas's file and slid it toward himself. Ramirez slammed her hand down on the file and Hunter's hand.

My partner didn't flinch. "Well, now, Ms. Ramirez. That's a little forward of you, trying to hold my hand already. I haven't even bought you dinner yet. But since you seem so intent on public displays of your affection for me already, I guess that's a yes."

She jerked her hand from Hunter's and reclaimed the file. "I can't let you see federal parolee files, Mr. Hunter, and I wasn't—"

He interrupted her. "Just Hunter, Tina. May I call you Tina since we're having dinner and drinks later? Ms. Ramirez feels a little formal."

She tried not to smile. "You can call me Tina if you want."

Clark Johnson would be proud, I thought as I watched Hunter play his game. If he could learn that crooked smile of Clark's, he'd be unstoppable.

"Well, you certainly haven't said no, so until you do, I'm going to assume it's a yes. What time shall I pick you up?"

She squared the files in her hands and bounced them on the desk before sliding them back into the box. "What is it you want, Mr., I mean . . . Hunter?"

"I thought we established that. I want to take you to dinner, and you want to hold my hand. I don't see any reason we can't make both of those things happen. Do you?"

"No, that's not what I meant," she said, a little flustered. "I meant, what did you want when you came in here?"

Hunter produced a credentials pack from his pocket and badged Ms. Ramirez. "Stone W. Hunter, Naval Criminal Investigative Service, and the gentleman behind me is Mr. Fulton, U.S. Secret Service."

I flashed my cred-pack.

We're interested in your client, Ms. Carla Thomas, and we have both the clearance and need to know to see what's in that skinny little file of yours."

She let out a breath, closed her eyes, and lowered her head.

"Don't worry, Ms. Ramirez . . . Tina. We're still on for dinner and hand-holding."

She opened her eyes, pulled Carla's file from the box, and tossed it on the desk. The look on her face was a cross between fear and "Oh, shit." I was sure Hunter noticed it, too.

It was my turn to play bad cop. "Is there anything you'd like to tell us about what we're going to see—or not see—in that file, Ms. Ramirez?"

She pressed her lips together and stared at the wall behind me as if she were deciding what and how much to say.

I made my hands into fists and propped them on the front edge of her desk. "Ms. Ramirez, what are we going to discover when we open that file? You're not doing yourself any favors by hiding things we already know. This would be a very good time to come clean."

She swallowed hard. "Listen, I thought I was doing the right thing, okay? I didn't do it on purpose."

Neither of us had any idea what she was talking about, but the psychologist in me had just climbed into the bouncy house with his shoes off. "Ms. Ramirez, are you saying what you did was an accident?"

A tiny tear formed in the corner of her left eye, and I made the decision to take full advantage of it.

I raised my voice. "It was either an accident, or you did it on purpose. Now, which was it?"

Her chin began to quiver. "I really wanted it to work, and I thought she was coming back. I wasn't going to do it again, I swear."

Clark had taught me to shut up and listen when someone started rambling under interrogation. Hunter had apparently been taught the same. We sat in silence, staring at Tina Ramirez as she crumbled under the weight of whatever she'd done . . . or not done. I just hoped she was going to spell it out for us soon.

She pulled two urine sample cups from her box. "Look! See, I didn't use them. I only did that once. I wasn't going to do it again. The Second Chance program is working, and I didn't want the only woman in the state of Texas to be released on the initiative to screw the whole thing up, so I peed in the cup for her one time." I tapped my finger on the edge of the desk, and she caved. "Okay, twice, but I wasn't going to do it again. Look. Here's the cups. They're still sealed. I was going to write her up this time. I really was. I can show you. I have the paperwork right here." She opened the file and clumsily fingered through the pages.

It was coming together for me. "How many?"

The tear escaped her eye, and it wasn't alone. "What's going to happen to me?"

Ah, the door was open, and I was happy to stroll right through. "That's up to you, Ms. Ramirez. How long has it been since Carla Thomas checked in?"

Her voice cracked, along with her will. "Today makes four weeks."

I pulled a pad from my pocket. "Four weeks. Hmm. And you only falsified drug tests twice in those four weeks. Something isn't adding up here, Ms. Ramirez."

She wiped at her eyes. "I only did it twice. Last week, I made my roommate do it, but I was done. I swear I was."

"Okay," I said. "So, you lied, you knowingly provided fraudulent drug tests, and you filed falsified federal documents. Spell your supervisor's name and verify her phone number for me."

I silently prayed her supervisor was a female, otherwise, I'd just blown the ruse.

She sniffled and caught her breath. "Angela Turner."

I pulled a second chair in front of the desk and softened my tone. "This doesn't have to result in jail time for you. In fact, it doesn't necessarily have to end your career, but that's up to you. Ms. Turner doesn't suspect you of anything . . . yet."

The tears were still coming, but a tiny glimmer of hope shined in her eyes.

I continued. "It's not our job to report your actions to your superiors or the U.S. Attorney, even though what you've done is, well, I'm sure I don't have to quote the U.S. Code for you, do I?"

She shook her head and wiped at her nose with the back of her hand. "No, you don't have to cite the Code."

Hunter came in right on cue. "Our interest is not in you, Tina. We understand how it is. You're fighting the good fight and clawing your way through a man's world. And until Carla Thomas messed it all up for you, you were winning that fight. We know, and we agree with you. The world needs strong women like you in positions of power. We don't want this to tarnish the work you've done and the strides you've made. And it doesn't have to. Do you understand?"

The tears had left long stains down her cheeks. She studied Hunter's words, but she seemed lost. "No, I don't understand."

Hunter took her hand in his. "It's okay. Really, it is. We're not interested in what you've done wrong. That's not our world. We're not here to trap the good guys, like you, in minuscule federal technicalities. That's not what we do. We want Carla Thomas, and when you help us find her, no one ever needs to know about the drug tests or the falsified reports you filed. We get what we want. You get what you want. A fugitive is brought back into the system, and all is right with the world. Right, Tina? You will help us find her, won't you?"

"Yes, I'll help you, but I have to file a report for today, and I'm not going to—"

Hunter squeezed her hand and tossed a urine cup over his shoulder toward me.

I returned two minutes later with an adequate, clean sample. If they checked the DNA, they'd find both an X and Y chromosome, but I doubted they'd do more than stick a test strip into the cup and wait for it to change colors.

I placed the cup on the desk. "See, Ms. Ramirez? We're on the same team now. Coconspirators in the business of bringing fugitives back to justice."

Chapter 26
Car Trouble

"So, about that dinner date. . . ." Hunter said.

Tina Ramirez looked up in disbelief. "You can't be serious."

"Oh, I'm quite serious, but it's probably not going to be as romantic as either of us would like. We've got a lot to talk about, and everybody's got to eat." He glanced at his watch. "What time are you expected back in Lubbock?"

Her expression softened, but only slightly. "I'm . . . I mean, I don't have to be back in Lubbock. I work a compressed schedule, but you already know that, I'm sure."

"Of course we do," Hunter said, "and we appreciate you not insulting our intelligence by trying to mislead us again. We know far more than you'd think."

Hunter's pretty good at improvisation. I don't think I'd want him conspiring against me.

Tina nodded. "Okay. What do you want me to do?"

My partner glanced over his shoulder, yielding the floor to me.

"Ms. Ramirez, we want you to go about your afternoon just as you would have if you'd never met us. File your reports. Seal the urine sample from your parolees"—I pointed toward my sample—"including Ms. Thomas's, and meet us back here at six o'clock tonight." My fists landed on her desk again. "You will be here at six. Your name on my report on the desk of the U.S. Attorney is not a good way for this to end. I'm sure you agree."

She swallowed hard and nodded her agreement.

Hunter reached for her hand again, and she placed her trembling fingers in his palm. "It's going to be over soon, and you'll be able to forget any of this ever happened. We're late for another appointment, but we'll see you at six. Oh, and dinner's on us."

"What about my roommate?" she asked timidly.

"What about her?" Hunter said.

"She knows."

Hunter once again surrendered the stage to me.

"Obviously, you trust her, otherwise, you wouldn't have involved her. I recommend you continue trusting her to keep her mouth shut. I'm sure she doesn't want to be covering the rent all by herself."

She nodded again but said nothing.

Hunter and I pushed through the front doors of the building like the feds we were pretending to be.

"Could that have gone any better?" I said, nudging my partner with my elbow.

He let out a nervous laugh. "I can't believe it worked."

"Neither can I, but I'm thankful it did," I said. "I'm even more thankful you held on to your NCIS creds when you resigned."

He looked at me from the corner of his eye. "I've been meaning to talk with you about that. Until very recently, I wasn't completely sure I'd be able to make my bills on what you paid, so I agreed to stay on with NCIS as a consultant until I knew for sure this was going to work out."

"What makes you think this is going to work out now, Mr. Millionaire?"

"Let's just say a little birdie told me everything was going to be okay."

"Was that little birdie bearing a little black plastic card from a bank in the Caymans?"

"Maybe," he admitted, and pointed toward the roof of the vacant building. "Look. The scope's gone."

We broke into a sprint, Hunter going left and me going right around the vacant building. I beat him to the backside by little more than a stride, and we both shot looks toward the top of the portico. The ladder was gone. We turned south and headed for the truck, and when we rounded the corner of the dilapidated building, my heart sank. The ladder wasn't the only thing missing. The white truck was nowhere in sight.

It was ten after twelve. If the man had abandoned his post the instant Hunter and I went into the court building, that would've given him only twenty-five minutes to come down, stow the ladder, replace the flat tire, and disappear.

I yanked my phone from my pocket and hit redial. Skipper answered almost immediately. "Yeah?"

"Skipper, I need to know where the truck is, and I need to know now."

"Hello to you, too," she said. "Patience, Double-Oh-Seven. I'm on it. I have two active trackers. One started moving almost an hour ago, and the other left exactly three minutes ago. Which one do you need?"

"The three-minutes-ago is our man. Where is he?"

"He moved about five hundred feet, stopped for six minutes, and started moving again. He's pulling onto the interstate now, northbound."

"That makes sense. We made sure he had a little car trouble. Don't lose him! Nothing is more important than tracking him. Got it?"

She huffed. "Yeah, yeah, I got it. Don't lose the white Ford truck that doesn't exist."

"Call me back if he stops."

"Okay, I will. But what about Penny's mom? Did she show up? How does she look? Did you talk to her? Is she the other tracker?"

"No," I said.

"No to which question?" Skipper asked.

"All of the questions. I'll tell you about it later. Forget about the other tracker, and keep your eye on that truck. Can you track my phone?"

She said, "Duh. Of course I can track your phone."

"Good. Keep an eye on me, as well. We're going after the truck. Let me know if it looks like we're losing him. I gotta go. I'll check in again soon." I hung up before she could ask any more questions.

Hunter stood with eyes wide, awaiting an update. "Let's hear it. What did *our* secretary have to say?"

"Oh, so now she's *our* secretary. I'll be sure to let her know she now takes dictation from you, as well."

He shook his head violently. "No, you won't either. If you do, I'll tell Penny I saw Anya leaving your room breathless and barely able to walk."

I glared at him.

"Too soon?" he said.

"Definitely too soon."

"Okay, I'd like to apologize for that. I'm not going to, but I'd like to. So, what did Skipper say?"

"I'll tell you in the car, smart ass. Let's go."

We raced west on Highway 70 toward the interstate. I hoped our credentials would work as well on a Texas State Trooper as they had on a frightened federal parole officer, otherwise, I was likely to learn how much speeding tickets cost in Northwest Texas.

I pushed the Camry as hard as it would go as I accelerated up the northbound ramp onto the interstate. I was pleased and surprised to discover we weren't the only speed demons on Interstate

27. Ninety miles per hour seemed to be the standard cruise-control setting for Texans.

"Where does this road go?" I asked as the needle stopped on one hundred ten miles per hour.

"I don't know. The closest I've ever been to here is Lackland Air Force Base in San Antonio for boot camp."

"Well, figure it out," I demanded. "We need to put together some ideas on where this guy could be headed."

He opened the glove compartment, apparently searching for an atlas, but came up empty-handed. He wasted no time continuing the search, and pressed the speed dial button for Skipper.

She answered at the same moment he turned on the speaker. "You're catching him, but not very quickly. How fast are you going?"

"One ten," I said over the road noise produced by pushing the car faster than it was ever designed to go.

She said, "In that case, he must be doing close to ninety."

"That's good news, but we don't have a map. Can you give us a little local-area orientation?"

"Sure," she said. "From where you are now, it's fifty-eight miles to Amarillo. The interstate ends at the I-Forty intersection, which runs east to Oklahoma City, which is about two-hundred-fifty miles east. Albuquerque is about the same distance to the west of Amarillo, maybe a little further."

"How about north of Amarillo? Are there any good roads continuing north?" I asked. "I think this guy may be heading for the mountains."

"I'm looking," she said. "Highway Eighty-Seven runs north out of Amarillo and then northwest. It's a pretty good four-lane highway most of the way. It meets Interstate Twenty-Five, and that runs north through Colorado Springs and on to Denver, but that's close to five hundred miles."

"Denver," I said. "It snows in Denver, doesn't it?"

Skipper laughed. "Yeah, a little."

"That's where he's headed. Keep on him, and call us if he makes a stop. He'll need gas sooner or later. Hopefully, we can outlast him."

"You got it," she said. "I'll call as soon as I see him take an exit."

Hunter hung up. "Have you thought about calling the police and reporting the truck for no tags? They'd pull him over, and that'd buy us some time to catch up."

I considered his suggestion. "I don't think I want the cops involved in this. If there's something wonky with his registration or if he's got a warrant, I don't want him getting hooked up and stuffed in some Amarillo jail. There's no way we could get to him in there."

"Yeah, you're probably right, but we need something to happen quickly. We can't chase this guy all the way to Denver tonight. I've got a dinner date back in Plainview."

It was time to make a decision. We definitely needed Tina Ramirez, and we probably needed the guy in the white truck. If I had to choose only one, it would have to be the parole officer."

"We'll chase him to Amarillo. If we don't catch him by then, we'll break off and focus on Ramirez back in Plainview, but I really want this guy."

"Me, too," Hunter said, "but Skipper can track him. We're relying on the lovely little parole officer to lead us to Carla Thomas."

Twenty minutes later, Hunter's phone chirped. He pressed the speaker button. "Yeah."

"He just pulled off the interstate south of Amarillo. It looks like the fuel stop you were hoping for. He's moving slowly to the west. Hang on. I'll have something more precise for you when he stops."

We leaned toward the phone, counting the seconds for her to come back on the line.

"Got him! He's at the Rocky View truck stop in Canyon."

"Great work, Skipper. Don't let me miss the exit."

She gave us turn-by-turn, high-speed instructions, and we slid into the gravel lot of the Rocky View truck stop. The lot was full of tractor trailers of every variety. There had to be two hundred trucks or more.

Hunter peered out the window, scanning furiously. "We may never find our needle in this haystack."

"We'll find him," I said. "His truck wasn't a diesel, so he has to be on the gasoline side."

We prowled through the lot and surveyed the seemingly endless rows of gas pumps.

"Well, looky there. That looks a lot like the needle we've been chasing."

I turned and followed Hunter's outstretched finger. "Well, aren't you quite the needle finder?"

The white truck with one mismatched right-front tire and an aluminum extension ladder strapped to the rack was sitting at a pump with the nozzle hanging from the fill hole. The man was nowhere in sight.

"He must be inside," I said. "You stay here and watch the truck. I'll check in the store."

He agreed, and we pulled our whisper-coms back into place.

I parked close enough to the door to make a quick exit, but also where Hunter could keep the truck in sight. Despite the number of cars and trucks in the parking lot, the interior was practically vacant except for the restaurant in the back of the store. Our guy wouldn't be having dinner with the nozzle hanging in his truck, so I kept scanning.

"I got him! He's heading into the men's room on the left side of the store. Get in here and cover the door. I'm going in."

Chapter 27
You Have the Right

The technique to subdue a subject in an enclosed space is done under countless conditions. I trained at The Ranch for this exact scenario more times than I could count, but that wasn't the end of my preparation for real life. Clark had put me through the paces of this exercise hundreds of times. I was well-trained, confident, and comfortable with what I was about to do. Done correctly, subduing an untrained subject in a confined space was relatively without risk for serious injury.

The protocol is simple.

Identify subject. There was no question the man who'd just walked through the door was my subject.

Post coverage at all ingress and egress points. The men's room had only one door, and I had only one partner, so the numbers worked perfectly.

Make either covert or overt entry depending on the situation. I would make my entry as covertly as possible to avoid spooking anyone else who might be inside the men's room or bystanders in the store.

Clear the confined space, if possible. I hoped my man was the only occupant of the restroom, but if he wasn't, I'd aggressively encourage anyone else to vacate the room without worrying about washing their hands . . . or even zipping their trousers.

Subdue the subject peacefully, if possible, and by force, if necessary. I fully expected the man to surrender without a fight, but if he wanted to press the issue, I was well trained to suppress his resistance.

Evacuate the area as quickly as possible. I would walk the man right out of the store as if we were old friends, unless, of course, he wanted to protest. In which case, I'd frog-march him or carry him out with my secret service credentials proudly displayed.

My theory about no battle plan surviving first contact with the enemy certainly wouldn't apply to this operation. This one would be a walk in the park, and I'd be one step closer to finding Penny and getting to the bottom of whatever I'd stumbled into.

Hunter came through the door, hustling toward me while scanning the interior of the store. "I've got the door," he said. "Remember to keep him alive and conscious, if possible. We need this guy to talk."

"Piece of cake," I said as I stepped through the men's room door.

What I saw inside served to only embolden my confidence. There were five urinals on the wall to my left, with three stalls beyond. All of the stall doors were ajar, and no feet were visible beneath the dividers. My target was standing in front of the second urinal and never made a move to check over his shoulder when I walked in.

I whispered, "Secure the door."

Hunter's one-word reply, "Roger," told me he understood I was one-on-one with no innocent bystanders to get hurt or get in the way. It also told me he wouldn't allow anyone else inside for the next few seconds.

Courtesy dictated that I announce myself and give the guy a chance to surrender, but my bank of courteous notions was overdrawn. I stuck a boot between the man's feet and a kneecap in the small of his back. The force of my two hundred ten pounds pinned his left hand between his hips and the cold, wet ceramic surface of the urinal. He was going to need a clean, dry pair of pants when this was over. I drove my left forearm between his shoulder blades and introduced his face to the painted concrete block wall above the polished silver plumbing of the urinal.

He tensed and groaned as the air left his lungs, but he made no effort to resist. He simply grunted, "I don't have any money."

"I don't want your money. I want to know what you were doing on top of that building in Plainview."

He relaxed his shoulders as if he were relieved to hear I wasn't there to rob him. Due to his face being pressed against the wall, his words were labored. "I'm a fugitive recovery agent. I was looking for a federal parolee who hasn't made it to a check-in in three weeks."

I'd just pinned a U.S. Marshal to a truck stop urinal, but unless it was on his ankle, he was sans-pistol.

I released the pressure I'd been applying and took a couple of steps back. "I'm sorry about your pants and about pinning you to the wall, but I think we're looking for the same woman."

He rotated his chin from side to side as if releasing tension in his neck, zipped his pants, and turned to face me. Before he'd planted his left foot back on the floor, I heard one of the most terrifying sounds one can experience in a close-quarters-battle: the telltale swoosh and click of a switchblade. My eyes instinctually darted to his left hand, where he held the menacing six-inch blade. His grip was relaxed and loose, and his right foot was eighteen inches in front of his left in a perfect fighting stance.

There's nothing I hate worse than a knife fight. Regardless of how well trained I was, there would be blood, and most of it would be mine if I didn't up the ante. I took two quick sliding strides backward and drew my pistol.

He hissed, "You're not going to shoot me in a public bathroom without a suppressor."

He had an excellent point. An unsuppressed nine-millimeter shot would sound like a cannon going off in the tiled surrounding of the bathroom. I didn't want or need that kind of attention, but I also didn't want my guts sprawling out on the floor from his blade.

I said, mostly for Hunter's benefit, "Put the knife away, and get on your knees. I don't want to shoot you, but I will."

Hunter burst through the door with his pistol leading the way, and the man's eyes darted between the two of us. Apparently believing Hunter was the more dangerous, the man shifted his stance to defend himself against my partner's charge, and then thrust his knife forward in a stabbing motion. Rotating my body ninety degrees to the left, I sent a bone-shattering right-side kick to the man's left knee, and he collapsed to the floor like a felled tree. Wounded, but not surrendering, he lashed out with his blade, aiming for our ankles and feet. There was no quit in the man, but he was facing two exceptionally well-trained, armed combatants. He might draw blood, but his chances of winning the encounter had vanished.

An electric hand dryer hung from the wall, and Hunter yanked it from its mounts, sending wiring and concrete dust flying through the air. He plunged his right hand into the metallic air duct protruding from the front of the dryer and advanced on the wounded animal scampering about on the filthy floor. The man tried to climb back to his feet, but his nearly demolished left knee wouldn't support his weight. That left him scurrying around with his back to the stall divider at the end of the row of urinals.

Hunter swung the heavy dryer through the air like an enormous, metal boxing glove, but missed the man's head by an inch.

He reacted like a striking scorpion, thrusting the point of the switchblade toward my partner's gut.

Shooting him would end the fight, but it would set in motion a long string of events that would result in Hunter and me being asked a lot of questions by a lot of cops we weren't prepared to answer. Hunter dodged the thrust with a juke of his hips that would've made Elvis proud. I took the opportunity to throw a kick to the man's knife hand. The blow sounded as if it broke several bones, and the knife skidded harmlessly across the tile floor.

Seemingly unfazed, the man lowered his head and shoved himself backward beneath the stall divider, temporarily separating us from him. Once inside the stall, he shoved the door closed and slid the latch into place. The next sound from inside the stall sounded as if he were tearing the toilet from the wall.

Hunter recovered from his missed attempt, tossed the hand dryer into the air above my head, and yelled, "Over the top!"

My height allowed me the perfect advantage. I snagged the dryer from midair with one hand, thrust it over the top of the divider, and downward into the stall like Michael Jordan on a slam dunk.

The man let out a wounded cry as the huge chunk of metal found its mark. In the time it had taken me to complete the alley-oop with the dryer, Hunter had moved behind me and aligned himself with the stall door. A mighty front kick sent the flimsy door crashing and off its hinges. He followed the door inward as the fight continued, and I stepped around the stall just in time to see the man crush the toilet seat over my partner's head as if he were wielding an axe. Hunter collapsed to one knee with stars circling his head, but he didn't go out.

I'd had enough. It was time to end the ridiculous battle.

With Hunter on one knee between the man and me, I reached across him, grabbed the man's collar, and jerked him forward with all my strength. His disabled knee left him with little balance, and Hunter's bulk made the perfect stumbling block. The man tumbled forward, assisted by my pull and gravity, until his chin met the cold ceramic floor. My partner may not have been unconscious, but our new friend certainly was.

Blood trickled from the man's nose and mouth as Hunter produced a pair of stainless-steel handcuffs and hooked up the knife-wielding fighter.

Hunter looked up at me. "You okay?"

I let out an exasperated breath. "Yeah, I'm okay, but I sure didn't expect that much piss and vinegar out of him."

My partner rolled the man over and pointed toward his soaking wet pants. "I don't know about the vinegar part, but I'd say you're at least half right."

I splashed some cold water on the man's face, and Hunter issued a few slaps to lure him out of the spirit world. He slowly regained consciousness, and we propped him against the wall. His eyelids fluttered as he appeared to come to the realization the fight was over—and he'd lost.

Hunter shoved his credentials inches away from the man's face. "You're under arrest. You have the right to remain silent, but if you do, I have the right to keep kicking your ass. I've got a date tonight with a beautiful girl, and you tried to mess up my pretty face with a toilet seat. Now, get on your feet."

We not-so-gently helped him to his feet . . . or rather, his foot. I'd done some serious damage to his left knee, so he wouldn't be walking anytime soon.

I bent over, stuck my shoulder in his gut, then hoisted the hand-cuffed man into the air like a sack of potatoes. "Lead the way, partner, but I recommend keeping that badge handy. We're going to attract a little attention on our way out of here."

Hunter yanked open the door and walked point while I carried the wounded man through the store. A few onlookers gasped and mumbled, but my partner set their minds at ease. "Federal agents. Step aside."

Judging by their Wranglers and filthy boots, what I assumed was a pair of rodeo cowboys met us at the door.

"Whoa. What'd he do?" one of them asked.

Hunter didn't hesitate. "Horse thieving. Reckon we're gonna hang 'im."

The cowboys stepped aside and held the doors for us. I deposited the man into the back seat of our rented Toyota and strapped him down with the seatbelts.

Hunter slammed the door, driving the armrest into the top of the man's head, and sending him back to the Land of Fairies and Unicorns. "I'll follow you back to the luxury hotel in his truck. He was nice enough to fill it up for us."

The man regained consciousness twice on the ride back to the Prairie View Inn. The first time he became belligerent and downright disrespectful, so the butt of my pistol to his temple sent his eyes rolling back in his head. The second time he woke up, he had learned some manners and exercised his right to remain silent.

Back at the motel, we progressed from carrying our new friend to helping him hop on one foot. We were both uncertain if he'd surrendered or if he was just biding his time and waiting for another opening to lash out. The optimist in me hoped he was willing to play nice, but the operator in me wanted one more shot at the guy for trying to stick a knife in my gut.

"Let's switch to nine-millimeter whisper mode," Hunter said as we shoved the man onto my bed.

I pulled a suppressor from my backpack and screwed it onto the muzzle of my Sig—a foot in front of the man's face.

My partner said, "Now, no one will hear the shot that creates a finger-sized hole in your forehead and an exit wound the size of Montana." He pulled the blanket and sheet from the corner of the bed, exposing the plastic cover on the mattress. "And would you look at that? The nice folks here at the Dew Drop Inn provided a plastic bag so we wouldn't get blood on their mattress. Wasn't that nice of them?"

The man's Adam's apple rose and fell as he gulped down what was left of his defiance. In a trembling voice, he said, "Who are you guys, and what do you want?"

I cocked the hammer of my pistol for dramatic effect. "We ask the questions. You give us answers. If you do that, and if we believe you, you get to live, and that broken knee will be the worst thing that happens to you today."

He blinked rapidly. "But you said you were cops."

Hunter gave him a slap. "No, we didn't. I shoved my wallet in your face and said you're under arrest. I never said we were cops."

He cringed. "Why are you doing this? Do you work for the cartel?"

Hunter jerked his head toward me, and I suddenly had a sliver of insight into what was going on.

I said, "We ask the questions, and you give the answers. Raul made it very clear what we are to do with you if you refuse."

His eyes narrowed. "Raul Jimenez?"

I pressed the muzzle of my suppressor to his forehead and forced him backward onto the bed. "There's only one Raul, and it only takes one bullet to stop you from asking questions. Is that clear enough for you?"

He arched his back as the cuffs and his fists dug into his spine and my muzzle pressed into the flesh above his eyes.

I glared into his face, leaving no room for doubt that I was willing to pull the trigger. "Get him on his feet."

Hunter yanked the man from the bed and stood him up. Unable to put any weight on his left foot, he balanced precariously on his right.

I took a seat on the edge of the bed in front of him and pressed my pistol into his remaining good kneecap. "We're going to start with something simple. Tell me your name."

He let out a jerky breath. "Anthony Davis."

"Where do you live, Anthony Davis?"

"Red Feather Lakes, about two hours northwest of Denver."

"And what do you do in Red Feather Lakes, Anthony Davis?"

He hesitated, and I added enough pressure to the kneecap to remind him I was running out of patience.

He stammered, "I, um . . . I don't do anything. I'm retired. I just fish."

I eased the pressure off the knee. "Why doesn't the VIN number on your truck match any vehicle registered in the States, Anthony Davis of Red Feather Lakes, Colorado?"

The stammering continued. "Uh . . . I . . . It's not my truck."

"Whose truck is it?"

"It's . . . uh . . . oh, God. I don't know whose truck it is."

"So, Anthony Davis of Red Feather Lakes, driving a stolen truck. . . . Retired from what?" I reapplied the pressure with enough force to start the knee bending the wrong way.

The pain, coupled with the fear, brought out the unconscious truth. "I'm a retired liquor distributor."

I un-cocked my Sig and stared up at the man. "Unhook him, Hunter. He's my father-in-law."

Chapter 28
A Little Privacy

Hunter removed the handcuffs and helped the man who'd called himself Anthony Davis sit on the bed.

I laid my pistol on the dresser by the television and turned back to him. "You're Mitch Thomas, Penny's father."

He looked up at me in terrified disbelief. "Did you say I'm your father-in-law?"

I sat on the edge of the bed, embarrassed and ashamed for what I'd put him through. "Mitch, my name is Chase Fulton. Your daughter, Penny, is my wife."

He shook his head as confusion overtook the sensation that had been fear. "Penny is married to a cartel hit man?"

I suddenly understood his confusion. "No, we have nothing to do with the cartel. I let you believe that during the interrogation. I'm sorry about that, by the way. I really am, but I'm determined to find Penny."

He interrupted. "What? I thought you said you were her husband. What's happened to her?"

"It's a long story," I said, "but I don't think she's in any danger. I believe she's somewhere here in Plainview, trying to do the same thing you're doing—finding her mother."

"And you're her husband?"

"Yes, I'm her husband, and we live on the east coast of Georgia."

He continued shaking his head. "Georgia? How did she end up . . ." His words trailed off as he obviously tried to rationalize everything he was learning.

"That's also a long story, but I'll fill in the blanks for you later. Right now, we have to get you to a doctor. After what I did to your knee, it's not going to fix itself."

"No!" he almost yelled.

I looked down at his knee that had already doubled in size. "You have to see a doctor."

"Yeah, okay, I get that, but I can't go to a doctor here in Plainview. I'm not supposed to be within a hundred miles of this place."

"You're in WITSEC, aren't you?"

He nodded. "Yeah, but that's a long story, too."

"I'm sure it is, but I understand. I guess that explains why your truck doesn't exist."

For the first time, he laughed. "I wasn't expecting you to ask me about the truck. I guess it belongs to the government. They gave it to me, and they bring me a tag every year. I've never even looked at the VIN number."

A look came over him as if a light had just come on in his head. "So, you guys are some kind of cops, then. You ran the VIN number of my truck. You knew I was in witness protection. You obviously know how to fight."

It was my turn to chuckle. "You're not bad in the boxing ring, yourself. It took both of us to take you down, and you're twice our age."

He smiled. "That's what fear will do for you. I was scared you guys were cartel, and I was fighting for my life."

I looked up at Hunter. "We've been there. We know exactly what you mean. By the way, this is my partner, Stone Hunter."

Hunter offered his hand. "I'm really sorry about all this."

Mitch grinned. "I can't really say it's nice to meet you, Hunter, but I am sorry about trying to mess up your pretty face with a toilet seat . . . especially since you've got a date."

I checked my watch. "I'm going to take Mitch back up to Amarillo to get somebody to look at his knee and maybe put a stitch in that chin. You're going to have to deal with Ramirez without me. Are you okay with that?"

Hunter put on a sinister smile. "I think I'll get by without you. Besides, three's a crowd."

I helped Mitch up and started for the door.

He said, "I don't know if Amarillo is far enough away. If the Marshals get wind of me being down here, I have no idea what they'll do."

"I'm the visiting team," I said. "I don't know anything about this part of the world, but I'll take you anywhere you want to go. We'll go all the way to Denver if that's what you want."

"Hey, wait a minute," Hunter said. "How far is it to Clovis, New Mexico?"

Mitch said, "Maybe an hour and a half or so. Why?"

Hunter pulled out his phone. "I've got an idea. Don't go anywhere just yet."

Mitch sat back down on the bed.

"I've got some morphine if you want it," I said. "It won't do anything to help the knee, but it'll ease the pain for a while."

He looked down at the badly swollen joint. "That's probably a good idea as long as you promise not to kill me if I fall asleep."

"I promise." I pulled a syringe from my bag, and two minutes later, Mitch was feeling the effects of the narcotic.

Hunter hung up the phone. "That was a buddy of mine. We went to Pararescue Indoctrination training together in the Air Force—"

I cut in. "I thought you were a combat controller, not pararescue."

"I was, but I started out to be a PJ. I switched to combat control when I figured out I couldn't stand the sight of blood."

"They let you do that?" I asked.

"Not usually," he said, "but I was doing really good in training, and they don't want to lose somebody who can survive that indoctrination phase. About eighty percent or more never make it through that first phase. Me and Doc were two-thirds of the graduating class. We started out with twenty-six and finished with just the three of us. Anyway, unlike me, he was really smart, and the Air Force ended up sending him to medical school. He's a doctor now out at Cannon Air Force Base with the Twenty-Seventh Special Operations Med Group. That was him on the phone. He says if you can get Mitch out there before midnight, he'll put him back together, and nobody will ever know."

"It's good to have friends," Mitch mumbled.

"Indeed, it is," I said.

It took almost two hours to get to Cannon Air Force Base, but Hunter's buddy kept his word and had my father-in-law stitched up and braced in no time.

Doc said, "It may be a torn ligament, but I don't think so. We'll have to take another look once the swelling subsides, but it's definitely not broken. Whatever happened to you—and I don't want to know—but whatever it was, I'm sure you don't want to go through it again."

Mitch looked at me. "No, I never want to do that again."

Doc tossed a bottle of pills to Mitch. "Take these every four to six hours before the pain starts kicking your ass. They'll make you sleepy, so no driving. Got it?"

"Got it. Thanks, Doc. I really appreciate this."

He shook Mitch's hand. "Don't mention it. And I *really* mean, don't mention it to anyone. And tell Hunter he owes me *another* one."

I shook his hand. "Will do, Doc. It was nice to meet you. Hunter wasn't wrong. You're all right."

Back in the truck, it was time for confession. I told Mitch everything I could about who and what I really am and how I met and fell in love with his daughter. In return, he told me all about Carla's involvement with the Jimenez Cartel.

When it came time to explain why he testified against his own wife, he couldn't hold back the tears. "They had Penny, and they were going to do things worse than killing her. I had to make the worst decision any man could ever face. I had to choose between saving my daughter's life and protecting my wife from prison. If I hadn't told the feds what was going on, God only knows what those animals would've done to my daughter. There was only one choice for me, Chase. I told 'em everything I knew and everything I believed. The FBI Hostage Rescue Team yanked Penny out of there, and the DEA arrested everybody in sight. I didn't have any choice. I had to save my little girl."

I tried to imagine the hell he'd been through, but I wasn't capable of putting it together in my mind. "I don't know what to say, Mitch. Your daughter grew up to be a fine woman. She's a writer now. She's got a screenplay that's under contract to make a Hollywood movie. You'd be proud of the woman she's become."

His tears continued. "What did she tell you about me and her mother?"

I could see the painkillers taking him. "She said she worshipped you, and that you two learned to fly together. We've got an airplane—a One-Eighty-Two-R-G—and Penny's a fine pilot. And a good wife."

"A One-Eighty-Two, huh? How about that? I had a Mooney, but I don't know what happened to it, and I haven't been in the front seat of an airplane for over ten years, I guess . . . No, longer than . . ."

He drifted off to sleep as I drove east, back toward Plainview, Texas, where his daughter, my wife, was trying to find the woman who'd destroyed their family.

* * *

I shook Mitch awake as we pulled into the Prairie View Inn. He yawned and stretched himself mostly awake before looking in every direction, trying to figure out where we were. "Oh, I guess this is home for now, huh?"

"For now," I said. "Do you need some help getting out?"

He pulled his crutches from beside him. "No, I can do it. Just drag me inside if I fall down."

He didn't fall down until we made it inside. Fortunately, the fall was onto one of the two beds in my room. He was back asleep before his head hit the pillow.

Hunter came in just before ten thirty with Tina Ramirez in tow.

I knocked on what remained of the wall between our rooms. "Mind if I come over?"

He flipped on a lamp. "Sure, come on in. The door's open."

I squeezed between the wall studs and took a seat in the fifty-year-old chair by the television. "Hello again, Ms. Ramirez. It's nice to see you."

She ducked her head, apparently embarrassed. "Hello, Special Agent Fulton."

"Yeah, why don't you have a seat? We need to talk about that."

Hunter chuckled. "We already had that talk, Chase. She knows the truth about us, and she's pretty pissed about it. Or, at least she was."

"Stone can be quite charming when he's not lying about sending me to jail and ending my career," she said.

"Yes, indeed, he can be," I said. "I'm sorry we had to resort to those lengths, but we have a mission, and you, technically, are in a lot of trouble if anybody finds out what you've been doing."

"Yeah, I know, but you two scared the hell out of me today. If you'd just told me the truth, I would've helped you. The truth, in this case, is a lot more compelling than the lie you told."

"We didn't plan it," I said. "It just sort of fell into place after we were in your office. You're terrible under interrogation, by the way."

"Don't I know it?" she said. "That's why I never joined the military. I would've caved the first day I got captured."

I smiled. "You never know what you're capable of doing when you're devoted to your cause."

"Like flying two-thirds of the way across the country to find your missing wife?"

"Yes, like that," I said.

She pointed through the custom doorway to my adjoining room. "Who's that in there?"

I turned to Hunter, and he shrugged.

I said, "He's a long story, but for now, let's just say he's on the same mission we are."

"That's Mitchell Thomas, isn't it?" she said.

"I can neither confirm nor deny that, Ms. Ramirez."

She rolled her eyes. "How did you find him?"

"He sort of fell into our laps."

"I see," she said. "That seems to happen a lot with you guys. Did you threaten to have him arrested, too?"

Hunter said, "No, we didn't threaten him. We actually put the cuffs on him, and Chase broke his leg."

"It's not broken," I protested. "It's just a strained ligament. Maybe torn."

Hunter checked his watch and then checked me.

I feigned a yawn. "Well, it's been a long day. I'm going to hit the sack. I'll hang the blanket back up over the hole in the wall, so you won't have to listen to me snore tonight."

He smiled. "Thanks. I appreciate that. A little privacy can change everything."

Chapter 29
Trading Up

Friday morning dawned over the flat, endless eastern landscape of Northwest Texas, and like most sunrises of my life, I watched it happen. A Styrofoam cup full of lukewarm black water masquerading as coffee rested beside me on the lowered tailgate of the pickup truck that didn't exist, and I reflected on the life that had brought me to this foreign landscape so far from the ocean, and, in every way, distant from a world I could recognize.

My wife—a woman I loved more than anyone in the world, and a woman I barely knew—was somewhere in this blistered, dusty corner of the Earth, and she was, most likely, scared and alone, running from something she had no reason to fear.

I pored over the possibilities in my tortured mind, and I couldn't create a scenario that would turn me against the woman I adored. No matter what she was doing, I had the financial resources and physical wherewithal to either help her accomplish her goals or to extract her from any situation she'd gotten herself into. Running from me didn't make any sense, but trying to apply logic to an emotional decision is like teaching calculus to a squirrel. He might pretend to listen in hopes of getting an acorn, but ultimately, he's still going to run in front of a car.

As I ran through the details of the previous days, I remembered the call log from Penny's phone and the call to Anya. Emotion screamed for me to call the Russian immediately and demand to know what Penny told her for six and a half minutes on that call, but I wasn't ready to run in front of any cars. I tried to swallow the muck in my Styrofoam cup and come up with a reasonable explanation for my wife to have a three-hundred-ninety-second conversation with my former lover in the days leading up to her mysterious exit from my life.

I needed more information before such a determination would be possible, so I dialed Skipper.

Her sleepy, morning voice came on the line. "You're up early."

"No, I'm up at my usual time," I said. "It's just that I rarely involve you in my morning routine. Are you awake?"

She yawned. "Yeah, I am now. What's up?"

"I've got a lot to tell you, and I need some information."

The sounds through the phone made it clear she was climbing out of bed and descending the stairs.

"Okay, sure. Let's hear it."

The sound of coffee being poured came next.

"First, we've got Tina Ramirez, the parole officer. We had to threaten her a little, but she came around. Carla Thomas hasn't made it to a meeting or drug test in three weeks, and Ramirez was covering for her."

"Why would she do that?" Skipper asked amidst swallowing her first sip of coffee.

"It's a convoluted story, but it seems she wanted the only woman parolee in Texas released on the Second Chance program to succeed, so she went to a lot of trouble to make it look like she was making her meetings and passing her drug tests."

"Okay, that's screwed up, but whatever. What else do you have?"

Envious of the good coffee Skipper was drinking a thousand miles away, I poured my black-tar warm water onto the gravel parking lot of the motel. "You're never going to believe who the guy on top of the building was."

"Come on. Spill it."

"It was Mitch Thomas, Penny's father."

"No way!"

"Oh, yes, but it gets better. He's asleep in my motel room right now. He was down here looking for Carla, just like us. Hunter and I roughed him up a little because he put up quite a fight. I now know where Penny got her feistiness. He was a handful, but we shook him up, and he spilled his guts. He's been in WITSEC up in the mountains of Colorado."

Skipper said, "So, in your first two days in Texas, you've got a federal parole officer and a dude out of witness protection working with you. Is that what you're saying?"

"Pretty much," I said. "Now, all we have to do is find Penny and or Carla. I have a hunch they're together."

She slurped another sip, and I grew more envious. "I've not checked any of the overnight reports yet this morning," she said, "but I'm logging in now."

I cleared my throat. "I have a crucial question about Penny's phone logs. When did she make the call to Anya?"

The sound of ruffling papers came through the phone. "It was the last call she made before she bolted."

"That's what I was hoping you'd say. Anything on the overnights?"

"They're coming up now. It's a lot of nothing so far, but it looks like I did get busted by the National Weather Service for messing with their satellite. That's okay, though, because I wrote a patch that'll make it look like a software glitch. They'll run diagnostics all day and discover a piece of space debris briefly interrupted the bird's orbit. It'll be fine."

"How did you learn to do all that stuff?" I asked.

"It's not that hard. Ginger taught me most of it, but some I just pick up along the way. It's all pretty simple when you break it down."

"No, it's not simple, and I'm thankful to have you on the team. I couldn't do it without you."

She laughed. "Yeah, I know. Major cog in a big machine . . . and all that. Whoa! Wait a minute. . . ."

"What is it?"

"Hang on. Hang on . . ."

The sound of rapid-fire keystrokes echoed in my ear.

"Oh, Chase, this is big. I put a twenty-four-hour hold on any withdrawals larger than five grand on the two Cayman accounts Penny has access to, and we got a hit. She tried to withdraw a hundred grand yesterday afternoon from the Merchant First Bank in San Antonio at four oh five p.m."

I jerked my arm up to check my watch. "That means I've got just over nine hours to get to San Antonio. How far is that from here?"

More keystrokes. "It's four hundred twenty miles. That should take a little over six hours if the interstate traffic isn't bad."

I leapt down from the tailgate of the truck. "Call the bank. Make damned sure they don't issue that cash before four oh five this afternoon. Tell them if they do, we're moving every penny of our money out of their vault."

Bursting through the motel room door, I yelled at Mitch. "Get up! We're going to San Antonio!"

Mitch stirred and forced his eyes open. "What?"

"I found Penny. We're going to San Antonio."

He swung his legs over the edge of the bed and wiped the sleep from his eyes. The brace on his left knee looked uncomfortable and robotic, but it was better than how the knee had looked the night before.

I yanked down the blanket covering the hole in the wall and stuck my head through. Hunter and Ramirez were entangled beneath the wafer-thin blanket. "Hey, guys. Get up. Skipper found Penny. She's in San Antonio. We've got to go—now."

Hunter's feet hit the floor before I'd finished, but Tina mumbled, "Who's Skipper?"

Fifteen minutes later, the four of us were crammed into our rented Camry and screaming south on Interstate 27.

"This ain't gonna work for six hours," Hunter said. "I think we need to get on the horn with your secretary and trade this thing in for something that'll carry four grown-ups."

"You call her, and put it on speaker," I said.

"That was fast," Skipper said. "I just got off the phone with the bank in the Caymans. The releases are sent electronically on the quarter-hour, so they'll notify Merchant First Bank of the authorization at four fifteen. The San Antonio branch closes at four thirty."

"That's beautiful, Skipper. You've just manufactured the perfect ambush point, but I need another favor. Get on the horn with the rental counter in Lubbock, and get us something that can carry four, no, make it six adults, and make it something fast."

She laughed. "You want a six-passenger sports car. I'll see what I can do. Hang on."

A minute or so later, she came back on the line. "Are you still there?"

"We're here," I said.

"You don't have to yell, Chase. It's a speakerphone, not a megaphone."

"Did you get us a car or not?"

"Not," she said. "I got you a Suburban. That's an SUV, not a car."

"Add one more forehead kiss to the tally sheet. Make sure they know we need a quick turn in Lubbock. I don't have time to mess around."

"I'm way ahead of you," she said. "The Suburban will be waiting at the curb, fully fueled, and I'm sending her an electronic signature. All you'll have to do is dump the Toyota and jump in the Suburban."

"What would I do without you?"

"You'd hire a team of analysts and secretaries," she said.

"You're probably right. Thanks, Skipper. I'll check in when we hit San Antonio."

Hunter clicked off.

Tina said, "I think I need a Skipper in my life."

"We all need a Skipper in our lives," I said.

The exchange was even easier than I'd hoped. The Suburban was running with all four doors open when we pulled into the airport parking lot.

"Hunter, you drive. I've got a call to make."

My partner climbed behind the wheel and adjusted the seat and mirrors while I helped get Mitch settled in the far back seat. Between the trauma his body had endured and the narcotics, I assumed he'd sleep most of the way. Tina Ramirez mounted the front passenger seat, and I situated myself in the plush second row.

We pulled out of the airport and back onto the interstate. The big V-eight engine accelerated the six-thousand-pound truck through ninety miles per hour in seconds.

Hunter rubbed the steering wheel in admiration. "We've got to get us a couple of these."

"I think you may be right," I said as I scrolled through my phone for Anya's number.

Tina reached across the front seat and took Hunter's hand. "I think all of us may be finding things we want to keep lately."

I met Hunter's eyes in the mirror, and he blushed. "I told you I've got a soft spot for dark-haired Latin girls."

I stared down at my phone. Logic had to prevail. I couldn't turn this into an emotional scenario. The conversation I was about to have with the former Russian SVR assassin could only end one of two ways. She would either deny having spoken with Penny and find a way to make me believe her, or she'd tell me everything. There would be no in-between with Anya.

My gut rumbled, and I wondered if it was hunger or anxiety growling up at me. I suspected it was the perfect storm of both. My thumb hovered over the send button until I finally overcame my hesitance and pressed it.

Anya Robertovna Burinkova, one of the deadliest women on the planet, answered on the second ring. "I have been holding phone in hand for two days and waiting for you to call, Chasechka. I have many things to tell to you."

Chapter 30
Only One Reason

"Hello, Anya. Apparently, you know exactly why I'm calling."

"Yes, I know why you are calling, but I am surprised it took you so long."

"We've been a little busy," I said, "but I need to know what Penny told you before she left, and I want to know why you didn't tell me when she called."

Anya sighed. "I made to her promise I would not tell until you asked. To me, promise is important."

"Yeah, well, so is my marriage, and you could've prevented a heap of trouble if you'd just told me what's going on."

"Do not be angry with me, Chase. I will tell to you all of it if you will listen."

I growled. "Fine, Anya. Tell me all of it. And whatever conditions there are on it, consider them lifted. No secret codes or waiting until I ask just the right question. Tell me everything you know."

She began without preamble. "Penny has been afraid to tell you truth about her family."

I interrupted. "But she's okay telling you?"

"No, Chase, she did not tell to me. She only said to me she was afraid for you to know truth. I do not know what is truth about her family. She told to me something happened, and I do not know what this something is. She said to me she is going to find answers about her family, and it could be dangerous."

I was losing what little patience I had left. "You let my wife go off on some dangerous quest to find answers halfway across the country, and you didn't tell me?"

"I do not have power over wife for you. I cannot make her go or stay. She is strong woman, like me, who is going to do what she wants. Maybe yes, I should have told to you this before, but Penny made me promise to tell only when you come to me and ask. She said if I do not promise this, she will not tell me what is happening, and is important for someone to know."

I clenched my teeth. "Okay, fine. You made a promise, and you kept it. Tell me everything."

"This is what I am trying to do, but you interrupt me. Is now for you to only listen and not talk. Yes?"

"Fine," I huffed.

Anya continued. "Penny believes you cannot love her if she does not get answers she needs. She could not come to you for this, Chase. She has to do alone. She knows you would do for her anything, but she cannot ask of you this thing. She believes something happened many years ago that is wrong, and maybe truth will now make everything better. I know all of this sounds like puzzle, and it sounds same to me, but this is what she said."

My anger was beginning to subside. "No, believe it or not, it all makes sense. Penny's mother was convicted of narcotics trafficking with a Central American cartel twelve years ago. Penny's father testified against her mother. That's the terrible truth Penny didn't think I could handle."

Confusion punctuated Anya's voice. "But this does not make sense. What are answers she could want now if this happened twelve years ago?"

"Her mother was released from prison back in February. I suspect Penny learned of the release and needed to find her mother and get answers to about a thousand questions, starting with, 'Why did you do it?'"

"I think is something more than this. Did cartel kill her father after trial?"

"No, but they would have if they could've gotten to him. He's been in the Witness Security Program since he testified."

Anya let out a sigh of recognition. "This is why she said if she does not come back, I am to tell you to contact United States Marshals and tell to them Mitchell Wade Thomas's daughter is missing."

I drew my hands into fists. "Anya, I'm serious. Tell me absolutely everything she told you. Every detail is important."

"There is only one more thing."

"Damnit, Anya. Just tell me."

"She loves you, Chase."

My brain wanted to explode. "Oh, she loves me, does she? So, she disappears, pretending to be mad about something that never happened, and then she calls you to let you in on the big secret. That's her loving me, huh?"

"I think you do not understand how women think."

"Oh, you're right about that," I almost yelled into the phone. "Nobody understands how women think. Not even other women."

Her voice remained calm. "I am not like other women, but I understand why Penny was afraid to tell to you truth about her family. I have felt same. You cannot believe me, but I loved you, and I was afraid for you to know truth about my past, also."

"You didn't make up some stupid reason and disappear, though."

"No, Chase, what I did to you was much worse than any of that. Do not be angry with Penny. She is your person, even if you do not know everything of her time before she came to you. You are her person, and she is yours."

I roared. "How about you leave the relationship advice to somebody who's not a communist spy, huh? Do you think you can do that?"

No one in the Suburban said a word after I hung up and let the steam boil off.

Finally, I said, "She called Anya and told her she was afraid for me to find out the truth about her family, and she needed to go find some answers. She said if she doesn't come back, Anya was supposed to tell me to call the U.S. Marshals and tell them she'd gone missing."

Tina turned in her seat to face me. "That's all she said, and that was enough to send you on that tirade?"

"Not that it's any of your business," I said, "but she told Anya to tell me she loves me."

Tina frowned and turned away. "I understand now. I'm sorry."

We rode in silence for an hour. Just north of some godforsaken place called Big Spring, Hunter said, "She knew you'd find the phone and figure out she'd called Anya. If she didn't love you, she would've just walked away without leaving the breadcrumbs."

He was right. Just like Clark, he'd pull me back from the edge more times than I'd be able to count in my life. I'd done exactly what I'd sworn I wouldn't do. I'd let emotion take over, and, just like the squirrel, I was running in front of cars without any hope of finding an acorn.

I laid my hand on Tina's shoulder. "I'm sorry I snapped at you, Tina. This is new territory for me. I'm not used to chasing people I love. My forte is pursuing low-life scumbags who I intend to kill."

"It's okay. I know you're upset, but it sounds like you've got a lot of people who care about you." She cast a thumb toward Hunter. "Especially this one."

"You're right, and I'm lucky to have them."

Mitch leaned forward. "Is everything all right?"

I explained what I'd learned, and he appeared to be relieved by the news. Maybe I should've taken some solace in knowing Penny left a few breadcrumbs just as Hunter had said.

My watch and stomach told me it had been a long time since a meal. "We're making good time, and I'm sure everybody's hungry, so let's grab a bite and hit the head."

Everyone agreed, and we pulled into a mom-and-pop, roadside diner in Big Spring. We ordered cheeseburgers and chili dogs to go and took turns in their single bathroom.

* * *

At just before two o'clock, on the outskirts of San Antonio, we came to a traffic stop on Interstate 10 at the Four-Ten interchange.

"This certainly doesn't look good," I said, peering between the front seats.

Hunter said, "Relax. The GPS says we're less than five miles from the bank. We've got plenty of time."

Tina spoke up. "It'll clear up once we get past the Four-Ten. This intersection is always like this."

"You seem to know a lot about San Antonio traffic," I said.

"My parents moved here from Brazil when I was two years old. I spent twenty-one years in this city before I moved to Lubbock. I know everything about it."

"What do you know about the Merchant First Bank?" I asked.

"It's the largest bank in South Texas. It's full of oil money and drug money. Many people say it's the same money. The building is beautiful, but that's all I know about it."

"That's actually good news," I said. "I hoped it would be a bank in which a hundred thousand dollars wouldn't cause a stir."

Tina started to speak but then hesitated.

"What is it?" I asked.

She shook her head. "It's just that your wife is taking a hundred thousand dollars out of your bank, and you don't seem worried about the money. I don't get paid until next week, and I've got like two hundred bucks in my account."

"Of course the money is important," I said, "but finding my wife and making sure she's okay is worth more than all the money in that big, beautiful bank."

Tina's curiosity piqued. "But, for real. You've got a hundred thousand dollars in the bank that she can just take out whenever she wants?"

Hunter intervened. "Like I told you last night, we're security contractors, and there's plenty of work for people like us, so we make a nice living while we're young so we can chill out when we get old."

"*If* you get old," she said.

She was right about that—and about the traffic. Once inside the Four-Ten, we were back up to highway speed. She was also right about the Merchant First Bank. The building was something right off the cover of architectural digest, but its size and the fact that it had six entrances and exits made it a nightmare for surveillance. There was no way Hunter and I could cover all the doors.

We drove around the building twice as he and I planned how we'd handle the ambush. "What do you think she'll do when she sees you?" he asked.

"I've been thinking about that. She did leave the breadcrumbs, so she had to know I'd come to find her. She may not love the timing, but I don't think she's going to freak out."

"What do you think the money's for?" he said.

"I can answer that one," Tina said. "If she found her mother, and she's in trouble, there's only one reason they'd come to San Antonio and need that much money."

We were hanging on her every word. "She's helping her run. With a hundred grand in cash and an international airport, you've got a lot of options. The only international direct destinations out of San Antonio are in Mexico, but if she hops on a flight to Miami, LAX, or Atlanta, she could be anywhere in the world in less than twenty-four hours. Do you think her daughter will go with her?"

I replayed the phone call with Anya over in my head. "No, she's not planning to go with her. Anya said that if she doesn't come back, we're supposed to call the Marshals Service. If she were planning to run off with her mother, she never would've left those instructions. She wouldn't want the Marshals to know anything about it."

"That's a good point," Tina said. "That means she's planning to put her mother on a plane and watch her disappear. That's called aiding and abetting a fugitive, and it's a felony."

"Are you going to arrest her?" I asked.

Tina bit her lip and didn't answer.

Chapter 31
Voice Over

"She doesn't have the authority to arrest anyone," Mitch said from the back seat. "There's no warrant, and she's not a cop. She could call the FBI or the Marshals, and maybe even get a warrant signed by a federal judge, but the wheels of justice turn slowly, even in Texas. Trust me, I know."

"He's right," Tina said, "but I can't just let a federal parolee flee the country without telling someone."

To my surprise, Hunter said, "In that case, we'll drop you off at the Greyhound bus station and buy you a ticket back to Plainview. You can pick up your car and drive back to Lubbock. When your office opens Monday morning, you can parade your cute little butt in there and announce to the world that you let a federal parolee go three weeks without checking in and how she's now in Switzerland or someplace."

She hung her head. "Look, I knew I'd get caught sooner or later and probably lose my job, but there's some stuff you don't know about the Carla Thomas case. Yeah, all the evidence at the time looked like she was guilty as Lucifer himself, but I've spent an hour every Thursday with her since she was paroled back in February, and I'm telling you there's more to the story than what came out in court."

I leaned toward her. "What are you saying?"

"I'm just saying she may not be as guilty as she sounds. That's all, but I'm not a lawyer. It's not my job to say who's guilty and who's not. It's just that I have a hundred and twenty-six cases, and I know for sure every one of them is guilty except Carla."

"I've got a new plan," I said. "Kidnapping is a federal crime, right?"

Tina nodded. "Yes, it falls under the jurisdiction of the FBI."

I said, "Good, we're going to try adding that one to our list. Are you in, or do you want the bus ticket?"

Hunter scowled. "What are you talking about?"

"I'm talking about forgetting all about trying to cover all the entrances and exits. There's no way we could do that even if Mitch *could* walk. But we don't have to cover all the doors." I pointed to porticos above each entrance. "There are cameras everywhere, and those cameras have to be attached to a computer system. Skipper may not be able to hijack a National Weather Service satellite and get any good video from it, but I'll bet she can sneak her way into the network that runs those."

Hunter still looked confused. "I'm sure you're right, but where does the kidnapping come into play?"

"It's simple," I said. "We don't want to cause a scene inside the lobby of that bank. Even if Penny doesn't freak out, her mother will. She's a fugitive, just like Tina said. She's got a lot to lose. She'll do whatever is necessary to avoid getting caught, and I don't want to be stuck in the middle of some kind of pandemonium in the lobby of the biggest bank in South Texas. I don't want to answer the questions that would inevitably follow that scene."

"Okay, I'm tracking so far," Hunter said, "but you've not covered the kidnapping yet."

I grinned. "We simply let Skipper watch for Penny and her mother to exit their car and stroll into the bank. We then know which car is theirs. We sit on it and wait for them to withdraw their money at four fifteen, then grab them up when they come back out to their ride."

"Brilliant," he said. "Now, you'd better call Skipper and get her on board."

I called, explained my plan, and Skipper said, "Sure, I can do that. Find some place to hide, and give me a few minutes."

We found a coffee shop across the street from Merchant First and pulled into the parking lot.

Before we could get out of the Suburban, Skipper called back. "Okay, I'm in. It was a pretty tight system, so it took longer than I expected, but I've got control of all the exterior and interior cameras. I even discovered a cheap, low-resolution camera in the ladies' room that's been patched into the system. I think I'll have a little fun with that one and mess with the security guard who installed it. Pervert."

"Great job, Skipper. We're looking for Penny and a woman twenty-five years older who probably looks a lot like her."

"I'm on it. They're expecting their money just after four o'clock, so they'll probably be early. Go ahead and have some coffee, and I'll call as soon as I see them."

"How did you know we were at the coffee shop?" I asked.

"Duh. The black Suburban I rented is parked across the street from the bank where I control the security cameras."

I said, "I'll shut up, and we'll be having coffee now."

* * *

It was impossible not to stare at my watch as the second hand ticked in slow motion. Cars and customers came and went in a non-stop parade around the bank. Even with the cameras, it was starting to look as though it might be impossible to pick Penny out of the crowd.

At the stroke of four, my phone chirped, and I stuck it to my ear. "Yeah."

Skipper said, "I'm getting concerned. I thought they'd be there by now."

"Me too. Are you sure this is the right branch?"

"I double-checked, and it's definitely the right place."

"We're getting down to the wire here, Skipper. Have you got any ideas?"

"Hey, I'm just the analyst. You're the big-time spy."

"I guess our only play at this point is to wait it out. If they don't pick up the money, they can't run far."

She said, "I think you're . . . Hang on just a second."

My heart pounded in my chest, and I pressed myself to the front window of the coffee shop. I scanned the front of the enormous bank building, praying I'd catch a glimpse of Penny's wild hair dancing in the wind. "What do you see, Skipper?"

"Got 'em," she said. "They're in a blue Nissan Altima. I'm running the plates now."

"Where are they?" I demanded.

"North side parking lot, about twenty cars down from the end. There's an empty spot directly across the aisle from them. If you go now, you can grab it."

I shot a look at Mitch's crutches and his leg and turned to the parole officer. "Tina, you stay with him. Hunter, come with me now!"

My partner didn't hesitate. He was on his feet and headed for the door in an instant. We mounted the vehicle and bounced out of the coffee shop parking lot without looking in either direction. Horns blew and tires squealed as furious drivers slammed on their brakes to avoid a collision with the big black SUV.

The spot was still open when we accelerated into the lot. I backed into the parking space and tried to catch my breath.

Hunter put his hand on my shoulder. "Calm down, brother. We've done this a thousand times. It's a simple snatch and grab. You take Carla, and I'll get Penny."

"Why are you taking Penny?" I asked.

"In case they resist, I'll let her go. You probably wouldn't, and there's no good outcome from that. You'll put Carla in the vehicle, and if Penny agrees, she'll come willingly."

I analyzed his plan and couldn't disagree, no matter how much I wanted to. "Okay, I'll take Carla. Penny may be armed, but she won't shoot as long as she recognizes who we are."

"I've already thought of that, but what about Carla? She's never seen either of us. What's going to keep her from shooting?"

"She's got no history of violence, and I don't think she'd risk getting caught with a gun while she's on parole."

He made a face. "She's willing to risk skipping three check-ins with her parole officer."

I shrugged and called Skipper. "You're on speaker. It's just Hunter and me. We're in the spot across from the Altima."

"Yeah, I know. I watched you jump the curb and almost kill half a dozen people."

"Oh, that's right. You're watching."

"Yeah, I'm watching. They're inside the bank now and waiting for their money."

The clock on the dash showed thirteen minutes after four. They say the last two minutes of a football game are the longest on Earth, but whoever said that has never waited for their wife and fugitive mother-in-law to come out of the Merchant First Bank building with a hundred thousand dollars in cash.

Skipper said, "They're coming out. They've got the cash in a brown leather bag. It looks like a big purse."

I scanned the mirrors, straining to see them come through the doors, but my view was blocked by a van and a pair of Japanese maple trees. "Keep me posted, Skipper, I can't see the doors from here."

"They're outside and coming down the steps toward you. You should have them in sight in ten seconds."

I could hear my heart beating, and my mouth turned to sand. It felt like I hadn't had a drink of water in days. Hunter leaned forward and stared into the mirror on his side while I did the same on mine.

"There they are! I've got 'em," I said as they came into view. "They're going to walk right past us."

Hunter said, "If they come down your side, give them time to get pinched between us and the van beside you, then open your door. I'll run around behind them, and we'll have them pinned."

I watched the two women approach, and I held my hand on the door handle, waiting for them to turn toward me. They disappeared behind the Suburban, and I turned to Hunter. "They're behind us now. Watch for them to turn down your side."

He slid his hand to the door handle and locked his eyes on the mirror. He watched for an interminable moment as my heart raced in my chest. Finally, he said, "Go now!"

I leapt from the driver's side and sprinted for the sidewalk. I covered the fifteen feet in three strides and ran around the rear bumper just in time to see the brown leather bag disappear beside the Suburban. The vehicle beyond was a huge black Lincoln Town Car, so there was no chance of them getting away. I stepped beside the Suburban and behind Carla Thomas just as Hunter threw open the front door and jumped from the seat. His boots hit the ground the same instant Carla turned to run. Instead of taking her first step, she froze when she saw my six-foot-four-inch frame blocking her exit.

"Who are these people, Penny?"

She'd asked my wife who we were, but she'd done it in Penny's voice.

The same voice said, "That one is your son-in-law, Mom," but Carla's lips hadn't moved.

It was impossible to tell their voices apart.

Hunter opened the rear door, and I said, "Get in. Everything's going to be all right."

Carla turned to her daughter for reassurance.

"Get in, Mom," Penny said. "If they say it's going to be all right, you can believe them. They know what they're doing."

Carla climbed into the second row of seats while Penny stood, staring wordlessly at me. Her expression was impossible to read.

That's when a sound I hadn't expected came from the opposite side of the Suburban.

Hunter turned, looking into the vehicle, and yelled, "She's running!"

Carla had crawled into the Suburban, opened the opposite door, and kept moving right out the other side.

I locked eyes with my wife. "Don't run. Everything's okay."

Without waiting for a response, I turned on my heel and sprinted for the rear of the Suburban. I hit the sidewalk moving as fast as my feet would carry me, and Hunter materialized beside me. Carla Thomas was ten strides ahead of us and running with the leather bag bouncing across her back.

She was in better shape and a lot faster than I expected. We were closing on her, but not as quickly as I wanted. If she reached the street in front of the bank, it would be impossible to explain why we were chasing a woman in downtown San Antonio with a hundred grand in her enormous purse, but our closure rate wasn't fast enough to beat her to the corner.

Just as I started trying to formulate a plan to stop her in the street without being arrested, a shiny aluminum crutch protruded from between a work truck and a mini-van. The crutch met Carla's shin, and my fifty-five-year-old ex-convict mother-in-law hit the concrete sidewalk like a ton of bricks. The contents of her oversized leather purse filled the air.

Hunter and I put on the brakes just as Tina and Mitch stepped to the sidewalk.

Tina knelt beside Carla. "You missed your check-ins and three drug tests. We've got some catching up to do."

Epilogue

Carla Thomas spent the next several hours explaining how she'd been forced into trafficking for the Jimenez Cartel fifteen years earlier through relentless threats against the lives of her husband and daughter. She'd done what they demanded until the day they abducted Penny and tortured her in ways no teenage girl—or anyone—should ever have to endure. Caught up too deeply to ever have any hope of escaping the cartel, she'd bowed her head and accepted the conviction following Mitch's testimony. He'd done it to save his beloved daughter, and Carla had done it for exactly the same reason. She believed if she was convicted and sent to prison, her husband and daughter would be taken into WITSEC and kept alive. The decision to make the sacrifice to save her daughter and husband came easily, and the nearly twelve years she served in federal prison was a price she'd been more than willing to pay for the safety of the two people she loved more than anyone else on Earth.

But when she was released from prison on parole, and the second generation of the cartel was there to greet her, everything had changed. Instead of trafficking in narcotics, the new cargo was human beings. The cartel showed her a stack of pictures of her beautiful daughter all grown up and living aboard a magnificent sailboat, and the threats continued. Swallowed by the same demons who'd consumed her over a dozen years before, she gave in and recorded the audio that was altered and delivered to Thomas Meriwether containing the warning about sinking his precious oil rig in the Gulf of Mexico. That had only been the tip of the spear the cartel was determined to bury in her flesh. The tasks grew more unthinkable by the day until Carla could no longer stomach the sacrifices she was asked to make to save the life of the daughter she'd lost so many years before. The phone call to Penny, followed by the desperate plan they'd concocted together to free Carla from the talons of the cartel, would cost everyone involved far more than any of them could have imagined, but ultimate freedom is sometimes worth unfathomable sacrifice.

Hunter and I never learned what Shirl, the waitress, thought the one thing we could be was since we weren't rodeo cowboys, oilmen, or roughnecks, but there would come a day, we vowed to each other, when we'd find her and ask the question.

Cabo San Lucas, at the southern tip of the Baja Peninsula, is the perfect place to learn to sail a sixty-five-foot catamaran and put the pieces of a shattered marriage back together. That's exactly what Mitch and Carla Thomas did before setting out across the wide Pacific Ocean for a place neither of them had ever heard of before former federal parole officer Tina Ramirez explained that the island nation of Vanuatu had no extradition treaty with the United States.

Hunter stayed in Lubbock helping Tina Ramirez determine where the rest of her life would be spent and what she would do after resigning her position as a federal parole officer.

After rewarding the manager of the FBO at Lubbock Airport with the ride of his life in the front seat of my P-51, Penny and I flew home with the Mustang's name, *Penny's Secret*, painted on the cowling, now meaning more than ever. That three-hour flight was the worst possible setting for the agonizing conversation that couldn't be delayed. My questions resulted in answers that only created more questions . . . and more doubts.

"What have I ever done to make you believe you couldn't come to me with the truth?"

The headset gave Penny's voice a tinny quality, sharpening her tone even beyond the harshness of her words. "The rest of the world is always more important when your phone rings. I'm always second."

I found her eyes in the mirror that was designed to give WWII pilots the ability to see their attackers closing from behind. "Why did you turn to Anya instead of me?" I said. "Of all the people on Earth you could've trusted, why did you turn to her?"

The lie she'd told herself and apparently believed, punctuated by what she said next, left me terrified I'd wake up every morning for the rest of my life defeated, broken, and alone.

Penny turned, staring into the endless sky. "Why did *you* turn to Anya instead of me?"

About the Author

Cap Daniels

Cap Daniels is a former sailing charter captain, scuba and sailing instructor, pilot, Air Force combat veteran, and civil servant of the U.S. Department of Defense. Raised far from the ocean in rural East Tennessee, his early infatuation with salt water was sparked by the fascinating, and sometimes true, sea stories told by his father, a retired Navy Chief Petty Officer. Those stories of adventure on the high seas sent Cap in search of adventure of his own, which eventually landed him on Florida's Gulf Coast where he spends as much time as possible on, in, and under the waters of the Emerald Coast.

With a headful of larger-than-life characters and their thrilling exploits, Cap pours his love of adventure and passion for the ocean onto the pages of The Chase Fulton Novels series.

Visit www.CapDaniels.com to join the mailing list to receive newsletter and release updates.

Connect with Cap Daniels
Facebook: www.Facebook.com/WriterCapDaniels
Instagram: https://www.instagram.com/authorcapdaniels/
BookBub: https://www.bookbub.com/profile/cap-daniels

Made in the USA
Columbia, SC
04 January 2023

75484245R00162